PHOTO FINISHED

Also by Christin Brecher

The Nantucket Candle Maker mystery series

Murder's No Votive Confidence

Murder Makes Scents

15 Minutes of Flame

PHOTO FINISHED

CHRISTIN BRECHER

Kensington Publishing Corp
www.kensingtonbooks.com

KENSINGTON BOOKS are published by

Kensington Publishing Corp.
119 West 40th Street New York, NY 10018

All Kensington titles, imprints, and distributed lines are available at special quantity discounts for bulk purchases for sales promotion, premiums, fund-raising, educational, or institutional use.

Special book excerpts or customized printings can also be created to fit specific needs. For details, write or phone the office of the Kensington Sales Manager: Kensington Publishing Corp., 119 West 40th Street, New York, NY 10018. Attn. Sales Department. Phone: 1-800-221-2647.

ISBN: 978-1-4967-3882-0 (ebook)

ISBN: 978-1-4967-3881-3

First Kensington Trade Paperback Printing: November 2022

10 9 8 7 6 5 4 3 2 1

Printed in the United States of America

To my Granny and Papa

PHOTO FINISHED

Chapter 1

My greatest joy has always been taking photos. Some people escape into books. I escape into my camera's lens. It's fair to say that a sealed metal box that does no more than capture light and turn it into pixels can inspire me to jump into things I might otherwise have no business tackling. Without it, for example, I might never have landed in New York City.

I never know where this town will take me, but I love sharing the moments along the way. Like an Instagram photo I recently took while wandering Soho. In this image, I was excited to capture two New Yorkers who happened to look, at the same moment, toward a multi-story mural painted across a building. One person's head tilted as if seeing true beauty; another folded his arms as if seeing the opposite. Together, they told a tale of people with different dreams, thrust together by happenstance, and captured by a passing stranger.

At the end of the post, I added my usual shameless plug: *Visit me @livspyersphotography or in person at my studio in the West Village to see my portrait work. I'm ready to capture YOUR story!*

A snapshot of me: The morning I posted this little gem, I was under layers of blankets in my chilly ground-floor apartment in the West Village. Thanksgiving was one day away, the tealights tacked to my ceiling were still on, and I realized I'd fallen asleep while watching *Bridgerton* for the third time. I had an important workday ahead and planned to celebrate the holiday season that night with my oldest friend, Maria Ricci, at her annual Wild Turkey party in Brooklyn. I was feeling both prosperous and broke, aglow and obscure; basically, I was feeling like thousands of other Manhattanites trying to turn their dreams into reality.

No sooner had I hit Share than I heard a knock at my front door. I slipped out of bed and threw on a bit of lip gloss, because you never know who might be walking down your street in New York City. I knew the face that would greet me on the other side of my front door, however, and it was not going to be Lord Anthony Bridgerton.

At the second knock, I headed out of my bedroom and into my office. Like everyone who works from home these days, my morning commute is an easy one. With only a step across the threshold of my tiny bedroom's door, I leave home-sweet-home and arrive at Liv Spyers Photography, my small portrait photography studio. All that divides my private life and my business is a silky red privacy curtain that I pull across my storefront's window when the workday is done. My studio is a modest-sized, rectangular room that Maria and I painted white from top to bottom the first week I moved in. After studying numerous DIY YouTube videos, I'd installed a piece of sheetrock between the unsightly entrance to my bedroom and my studio space that also worked double-duty as a backdrop for my clients' photo shoots. Add a couple of catchlights to give my clients' eyes a little sparkle, a small desk with a visitor's chair, and a compact kitchen and counter space along the opposite wall, and you have arrived at Liv Spyers Photography.

I don't mind living like a size-ten foot in a size-five shoe, because a year ago I was still in my quiet, hometown suburb of New Jersey off Exit 83 on the Garden State Parkway and working at Starbucks after having had to drop out of college. For the record, abandoning my education was for financial reasons. But even with a head start over my peers on joining the "real world," I found very few outlets for my photography ambitions. Before I knew it, my friends from home had tucked their diplomas in the back of their closets, moved out, and had even started to indulge in things like craft cocktails instead of White Claws. I scraped and saved but joining them seemed impossible on a barista photographer's income.

My fate changed, however, when my grandparents moved their ground-level storefront, Carrera Locksmiths, to a converted space on the first floor of their townhouse. Granny and Poppy had bought their four-story brownstone way back in the 1970s when New York City was bankrupt, and you could buy real estate in their area for next to nothing. These days, the buildings around them were gloriously renovated and the streets were filled with high-end restaurants and boutiques, but neighbors still needed basic services that were less glamorous.

With a neon sign that reads KEYS in their front window, they'd run a well-oiled enterprise for decades, but when the cost of never-ending home repairs became too much, they decided to seek the extra income.

Enter: Me. Taking a page from their enterprising spirits, I convinced them to turn a blind eye to zoning rules to allow me to both live and work in their original commercial space. In exchange for a small family discount on rent, I watched my grandparents' store for them when they needed an extra hand.

I consider myself fortunate that my family all think they are getting a great deal in this set-up. In addition to living in a city that inspires my imagination at every step, I have hung my own shingle and declared my ambition to be a portrait photographer. Yes, my savings were nearly depleted, and I still had a long way to go before Liv Spyers Photography was New Yorkers' go-to place for portrait and events photography. And no, I hadn't had time to attend all the A-lister parties and fabulous clubs I'd hoped I might have by now. But due to my studio's street-level window display, I'd booked five family portraits for holiday cards during September, four yearbook photos in October, and when this particular morning began, I had high hopes for growing my head-shot business.

Unlatching the deadbolt, I opened the door. As I suspected, my grandmother, with her thick black Italian hair, still its original shade at eighty, was waiting for me.

"I made cinnamon muffins," she said, holding up a tin with a beaming smile. "You look skinny."

It truly wasn't until my first childhood sleepover with Maria, in my suburban New Jersey town of aboveground pools and Instagram-worthy holiday lawn décor, that I realized that waking up to a family member reeling off breakfast options is unusual, but this is what we do. The occasional forfeiture of privacy in exchange for good food is a solid family tradition.

"I have never looked skinny in my life," I said.

"Thank you again for opening the store for us this morning," said Granny, walking right by me and buttering a muffin, which I devoured. "Poppy's moving slowly these days, and I want to get to Yonkers for a good Stew Leonard's turkey before the rush, and then to the Bronx to pick up the sausage from Arthur Avenue for my stuffing."

"Take your time," I said, beginning to pack my camera bag with items for my morning's shoot, including a portable tripod, light reflector, and an external flash I'd recently invested in for location jobs. "I'll be back here with time to spare."

"You're an angel," Granny said, giving me a kiss and a pat on the cheek before tying the sash on her housecoat for the short walk back upstairs. "Poppy's opening that old safe we got in a couple of days ago. The owner is convinced he's inherited something special. He'll be focused, so remind him to eat."

"Does anyone know what's inside?" I asked, always curious when these jobs came along.

"You never know what you'll find," she said, an adventurous smile stealing over her wrinkled face.

"Maybe an old baseball card worth a million dollars?"

"Or a love letter," she answered as I gave her a hug and shut my front door behind her.

Two more muffins later, I released fourteen pounds of hair from a ponytail, not really, but really, and scuttled to the shower. As the first dash of cold water from the old pipes slapped me awake, I focused on my morning's headshot session with a client who was climbing the ladder in the financial world. I'd landed the gig through OneShot.com, which I'd joined a couple of weeks earlier. It's a one-stop-shop for people to find and book photographers. In exchange for a cut of our fees, I had access to their customers and a web page upon which I could showcase my work. This was my first booking through them. With a good review from this morning's client, I hoped to build a new source of income. Now that December was around the corner, I was banking on bookings through the service to get me through the winter.

I dressed in my usual black leggings, which I paired with a white button-down. The blouse looked smart with the collar flipped up and my camera strap around it. I slipped on my Doc Martens, which hold me up better than any shoes on days I'm on my feet for hours. Adding a welcome couple of inches to my overall height, they also give me an average sight line when I navigate the subway.

With only minutes to spare, I pulled back my red silk curtain so that passersby could see the inside of my studio. I grabbed my parka from the floor, threw my camera bag over my shoulder, and opened the small, wrought-iron gate that led to the sidewalk. I breathed in the late autumn air. Fall, with its billowing clouds, call for sweaters, and its scent of leaves is my favorite season. I smiled as I noticed that the flaming yellow leaves from the trees on my block had fallen by the thousands during a rain shower the night before and had transformed bags of garbage and discarded Amazon boxes into autumnal bliss. It was as if someone had splattered paint across the world with an enormous paint brush.

By the time I hit the 1 train at the height of the morning rush, I was jostled between corporate types, couriers, school kids, folks heading home from night shifts, and others heading out for day shifts and looking tired already. English, Spanish, and languages I couldn't identify floated up and down the train's car. Most of the comments were on their phones. Some nodded off for a few precious minutes. Others were checking the time and looking nervous.

Without warning, the train made a turn and I almost fell into a group of school children on a field trip gathered beside me. I noticed one boy pull out a rubber band from his pocket while his friends began to tear small pieces of paper and roll the fragments into pellets. I wondered who their targets were going to be. Their classmates sandwiched around them seemed to be the easiest marks.

It's not that I was condoning bad behavior, but I was impressed with their aim and their clandestine moves. Their victims did not notice they had been attacked, and I could see that the boys felt wonderfully rebellious. I'd basically decided not to rat on them to their teacher when a man who was standing by the door to our car cried out.

All eyes turned to him as he slapped the side of his neck. He was quite a vision, and instinctively my camera crept up to my chin. At least a full head taller than the rest of the passengers, he was dressed in a tuxedo. And not the rent-a-tux kind. He gave off a vibe that didn't fit with the rest of us plebes. I don't usually take photos on the subway—our shared space is already about as intimate as most people can handle—but the contrast between this guy and the early morning work rush was gold. Risking it, my finger casually clicked the shutter button. Then I lowered my camera like a submarine's periscope that had gone back below sea level.

Meanwhile, the man rubbed his neck and scanned the crowd for the culprits, who had already shoved their missiles back into their pockets. His eyes landed on mine, and I was frankly shocked that he could think I, a grown woman en route to a job, would have flicked him with a rubber band. I hadn't been on a lot of dates lately, but I would never stoop so low for a man's attention. Rather than return his look with the evil eye, however, I cocked my head toward the boys. I was pretty fed up with them, too.

At that, the guy winked at me. Seriously. Of all the brazen moves. Don't get me wrong. His perfectly trimmed hair, and dark eyes, offset by a nose that leaned slightly to the left somehow worked, but I knew enough not to pick up guys on the subway. Especially those who looked like they still hadn't been home from the night before.

To make matters worse, when the train pulled up to the Eighty-Sixth Street stop, I had to pass the guy to get out.

"Excuse me," I said, pushing my way toward the exit.

As I elbowed through the crowd, I put on my best *don't mess with me* expression. Unfortunately, as I reached the door a stampede of new passengers began to board the train, shoving me into him. After our awkward eye catch, it was the last thing I wanted, but there I was, smushed against him.

"Hey there!" he said.

To be clear, his words were not a come on. They were a cry for help because, due to our close proximity, my unruly hair had become tangled around the guy's coat button.

I pulled my head, which only served to make things worse

while sending shooting pain to my skull. The two of us then twirled around each other with a couple of rounds of "*Sorry*," "*Ooops*," and "*How did that happen?*" to try to separate from each other more delicately, but of course that only made things worse. As we negotiated our hair-vs.-button debacle, the other commuters began to audibly express their impatience with us.

I don't like it when people push me around or get one up on me, so I shouted out a general *"Give us a minute!"* to the crowd. Inside, however, I was feeling a little rocked. I heard the doors beside us begin to close. I couldn't be late for this job. I pulled the last, stubborn strands away with a tug that made my scalp feel on fire. Then, I spun around and leapt from the car to the platform as the doors slid toward me from both directions like a guillotine.

Immediately, I knew something wasn't right. I felt lighter and it wasn't because of the strands of hair I'd lost. I quickly ran my right hand down my side, my gut sinking as I did. I realized the worst had happened.

My camera bag was gone.

"No!" I screamed, chasing the subway car as it pulled away and banging on the doors as I did.

Through the car's window, I saw Tuxedo Man holding my bag. I was always so careful on the subway, but in one stupid move, I'd lost my precious, precious camera and my valuable equipment with it. Although I had a backup camera of lesser value at the studio, every other important accessory for my location shoots was in that bag. Even if I found a good deal online, I was in no position to make the investment to replace them.

Feeling as if I'd been physically shot, I walked up the stairs to Eighty-Sixth Street to put my head back on straight. Standing on the sidewalk with trucks and busses whizzing by me, I called my client.

"I won't be able to make it this morning," I said.

I began to explain what had happened, but he cut me off.

"It is what it is," he said, "but if you want to make it in New York, you have to have balls and be willing to use them. Nobody has patience for sloppy work or cancelled appointments."

It was low—and crude, and maybe even a bit sexist—but he was right. There was no room in this great, big, wonderful City for excuses. If I wanted to be in the game, asking for pity would get me nowhere, even if my ingenious idea to expand my clientele through OneShot.com had died before I'd met my first client.

I headed back down to the tracks and stopped at the ticket booth to file a missing-property form. A sign told me that the booth agent would be back in fifteen minutes. I waited thirty, and then waited another twenty minutes while the agent called his colleague at the next station. To my dismay, no one had dropped off my camera. I was told to fill out a property-loss form online, but from the expression on the agent's face I could tell he didn't hold out much hope.

When I finally reboarded the train back home, the downtown subway cars were much less crowded. I got a seat and checked my phone. Sure enough, my morning's client had already given me a negative review. When the doors opened at my stop, I exited and headed home. My heart was heavy as I walked up the stairs to open my grandparents' store.

"Finally. I've been waiting here forever," said a female voice behind me. She had a British accent. I love a British accent, but this one didn't exactly sound like the Queen of England.

I turned around, in no mood for a lecture from a stranger about being five minutes late to open the store. I found below me a woman in a bright red, floor-length kimono, topped by a fur bolero and finished off with pointy white booties upon which not one yellow leaf from my sidewalk had dared to attach itself. Some sort of fancy, old-school, cigarette holder was glued to her bottom lip, and I could see that Botox was her friend. She was a portrait photographer's dream subject. She also looked familiar, but I could not make out how I knew her, which was odd given her unforgettable appearance.

"I need a copy of this key," she said, waving a key that hung from an ornate gold key ring, adorned with a lion's head.

Before I could invite her up, her phone rang. Rather than climb the stairs to follow me into the store, she began to pace the sidewalk.

"This is Regina," she said. She pulled out a pack of cigarettes with the name Gitanes across it, popped one into her holder and lit it. "Talk to me, Manjeet."

Regina Montague. Of course.

I'd seen her face when I'd browsed the websites of the most successful commercial photographers in town. In my defense, she looked a good fifteen years younger online.

"Bollocks!" said Regina into her phone. "What do you mean she quit? The bloody fool. What about Alfredo or Simon? They might do."

Hearing her words, the heart-thumping rush I'd felt when the train had pulled away with my camera bag returned. This time, however, I felt excited rather than panicked. My ex-client had reminded me this morning that I had to have balls. Up my ball game, I'd venture to say. My future with OneShot.com didn't look bright, but who needed that side-hustle when Regina Montague had just stepped into my life? I willed myself to ignore the fact that when I'd arrived in New York I'd sent my portfolio to every reputable studio, including hers, without receiving even the courtesy of rejections. If I could add Regina Montague to my résumé, my credentials would skyrocket. I knew that within the span of an hour, I'd gone from losing my equipment to envisioning myself taking photos for the Met Gala, but I also knew I had nothing to lose by trying.

As Regina continued to groan into her phone, I hopped down the stairs and headed to my studio. I unlocked the door to the scent of freshly brewed coffee and Granny's cinnamon muffins. The inviting aromas bolstered my confidence. I'd been in a hurry this morning, but I was glad I always left the studio looking suitably professional.

"Met Gala, Met Gala, Met Gala," I said, projecting my dreams into the universe.

After a few minutes, which I spent trying to look busy, Regina finished her call. Remaining in my studio, I waved at her through the window. There was a terrifying second when she looked as if she might walk away, but then she sighed and plunged her phone back into her pocket. She opened the gate as if touching the entrance to a sewer and forged ahead in what seemed to be brave steps for her, down the two stairs to my humble workshop.

She paused at the front window, which was a breathtaking moment, but which also made me feel smaller than I'd expected. Through her eyes, I became painfully aware of how modest my business was. The window's display was filled with baby photos, family photos, and several portraits that showed off my skill. The six more artistic photos I had indulgently hung along the wall behind my desk now seemed oddly out of place. The images were of people I observed in Manhattan, both day and night, living their lives. I liked to think of them as spontaneous portraits in contrast to the more structured work I did with clients.

Nonetheless, Regina needed a key and, therefore, she needed me. She opened the door, my door chimes jangling with her.

"I thought you were the key girl," she said.

"I'm just filling in this morning at my grandparents' store," I said, pointing upstairs and cringing inside. "It's not hard to copy a key once you learn how to use the machine. But I'm a photographer. This is my studio."

At first, she looked at me as if I was one of those photographers in Times Square who rips off tourists, but then, my heart fairly dropping, she headed to my small collection of street-life photos.

"Huh. I like these," said Regina. She waved her cigarette in their direction and made general circular motions. "You have some style. The people look natural, the lighting is excellent, and there's energy in them. And your subjects clearly didn't know they were being photographed. These cheesier studio things over here"—she now waved toward the bread and butter of my life—"they suggest that you have what it takes to make anyone look good."

"Thank you?" I said. "Pish," Regina said.

"I couldn't help overhearing your conversation outside," I said, swallowing hard. "Are you looking for an extra staff photographer? Because, you know, I'm available."

Regina crossed her arms and flared her nostrils. I fought every impulse to offer her a muffin. Instead, I flipped up the collar of my shirt to the ceiling and put my extra camera around my neck. Going for it, I raised my camera and snapped her photo.

"So, you go for the shot, do you?" she said, tapping cigarette ashes on the floor. She sized me up again and then smiled. "I like that. As it turns out, yes, I am short a photographer on a particularly important night. One of my staffers ran off with her boyfriend to the South of France. Aside from ruining her career in this town from this point forward, she's left me high and dry to cover a coming-out ball tonight. It's one of the biggest events of the season."

"Good for the LGBTQ community," I said, trying to follow her. "Come out in style, I always say."

Regina snorted.

"No, like a debutante ball," she said. "You know, high society girls get officially introduced to Society. I pay fifteen hundred dollars a night for junior staff, and I have full rights to all the photos. I'm sure I don't have to tell you that your camera should be a bit higher end if you're serious about this business, but it will do."

Even with that salt in my fresh wounds, I was giddy. Fifteen hundred dollars plus a job at one of the season's biggest events was a dream come true. With a few jobs like that, I might even be able to replace my lost camera equipment.

Regina dug into her pocket and held a business card out to me.

"Thank you," I said, taking her beautiful, heavy stock card from her. Regina Montague's card! Yes, I was fan girling and I knew she could tell but I didn't care.

"Call Manjeet at the office for details," she said and then eyed my outfit. "Dress code is black tie. And not the T.J. Maxx kind."

Suddenly, the room was filled with a ringing noise. It was as if I'd won the grand prize in a game show, but then I realized this part of the scene had nothing at all to do with my rich imagination. Indeed, a blaring alarm was sounding off at rapid intervals.

"Oh my God," I said, heading to the door. "You'll have to excuse me."

Every month, at least one of us accidentally sets off the alarm in my grandparents' home. Why it had to be at this moment, I could not even begin to understand.

"I'll leave you to whatever this is," said Regina, following me out the door and to the stoop of my grandparent's building.

"I can make your key for you," I said over the noise. "I'll just be a sec."

"I don't do well with sirens, luv. Why don't you bring them to me tonight?"

Regina handed me her lion-headed key ring, then turned on her pointy-toed heels and hightailed it down the sidewalk.

"See you tonight," I said to her retreating figure.

"Don't screw things up," she said.

"I won't let you down," I said, close to skipping up the stairs and into the building with excitement over my change in fortune. "Poppy?"

The vestibule of my grandparents' remodeled entry includes a windowed door immediately to the left, which opens into their key store, and another of solid wood straight ahead that leads to their private residence. The door to the store was ajar, but the sign that hung from it was still flipped to CLOSED. I turned off the alarm in the small vestibule. I thought I heard something move inside the house.

"Poppy," I said again, letting myself in to my grandparents' home in case my grandfather had gone to the kitchen for some coffee. "It's me. I was about to open for you."

No one answered, so I poked my head into the store.

"Poppy?"

I did not find Poppy, but I did notice his days' work. In the middle of Carrera Locksmith, the old safe, which had been dropped off for my grandfather's expert hands to tackle, sat with its door open. Nothing was inside.

"Poppy? Where are you?"

A tap on my shoulder from behind made me jump. I turned to find behind me the soft gray eyes and wrinkled face of Poppy, who was leaning on his wooden cane and bundled in his dark wool overcoat with a *New York Post* under his arm. He took one look past me and into the store.

"*Ma donna*. Did you open that yourself?" he said, his bushy eyebrows raised.

I followed his gaze to the safe. I'd never opened a safe in my life, but these days Poppy got things confused, a lot. This time, however, the safe was open and the alarm was ringing. There was only one conclusion I could make. Carrera's had been robbed on my watch.

Chapter 2

New York is a place where you need to be ready for anything to happen at any given moment, but I'd never had so much transpire by ten in the morning on a Wednesday. Standing in the small key shop, my new career opportunity took a back seat to the yawning door of the old, chipped and scratched, forest-green safe. I didn't know whether a baseball card, a love letter, or anything had been inside, but my immediate instinct was to go after the offender. If you mess with me or my family, be ready for a fight.

I ran out the door in hopes of seeing someone who looked as if they were fleeing the scene of a crime. Hopping down to the sidewalk, I walked briskly along the street, knowing deep down it was a long shot, but I needed to at least try. People were going about their days. Regina Montague, a couple of blocks away, was on the top step of a small building with a bright, blue door, chatting with a neighbor. I was more than a little thrilled to realize I lived so close to her. I allowed myself the split second of a fantasy that we could share rides to work events if things went well.

When I accepted the fact that there'd be no fight to pick with anyone, I headed home to check on my grandfather. There, I was surprised to see Poppy had switched the store's sign to OPEN. I also saw that he had shut the safe's door.

"Where've you been?" said Poppy, wiping off the counter with some Windex and a paper towel.

"Looking for whoever broke into the store. Have you checked the cash register?" I said, my palms still sweaty.

"It's all here," he said, tapping the register's drawer with a confident hand. "We need a new alarm system one of these days."

He was right about that. The alarm's erratic behavior was one of the reasons I did not mind that my grandparents had accidentally disconnected the alarm when they'd move their store upstairs. I glanced around the store. The dummy keys which hung along the back wall behind the counter hung motionlessly. The glass case atop the counter was filled with its usual padlocks for sale. The seat cushion on a small club chair that sat in the corner of the room, an item which had not found a new home when my grandparents converted their den to their store, was still plumped from the night before. As the morning light streamed through the window, I could see small dust particles floating quietly in the air, as if whispering to me that nothing had disturbed their leisurely existence, especially not a trespasser.

"What about the safe? The open door?" I asked, not entirely ready to let it go.

Poppy walked across the creaky wood floors, his cane thumping at every other step.

"You worry too much," he said with a gentle pat on my cheek. "I opened the safe this morning. It was empty."

He shrugged and switched on the neon light in the window so that the single word KEYS competed with the sunlight on the street. I decided Poppy's story made more sense than a break-in to our key store in broad daylight, especially when I noticed a Post-it sticker stuck to the side of the safe with three numbers separated by dashes written in my grandfather's shaky handwriting. They looked like a lock's combination.

"Well, what did you expect me to think? You can't leave the store's door open like that, Poppy," I said, turning on the duplicating machine to both calm down and make Regina's key. "I almost had a heart attack. Granny's not going to be happy."

"Let's not bother Granny about this," he added, settling onto his decades-old stool behind the counter and opening his *Post*. "She has enough worries these days."

I probably should have paid more attention to his comment about my granny having troubles. In retrospect there were probably a lot of things I should have paid more attention to that morning, especially given what was to come by the day's end, but after keeping an eye on Poppy a bit longer than I'd planned, I knew I needed to focus on my new job. Once I'd given Poppy his lunch, I called Regina Montague Studios.

"RMS this is Manjeet speaking. He/him," said a man who sounded busy, impatient, and yet thrilled to have me on the line.

I began a friendly-yet-professional hello to Regina's assistant, Manjeet, but I was interrupted by his recital on when and where I should arrive for my gig: five p.m. at the side entrance to the Pierre hotel on Fifth Avenue and Sixty-First Street. He also reiterated Regina's request for subtle, yet classy formal attire, and he highlighted that I should under no circumstances wear white.

"You must have impressed Regina for her to hire you to work the Holiday Ball," he said at the end of his speech.

I hadn't realized the ball had a name.

This was the only personal comment Manjeet had made, and it halfway made up for his condescending remark about what colors I could and couldn't wear. White in November? This was a totally foreign world to me, but I wasn't crawling out from under a rock.

"If you want to succeed tonight just remember a couple of things," he said. "The client is the star; you are there to either be invisible or remind them of their status. Also, be ready to help anyone on the RMS team during the night. Our success depends on all of us doing our best."

Manjeet's other line rang in the background, and he signed off, which was fine with me. I had to attend to my nails, my hair, an outfit, my camera bag, and the shoe debate so that I could be my best for the night. The biggest issue, of course, was my dress. The two fancy gowns I owned were buried and wrinkled in the back of my one closet. I hoped Nordstrom's Rack was a step up from Regina's bias against T.J. Maxx because both had come from one of their clearance sales a couple of years ago.

I decided the red, strapless number was too flashy for the hired help, even though it was the dressier of my options. My other choice was a navy silk spaghetti-strap gown with a slit up the back and a line of buttons cascading down the front. Last time I'd worn it was to my cousin's wedding, and in its favor, I'd gotten lucky in it. Admittedly, that was also the night each member of my family had found a moment to share their condolences about my dropping out of college. After hours on my feet and a job offer from my Uncle Frank to work the ticket booth at his garage, comprised of three blank walls and one small window, the back of Bobby Faltone's van had seemed like heaven. Bobby was the venue's maître d' and also my ninth-grade boyfriend. Honestly? It was one of the nights that made me both love my family and hate my life's path.

I now willed my dress to be couture, but the thing was the plastic buttons were, well, plasticky. Not wanting to give Regina any reason to regret her decision to hire me, I rifled through the mountain of clothes spilling across my bed until I found a blouse with rhinestone buttons. Without pausing to think about it too much, I cut them off, one by one, and did the same on my dress. I subsequently learned it takes a surprisingly long time to sew buttons, but once I'd swapped in the sparkly ones, I had a dress I felt would be perfect for the night. Elegant and sharp. Just like Regina Montague Studios.

At four o'clock, I checked again on Poppy, who was helping

a customer. I called Granny, who assured me she was almost home. Then I took a deep breath and let Maria know I might not make it to her party. Thankfully, she was cool about it. She knew how much I needed a break. I promised I would show up late if I could.

I grabbed my heels, oh dreaded heels, tossed them into my old camera bag, which was not as snappy as the one I'd lost this morning, and threw on some flats for the trip uptown. I knew I'd cleaned up nicely from a few stares I got on the subway.

At Madison Avenue and Sixty-First Street a white-and-gold awning cantilevered over the sidewalk off Fifth Avenue. This was the side entrance, which I'd been instructed to enter, but THE PIERRE was written across it in the kind of script you see at the opening of fairy tales and on wedding invitations. The glow of the hotel's heat lamps beckoned to me, promising warmth from the wind, which was doing its best to spoil my carefully blown-out hair. After months of imagining what went on behind the bright lights and fast pace of a New York I'd yet to crack, I was on my way straight to the top.

A few steps from the doors, I noticed two women and a man at the side of the building, dressed in formal attire. I nodded politely in case they would be guests at the ball.

"Who do you think will cry this year?" I heard one say as another laughed. "Shh . . ." said the third.

I wondered if the gossip had ended because they thought I might be a guest. They'd soon know I wasn't, but I entered the building with my head held high as a couple of attendants opened and closed the doors for me. A few steps in, I reached into my bag and pulled out my heels. While I was doing the hop-and-switch dance of a public shoe change, I felt a gush of wind fly through the hotel's doors, which had been opened once more.

"Excuse me," a woman's voice said from behind.

The woman strode ahead and almost bowled me over as she

passed. About the same age as me, her gait had purpose. She was pulling off black gloves, tugging one finger at a time as she headed up a set of stairs in a cordoned-off section to my right. I was surprised when I noticed she had a camera bag strung over her black wool coat. Realizing she was most likely part of the RMS team of which Manjeet had raved, I took two stairs at a time to catch up while also ripping off my parka, which felt wildly out of place in my opulent surroundings. At the top of the stairs, I arrived at a large reception area covered in a blue rug adorned with a yellow pattern that seemed like a royal seal.

"You must be the new photographer," said my colleague with half a glance in my direction.

Fancy Pants, whom I decided I did not have to like even though she had immediately earned my respect, made a beeline for another woman who held a clipboard in front of her black silk dress and wore a headset over her shiny, silky, long red hair.

"Hey, Jinx," said the clipboard holder.

"Hey, Elizabeth," said my colleague while seamlessly taking a small pass from Elizabeth and pinning it discreetly to her dress. "You should have an extra pass tonight for our new photographer."

Jinx's team spirit extended to a nod in my general direction before she headed into a room adjoining the reception. Elizabeth, who I noticed from the subtle but eye-catching logo on her clipboard, was Elizabeth Everly of Elizabeth Everly Productions. The evening's party planner handed me a badge with my name on it without asking me who I was. Clearly, I was the only newbie tonight in this elite world of party events.

"Follow Jinx," Elizabeth said before returning to her clipboard. "The debutantes will be arriving in half an hour, so hustle. And give me your coat and that bag. I'll have them put in the check room."

Rather than enlighten her to the fact that I'd been hustling since I could walk, I unloaded my camera bag for the night. I'd thought I'd be able to keep it with me, but quickly realized how discreet we photographers were expected to be. While Elizabeth held my puffy parka at a judgmental distance from herself, I attached my lens, grabbed a few emergency supplies, and stuck them in my bra. When I pulled out my phone, Elizabeth waved her long index finger.

"No phones," she said.

"I don't understand," I said, my jaw slackening.

"This is a private event for people who value privacy," she said, taking my bag before I could have one last check of my phone. "No one wants candid shots of the night popping up on Instagram. Even the security cameras are off tonight."

Elizabeth passed my belongings to a stout, middle-aged woman at a coat check station a few feet from us who received my personal effects with equal solemnity.

I'd only taken a couple of steps toward my assigned room when I realized I'd left the key for Regina in my bag. Opting to avoid further confrontation with Elizabeth and the coat lady, I decided I'd have to wait until the end of the night to give the key to her. I joined the party and began to focus on the people, the space, and how they would come together to tell the story of the night.

Again, I wish I'd known what was really important to look at, because had anyone told me that story would include the murder of Charlie Archibald, billionaire/founder and managing partner of Lion's Mane Capital, I would have thought the crystal light fixtures and that gold gilt that followed wherever I looked had gotten the better of them.

CHAPTER 3

Murder being the furthest thing from my mind at that moment, however, I was not aware that the people I met might soon be suspects, or that the way they circulated through the party might later reveal their motives, or that the objects around me were the stuff of murder weapons.

Instead, thirty minutes later, I was circulating among a dozen or so perfectly groomed women in white, formal gowns, about nineteen or twenty years old, who sipped champagne and nibbled on hors d'oeuvres. As it turns out, attending a ball that at least originally had something to do with meeting husbands somehow included dressing like a bride-to-be. I've watched enough *Say Yes to the Dress* to know these truly beautiful women and their equally breathtaking gowns could have all been featured in Brides.com. At least I now understood Manjeet's comment about not wearing white. Even more impressive, the ladies here had *two* escorts, one for each side, who were dressed in what I learned was white tie, like genuine Disney princes.

As for the RMS team, this included Jinx and the gossipy crew I'd spied earlier outside the hotel, all of whom were now a chorus of smiles. Regina, who exuded both order and fun in a low-cut emerald-green velvet dress, hair in an updo, fabulous, gaudy jewelry only she could pull off, and her signature pointy shoes, divided the debs into groups for the individual portraits to keep things moving. Seeing Regina in action, I understood why her studio was the go-to place for capturing society's most glamorous events. She had a skill of managing type-A personalities with diplomacy and discretion, something the guests seemed to value highly.

My new boss gave me a nod after instructing our team on the plan for the evening, but I knew I was in a sink-or-swim situation. The RMS team was on familiar terms with many of the girls. They caught up with them on love lives and summer trips. When the girls and their escorts were heading out to form a reception line for the guests, even the predicted tear was shed when a woman in one of the most beautifully fitted gowns of the night somehow scraped the side of her hand against one of the crystal combs that held up her exquisitely adorned hair.

"Elizabeth? Can you help?" she said, looking for the party planner.

As it was, Elizabeth Everly was back in the reception hall, helping the debutantes assemble to greet the guests. In her stead, Regina beelined over to be of assistance. By the time she arrived, blood had started to pour at an impressive rate for a hair-accessory injury. The girl extended her hand as far from her gown's full skirt as she could as her tears began to well. I could see she was debating which would be worse, a bloody spot on her pristine dress or a puddle of mascara down her cheek. I felt for her. I don't know which I would have chosen.

I assumed the injured debutante would be in good hands with Regina. That is, until my new boss reached her. At the sight of the woman's blood, Regina retched. If the stakes hadn't been what they were, it would have been comical. Her gag was one of those gut spasms accompanied by a baritone *"huh"* from the throat. There wasn't even time for a ladylike hand to the mouth. I saw Regina was in serious trouble, blood not being her thing, so I grabbed a few cocktail napkins from an abandoned champagne tray and sidled up beside them.

"Let me help you," I said.

I pulled out a Band-Aid that I'd tucked into my bra. Regina, looking pale behind her makeup, mouthed a thank-you to me and scooted.

"Here you go," I said, hastily putting the bandage on the wound. "Just hold your hand up for a few minutes and you should be good to go. And here's an extra napkin to put in your glove, just in case."

"Thank you," she said and patted under her nose for good measure. "You're so kind. I'm Angela Archibald."

"Liv Spyers," I said.

Together, we headed to the reception room where the debutantes were shaking hands and introducing themselves to each arriving guest. I took my place in the adjacent garden room, which was located to the left of the stairs I'd originally climbed to the reception area. In this exquisite party space, every wall was painted to look like the grounds of a manicured French estate. A server, stationed at an open bar to the left of the room's entrance, poured drinks while most mingled among the shimmering lights. I quickly got to work, photographing gowns and bow ties and shiny smiles. Ranging in age from teenagers to some of the oldest people in, maybe, the world, everyone socialized cordially.

Although Angela Archibald was a guest of honor, I noticed it was her father, Charlie Archibald, who was the real star of the night. He was the alpha male of the ball with his elegantly tailored tuxedo, and gelled, dyed-black hair. As I moved through the cocktail hour, I was able to pick up from bits of conversations that he was at the helm of Lion's Mane, a leading venture capital company. He was, moreover, a *fintech guru*, that was the term everyone used. This seemed to be a haloed calling due to a new fund he had recently débuted called the LaunchTech Fund. He radiated confidence but was humbly charming to everyone. I decided it wasn't only his fintech savvy, but also his people skills that had gotten him where he was. I've worked my fair share of jobs, and I knew exactly where his real skills lay. Salesmanship.

When it was time for the party to dine, we made a pilgrimage the length of a football field to a flight of stairs at the other end of the reception hall. Descending, we headed through an oval room with more French garden murals, and up another staircase to arrive at an elegant dining room. Here, an elderly but strong hand touched mine.

"Excuse me," said a distinguished-looking gentleman in a velvet tuxedo jacket and holding a polished wooden cane. He had the posture of a soldier, in spite of his age. "I'd love a beautiful escort to help me find table four."

"My pleasure," I said, painfully aware that he did not need my help as his hand stayed on mine. I thought it fitting that his cane was carved into the shape of a snake, quite different from Poppy's, which was cushioned by tennis balls in DIY fashion.

When we arrived at table four, the table's host and hostess were busy helping their daughter gather her ambitiously full skirt around her seat. An elderly woman instead came to my rescue and extended her hand toward us. Her eyes were as bright as a twenty-year-old's while her body seemed as fragile as a China tea cup.

"Giorgio," she said. "You're late, as always, but I'm glad you made it on such short notice. A lady needs a date to these things."

I'd heard the woman say that the man was a late arrival, and I knew I was supposed to make sure that everyone was photographed tonight, but rather than raise my camera, my eyes became glued to one of the other guests at the round table. With his trimmed dark hair, offset by a nose that leaned slightly to the left but somehow worked, he was none other than the tuxedoed man from the subway whom I'd left holding my camera bag that morning. The boutonniere in his lapel had been refreshed to include a crisp, white rose. His face was clean-shaven. But it was him. He was seated next to a blond woman in a shimmering dress that plunged deeply, revealing her gorgeous décolletage. I found her immediately irritating.

I wasn't sure if I should hug him or slug him, but the coincidence proved that I was in a magical place. Or, if more realistically inclined, I'd walked into a society of people who probably wore formal evening attire as often as I wore pajamas, so odds were that if I were to ever see him again, it would be here. It was damn shocking, nonetheless. The thing was, he clearly recognized me, too, but made no motion to acknowledge our morning's mishap. Maybe losing equipment wasn't a big deal for him, but it was a game-changer for me. Unfortunately, I had to keep my mouth shut. I was the help who was expected to fade into the background, and I needed my job as much as I wanted my camera back. Given that confronting him was not an option, I slowly raised one eyebrow, a subtle but spine-chilling message my mother used to use on me when I was a kid to let me know when I'd crossed a line.

For a moment, he looked amazed. Then, to my astonishment, he smiled and raised an evil eyebrow right back at me.

"My dear," the hostess of table four said to me, her daughter's dress crisis now under control, "let's get our group photo out of the way, since we're all here. Giorgio, Harry, Allegra, Bernie, everyone, let's gather around Louisa."

Harry. I had a name.

As I raised my camera and focused my lens, a woman from table three beside us tugged at my dress. "Can you get us next?" she said.

Regina had divided the RMS team into five groups for dinner photos. I was not in my assigned area, but I did have a strategic proximity to Harry, which I wasn't ready to abandon. After finishing with table four, I moved on to table three.

"I'll speak with you later," I said to Harry, pretending to fix my dress as I passed him so that no one else heard me.

"Sure thing," he said with a cough into his napkin.

When I finished the photos at my next table, I saw Jinx at my assigned area of the dining room, at far-off tables that looked like they were in exile. I waved but she flashed me a look that rivaled the one I'd given Harry. I'd made no friends at RMS.

Fortunately, I'd worked my cousin's wedding, so I knew how to pace myself. Moving on to table five, I complimented dresses to loosen up guests, reminded them how beautiful their smiles were, and made sure no one looked too tall, or too small, or too fat, or too skinny.

I also strategically delayed photographing table eight, which was the Archibalds' table. I didn't want to interrupt the continued flow of handshakes, hugs, and kisses, but when I finally saw a lull in the action, I approached their table. A woman I decided was Angela's mother, from her striking resemblance to her daughter, was in the middle of making a toast. The group had finished raising their glasses in Angela's direction, and I was pleased with my timing. That is, until I realized she hadn't finished. She shifted her still-raised glass to Angela's father.

"Charlie," she said, "I have a word for you, too. Unlike the sycophants here tonight, I know you for who you are. And I love you anyway."

A half-hearted laugh went around the table as she reached her hand to her husband and enthusiastically kissed him on the lips. Although she did not seem to be drunk, it was a bolder gesture than the moment called for, and one I'd seen her repeat throughout the night. Angela glanced at me with a pained expression.

"Hello, can I get your photo?" I said, launching into my

routine and rounding up the crew. There were ten people at the table, two who were older, so I didn't want to disturb their seating.

"Let's gather around Grandmother and Grandfather," Angela said, seeming to agree with me. Angela reached out to include her grandparents' nurse, who had stepped to the side while the party gathered for their photo. She was a class act, and the only person at the ball to introduce me to her guests. In addition to her immediate family, they included two couples: Bill and Anne Topper, plus Miranda and Phil Headram.

"OK, looking good, everyone," I said, and raised my camera.

Through the frame of my tightly focused lens, I realized that the guests at table eight did not look particularly joyful, despite the love that everyone at the party had bestowed upon Charlie Archibald throughout the evening. Bill Topper, a man about Archibald's age but with sparse gray hair that stood so upright it defied gravity, steadfastly refused to smile. His wife, Anne, a forty-something woman with a crown of blond hair glued back in an array of embellished hair accessories, stood next to him Although Anne smiled broadly and Bill stayed by her side, there was a space between them that none of my coaxing could bring together. They were like two opposing magnets that could not connect. As hard as they tried, there was something keeping them apart.

On the other side of Angela stood Miranda Headram, heavy set and covered in diamonds that were as overdone as her makeup, with her lips set in a thin line.

"Let's make sure everyone smiles," I said.

Her lips got thinner. Her husband, Phil Headram, grinned peevishly beside her. Given the loose fit of his tuxedo, the out-of-date size of his lapels, and the slight shine to his suit's fabric, I decided his wife's diamonds were probably fake.

Even Mr. Archibald, all smiles until then, briefly lurched out of the picture frame as if he'd been caught off guard by something. I wondered if the challenge of this unruly group was why Regina had assigned the more seasoned Jinx to this area of the dining room. I did my best, but they were my most challenging table.

When I finished my last table's portrait, table six, a markedly more cheerful bunch who smiled on command, I inhaled deeply and stretched my shoulders back. I was handling the night well.

What followed was a collective "*Uhhh*"-slash-"*ooh*"-slash-"*oh honey*" chorus and immediately I realized it was directed at me. The mother of table six's debutante reached into her empty wine glass. She retrieved something from it which she handed to me. I saw immediately that it was one of the crystal buttons I had sewn to the front of my dress. I humbly thanked her for returning it to me and sidestepped out of the room.

Once again I was down the stairs, across the romantic oval room, and up the other set of stairs. This time, I was clutching the bodice of my dress. Worse, Charlie Archibald left the dining room at the same moment. Our steps fell into sync.

The same journey that had been dazzling an hour earlier was now excruciating. I could think of nothing to say to Charlie Archibald. Thankfully, he did not appear to have anything to say to me. He seemed to be thinking, his charm on autopilot while his smile was tucked away. As we made our way down the finish line of the reception room, Archibald finally looked up.

"Bess," he said with a nod to Elizabeth Everly, who was conversing with the coat check lady.

"Mister Archibald," she said with an icy tone and without making eye contact.

I opened the door to the restroom, but something made me stop, the door handle still in my grip. I thought Archibald's familiar greeting and Elizabeth's cold reply was odd given the help's goal of making all guests feel special. I watched as

Archibald continued to the end of the garden room and to a set of doors that were ajar, revealing yet another ball room that was to be the next part of our night.

"There you are," he said to someone behind the door. I was surprised to hear a menacing tone in his otherwise silky voice. "We need to talk. I have a business proposition for you."

I wanted to take a photo of how the light bounced off his shoes and added a flash of danger to his already intimidating transformation. I also wanted to know who had prompted him to use that tone. Instead, Archibald stepped into the ball room and disappeared. And I, in the spirit of RMS's protocols, remained in the background. I continued into the ladies' to repack my boobs.

Chapter 4

"Aaaarrrgh," I said, staring at my wardrobe malfunction in the mirror.

The button that had popped off my dress had been located halfway down my bodice, leaving me looking as if I'd forgotten to pull myself together after canoodling with someone in a coat closet. I reached into my bra and felt around for a safety pin I'd tucked away, but it was gone. I realized it had probably fallen out earlier when I'd given Angela her Band-Aid.

"Crap, crap, crap," I said.

A toilet flushed. I hadn't even looked to see if I was alone, and immediately regretted my outburst. I was appeasing myself that my choice of four-letter words could have been a lot worse when the door opened, and Jinx's image met me in the reflection of my mirror. I smiled sheepishly and nodded.

Jinx nodded back, washed her hands, added some hand sanitizer for good measure, and wordlessly leaned against the wall. I knew she was sizing me up, and it didn't help that I was futilely trying to make the pin of my ID card work as a fastener across my chest. I decided, however, that I'd about had it with the hazing routine.

"Shouldn't you be in the dining room?" I said.

"I like to be in the ballroom when they arrive," she said. "The entrance photos are usually pretty good."

I looked back at my reflection and took a deep breath to test my ID card solution. It flew right off. Jinx sighed as if I was utterly useless.

"I can't imagine how many nineteen-year-old boys are salivating over your mishap right now," she said.

In a move that suddenly made me feel like an absolute jerk for any ill-will I'd harbored toward her, Jinx pulled out a small pouch from the cuff of her long-sleeved dress and handed me a safety pin from inside it. My button easily slid through the needle, and I fastened it to my dress. Success!

"Thanks," I said, penitently. "Listen, I'm sorry about taking your area of the dining room. An old man asked me to escort him."

"I saw. He's a letch," she said. "So, what's your story?"

Jinx hiked up her dress and retrieved her lipstick from a garter underneath. She joined me at the mirror and began to reapply.

"Regina's giving me a shot tonight," I said. "Carpe diem, right? What about you?"

"I'm looking for a rich husband." she said very matter-of-factly. "Meantime, the job pays well, and there are extra perks. Someone always sends back their entrée for a vegetarian meal, so if you swing by the serving trays near the kitchen you can get yourself a free steak or chicken dinner. And you'll be shocked with what you can sometimes pick up from these parties. I saw someone toss a piece of jewelry in the trash. I guess it was a copy, and someone else was wearing the real thing, so out it went before anyone noticed. But, as they say, one man's trash is another's treasure."

She tucked her lipstick back into her garter. "You ready?"

"I've got to . . ." I nodded toward one of the stalls.

"Don't dawdle," said Jinx.

I didn't. And when I stepped back into the reception hall, I could hear the echo of dinner guests beginning to leave the dining room. Following my new friend's recommendation, I walked through the garden room to the even more beautiful ballroom, which was filled with tables around a large dance floor. Jinx was not inside. Neither was Charlie Archibald. I positioned myself by a pillar not far from the doors so that I had a great angle as the guests entered the room.

I stood there for about a minute. No one came and I was starting to think that maybe Jinx had messed with me, when I heard noise from behind a pillar at the other end of the room, followed by a muffled curse.

Regina, eyes glued to her phone, stepped out from behind the obstruction and marched across the ballroom as I tucked myself behind the column so she could not see me.

"*You'll never get it*," she said, while appearing to text her words into her phone. Her expression as she typed was both defiant and smug.

I wondered what had caused her outburst, but Regina's face turned from one of general disgust to one of gracious smiles as the guests reached the door. Along with her, my focus switched to their excited faces as they entered the dazzling room that awaited them.

Once the company found their new tables, my shutter worked at a furious pace to capture the presentations of the debutantes, followed by a traditional waltz with their escorts, and, finally, a father-daughter dance to "Thank Heaven for Little Girls." I was happy to see Angela and Charlie Archibald enjoying their dance after having sensed some tension at their table earlier.

When the band broke into "Don't Stop Me Now" by Queen, I was surprised to see everyone, young and old, pour onto the dance floor. In no time, I found myself essentially at a college party, albeit a very expensive one. The drinks flowed. The elegant lighting during the presentations changed to colorful hues. The importance of keeping white dresses pristine was replaced with the debutantes' appetite for fun.

I decided it was the perfect time to discuss the return of my camera with Harry, who I saw at the edge of the dance floor. As I approached, I passed the Archibalds' table. I noticed Angela's grandparents and nurse had left early, and most of their crew were now on the dance floor, but Charlie Archibald and his friend, Bill, remained at the table. They were having a heated conversation despite the loud music. Archibald patted Bill's arm, but his friend gritted his teeth and fiddled with an object in his left hand, as if trying to contain his irritation. Their dynamic was distinctly at odds with the social mores of the party.

"I was wondering when you were going to find me," Harry said with an easy smile when I reached him.

"I don't want trouble," I said. "I just want my camera back. I saw you with it as the train pulled away."

"Trouble?" he said, looking genuinely surprised by my direct confrontation. "I feel like we haven't gotten off to a good start. Can we try this again?"

He stepped forward, which put him on the dance floor. I really had no idea what to make of this guy, but I followed. The music changed tempo, as if knowing the man's every whim. He slipped his arm behind me as an old-timey Gershwin song my granny likes to sing while doing the dishes began to play. Fortunately, my camera acted as a barrier to keep me from getting too close to him.

"It's Liv, right?" he said.

"How do you know that?"

"I found one of your cards with your belongings and texted you before I left tonight to say I'd be happy to drop off your camera. Sorry it took me so long to reach out, but I was in meetings all afternoon," he said, gliding me into a waltz I had no trouble following. I felt my blood rush and my cheeks redden.

"They made me leave my phone at coat check, so I haven't checked it in hours," I said. "My equipment means a lot to me. Losing it was a big deal. It's Harry, right?"

"Harry Fellowes," he said.

"Do you rotate through these parties, day and night?" I said, shifting the subject away from my accusations of theft. "Your dry cleaner must work fast."

He laughed. It was a nice laugh. Genuine; not practiced.

"That was my aunt Bernie you met at our dinner table," he said. "She was hellbent on me coming. I had no idea I'd be bumping into you here. Turns out, it's not the worst party I've ever been to."

It wasn't the worst party I'd ever been to either. I was painfully aware that I was in a ballroom, in a silky gown, with a handsome man.

"What happened to your date?"

"Allegra? She's Bernie's goddaughter," he said. "It was my job to escort her tonight, but I didn't need to. She found her ex-boyfriend. They left together about an hour ago."

As much fun as I was having, I also knew I'd be in big trouble if Regina saw me fraternizing with the guests, so I pulled away.

"I'll see you again," I said. "To get my camera."

"I'll get it to you as soon as possible," he said. "I'm sure as a photographer that was an incredibly upsetting accident."

The music shifted back to a more spirited song, and Bernie appeared at the edge of the dance floor. I offered my hand to help her. I had a feeling she'd been coming to this party since she was the current debutantes' age.

"Come on, Harry boy," she said. "Be a good nephew and dance with me."

She dove onto the dance floor with her nephew, and I watched some of the debutantes gather around them. Additionally, I saw Charlie Archibald once again under fire, this time by Miranda Headram. Charlie looked annoyed by her, as if she were a gnat flying around him that he wanted to swat. Miranda seemed to sense his desire to get away from her, too. I saw her take Archibald's wrist in her hand and squeeze it hard. She had a smile across her face for appearance sake, but I could tell that whatever she was saying cut like ice. When she finished, she left Archibald on the dance floor. Angela came to his rescue, and I could see that he was truly relieved and happy to dance with her. I took the opportunity to take their picture.

"Well done," said Jinx, sidling up next to me and nodding in the direction of Harry. "I've never seen him before. He's cute."

"Oh, Harry? I know him from before tonight," I said. It wasn't entirely a lie.

I took a sip of water from a passing tray and dabbed my lips. I needed a breath of air at this point and headed to the garden room, which I knew would be empty. I stopped at the doors though because a scene was unfolding right outside the ballroom. A woman dressed in a dark gray pantsuit that was very chic but completely inappropriate for the night's festivities was making a beeline down the reception hall and toward the ballroom.

Elizabeth Everly ran behind her until she was on the woman's heels.

"I have to speak to him," the woman said to Elizabeth. "This is urgent. Or if you could just tell him I'm out here, I know he'll come speak to me."

"Miss Cromwell," said Elizabeth, once again supporting my theory that I'd stepped into a very small world where anyone who was anyone was known. "I'm sorry, but you'll have to leave. I can see you are upset, but you will have to wait in the lobby or speak to him tomorrow. The guest list is very strict. I'm sure you can understand."

As she spoke to Miss Cromwell, I noticed security guards were arriving. I felt sorry for her, but I understood Elizabeth's position. Miss Cromwell had trouble written all over her, and this was not a night for real-life worries. I had a hard time imagining the woman would wait in the lobby, however, because the party raged on until well after midnight. And even then, although the older folks hobbled home, the younger crowd left for after-parties.

I was relieved when my work was officially done. I'd taken some good photos, survived on my heels, made a work friend in Jinx, and had even rescued Regina from Angela Archibald's bloody hand. I had a feeling I was going to be a regular at RMS and it felt good. I still owed Regina her key, so I reclaimed my coat and bag where I left them. The thing was, I could not find Regina. The rest of the RMS team had left as well.

I figured Regina would stay until the ballroom had emptied out entirely, but I knew she smoked. Perhaps she'd taken advantage of the party winding down to slip out for a quick nicotine fix.

I wondered if I should pack up and go looking for her. I decided not to. What would my elegant, new boss think if she found me in my big puffy coat at a black-tie event? I returned to the dining room and sat at an abandoned table at the far end of the room. I'd wait it out.

Charlie Archibald and his gang, minus Angela and her grandparents, still lingered in the mostly empty room. I had a feeling each of them was waiting for the others to leave so they could pick up whatever arguments they'd had brewing with Archibald. In addition to the Archibalds, there were a few other stragglers. The old man with the snake cane was still there. Maybe Bernie had been joking when she'd referred to him as her date, but either way he hadn't escorted her home. Not everyone here had good manners. Instead, he finished a large drink and thanked a waiter for bringing him a doggie bag of party leftovers before leaving.

The rest of the stragglers, except for the Archibalds, left, too. In a little while, it was just me and the waiter, who seemed to have pulled the short straw for overtime and stood by a wall in case the Archibalds needed his services.

While I was waiting, I fished out my phone from my bag. Appreciating the privacy the table's flower arrangements afforded me, I broke the no-phone protocol and sent a photo of the empty room to Maria with an apology that I would not be making it to even the tail end of her Wild Turkey party. She replied with a photo of her small apartment. A couple of people, mouths hanging open, were passed out on her sofa and behind them someone was doing a shot. I'd clearly missed a great night at Maria's, but I had no regrets. I next checked the texts Harry had left me. They were friendly and polite. There was something very charming about the guy.

When will you be free for the camera handoff? I typed.

Immediately, three dots flashed at the bottom of my screen. I was deeply focused on those dots, but I looked up when I heard movement from the Archibalds' table. Charlie Archibald rose and swiftly withdrew from the room, leaving the rest of his guests looking confused, irritated and ready to leave, too.

With what looked like a reassuring word to the table, Mrs. Archibald left the room as well. Their party was like a good reality show, and I found myself becoming more and more fascinated by them. Plus, Harry had left me hanging. The dots had disappeared without a note.

When Mrs. Archibald finally returned a few minutes later, she was alone. The guests looked at each other uneasily, and then Phil Headram rose and left the dining area. He limped, which I hadn't noticed about him when I took his photo earlier. His wife followed him out of the room shortly after. Phil returned without Miranda, at which point Anne Topper left. I supposed they were all using the facilities until I heard Bill call after his wife.

"Anne," he said, as if he'd done something to set her off.

Following suit, Bill rose to seek his wife, but in their continuing circus of entrances and exits, Anne returned without her husband.

Finally, Elizabeth Everly entered the room and cleared her voice. She approached the Archibalds' table and whispered into Mrs. Archibald's ear. I assumed she was hinting that it was time for everyone to go. I had to agree.

"I texted him." I heard Mrs. Archibald say this to those at the table, looking as frustrated as they did. "I don't know where he's gone. Whoever knows with him?"

"Well, if he doesn't come back soon, we're heading out," said Miranda. "You can tell Charlie that the party was lovely, no thanks to him."

"You know I'll say nothing of the sort," said Mrs. Archibald, staring at her phone as if willing a sign from her husband to appear.

There was still no sign of Regina, either. Delivering the key to her was beginning to feel less pressing. Deciding to call it a night, I rose from my hidden corner and slipped around the perimeter of the room to make my escape. When I reached the ballroom doors, Bill passed me on his way back in. At this hour, his hair now fell flat on his head and across his forehead. I realized that no one wanted to ditch Mrs. Archibald, but everyone wanted to leave. We'd all had a long night, but at least I'd be paid for mine.

As I crossed the garden room one last time, I heard a sound. It was a familiar retching noise I'd heard once already tonight. I looked over to the empty cherry bar and saw Regina, holding herself up with one hand.

"Hey," I said. "I've got your key."

I hadn't seen Regina drink during the night, but something wasn't sitting right. She looked like she was ready to let go of her dinner. Maybe it was food poisoning? I knew she would not want to make a mess on the carpet of the Pierre, especially with clients like the Archibalds still on the premises.

I looked back into the dining room and cleared my throat to catch the waiter's attention. When he looked at me, I made some universal gestures regarding the situation so that I did not call general attention to Regina. The man, still crisp in his uniform after a long night, must have been through this drill before because he nodded and waved his hand to let me know he understood and had me covered.

With help on the way, I headed to the bar to keep Regina company. When I arrived, I noticed that Regina was staring hard at the floor. Out of curiosity, I peeked over the bar and immediately realized Regina was not retching because of alcohol or food poisoning. A man lay prone beneath us. I recognized him as Charlie Archibald from his smooth black hair.

I've passed out in an inopportune spot or woken up with an arm or a leg hanging off of me as if it didn't belong to my body but I'd never seen anyone as wrecked as Archibald was now. He faced the hollow interior of the bar with one arm flung backward to Regina's pointy shoes while his feet faced straight up in an unnatural direction.

"Mr. Archibald, everyone is looking for you," I said.

I came around the bar to where Regina was standing and touched his shoulder. The phrase *dead drunk* came to mind. As if in slow motion, Mr. Archibald rolled toward me. His body made a thud so that he was now facing the chandelier above.

I have a stronger constitution than Regina Montague when it comes to blood, but when I got a look at Mr. Archibald's face I recoiled at the sight of his left eye. His lid was shut, but it was gruesomely swelled, and blood leaked out of the corner and down his nose. He looked like he had boxed ten rounds.

"Oh, shit!" I bellowed.

"Quiet," Regina snapped at me in a hushed but frantic voice.

"Look at him!" I said. "What the hell?"

I prayed he would take a breath, but he lay there, extremely still. I took a step back with the intention of getting help, but Regina grabbed my arm.

"What are you *do—*" I stopped. Regina's hand, which gripped my arm like a vise, was covered in blood. Wet, sticky blood. I looked at her other hand, which was also streaked in red. She did not seem to have any injuries herself.

"OK," I said. I felt my breathing pick up. I think I was talking to myself as much as Regina. "It's OK. It's OK. This is OK."

As I repeated this mantra, Regina dropped my arm. Free from her hold on me, I backed away across the garden room. The waiter was walking toward me with an empty champagne bucket that was presumably meant to help her if she got sick.

"Do you know CPR?" I said.

The man shook his head.

"Does someone know CPR?" I shouted into the ballroom.

Not waiting for an answer, I ran back to the body, where Regina was still standing over Archibald, staring at her hands and breathing erratically.

"He's dead," Regina said, suddenly looking at me with saucer-like eyes. "I . . . I . . ."

"You what? What did you do?" I said to Regina. "How did this happen?"

"I don't know," said Regina. "I don't know. I've got to get out of here. Let me get out of here."

The waiter leaned over the bar.

"Jesus, lady," he said, making the sign of the cross. "What did you do? Hey, I'm not going to get messed up with murder. What are you, crazy? Jesus."

"She didn't murder anyone," I said, and turned back to Regina. "Did you?" I hated the accusatory tone in my voice.

"Did she do what?" I heard Bill Topper say from behind me.

"Murder," the waiter said. "I've got nothing to do with this. Nothing. I didn't see her do nothing."

"What's going on?" Miranda Headram now said.

I didn't need to turn around to know that the Archibald party was joining us.

Regina tried to take a step away from the body, but her legs buckled. She put her hand on the bar to steady herself and clutched the champagne bucket the waiter had brought to her chest. In doing so, it slipped from the bar and she raised it erratically to steady herself.

"Watch out," said Bill. "Stand back, everyone. Put it down, Regina."

"Damn you, Charlie," she said.

"Oh my God, what did you do, Regina?"

"Stay back, Donna."

"Don't look."

"Thank God you found her before she escaped."

I'd stopped following who was saying what, but I had a feeling the last remark referred to me. All at once, the voices around me faded. Shock was setting in and to soothe myself, I did what I know best. I studied the setting as if it was a photograph, frozen in time. Instead of adding to the growing screams and panic in the room, I instinctively surveyed the area around Archibald.

Not surprising, beside Archibald's head was a pool of blood that seemed to come from his eye. Near Archibald's midsection I noticed shards of glass and a puddle of red wine. Given his eye injury, it followed that a piece of glass somehow lodged into his eye in a way that could kill him. Unfortunately, the broken pieces lay by his torso, not his face, which would make it hard for anything deadly to have reached his eye.

I looked for a protruding object near his head that might have caused the injury; maybe a nail, or a pointy edge of the cart, or some sort of peg to hang a rag from. I prayed I'd see something, a simpler explanation to Archibald's death than murder. Unfortunately, the edge of the bar was curved, and the empty, interior space was finely finished without any jagged projections to catch on. I shivered as I noticed a petal from Archibald's boutonniere, which lay beside his shoulder. Half of the petal was curled from the weight of his blood.

The voices in the room began to return. I noticed Phil Headram and Bill Topper had moved to the two exits in the room to block any means of escape for Regina.

I clutched my camera to me like a safety blanket and felt my head grow light.

CHAPTER 5

"Hey," I heard a man say.

I felt someone tap my hand and then my cheek.

"Come on now, you're OK," the voice said.

I opened my eyes long enough to see a stranger in an EMT jacket, and then I closed them.

"She's OK," the man said. "Coming out of it."

"Detectives'll be here soon," said another man.

I thought of Archibald's eye while I kept my own closed. I'd never fainted before, but apparently, I now had. The smell of a full-bodied red wine filled my nostrils and I swallowed hard. I touched the back of my head and felt a lump where I must have hit the floor. After another moment, I surrendered to curiosity. I opened my eyes.

Fortunately, I'd had the good sense to take a couple of steps back before I'd blacked out.

I pushed myself up against one of the beautifully painted walls. Charlie Archibald's face was turned toward me with his swollen, bloody eye. The guys from the EMS team stood beside him, but they were making no attempt to resuscitate.

I looked away, across the sparsely populated room. The waiter was by the ballroom's doors drinking a large glass of wine. The others, those who knew Charlie Archibald, looked both shocked and frightened. Mrs. Archibald sat in an alcove within the garden room with Anne Topper and Miranda Headram. She rocked quietly back and forth and cried soft, pained tears while her companions comforted her.

Regina appeared more sedate now. She sat alone, drinking a glass of water. I could see she'd tried to wipe the blood from her hands but her fingers were still red, as if she'd done a bad job at removing nail polish. Everything that was once bright about her seemed to have dulled, down to the emerald of her dress and the light of her dazzling accessories. A security guard was stationed beside her. I got the feeling from his frozen stance that he felt he was as in a jungle and standing next to an angry lioness, rather than at the Pierre beside a shaking woman ornately bejeweled in a formal gown.

I stood and made my way to her, hoping she could tell me what had happened now that the initial shock and panic had subsided. Before I could speak, Regina raised a hand to me.

"You're new," she said in a quiet voice of steel. "I know that. But I made myself very, very clear. You were here to be invisible while making the guests feel important."

"What?"

"Putting me at the scene of a dead body with blood on my hand. Inviting a waiter to witness the scene and announce that I'm a murderer. Fainting on top of it . . . well, does that fit the bill? I don't think so. Here's some free advice. In the future, leave dead bodies for someone else to find."

It wasn't advice I'd ever expected to receive from anyone. How often did photographers stumble across corpses in New York?

"Thanks to your lack of discretion, Regina Montague Studios will be cancelled," Regina continued. "People like a good scandal, but they also know better than to hire the woman who's been accused of murder."

"I'm sorry," I said. "I'll explain everything to the police. Of course, you didn't kill Mr. Archibald."

Regina had been found with blood on her hands, but I'd seen her shock, fear, and bewilderment. I didn't have any experience with homicide, but she hadn't looked like someone who had just killed a man in cold blood.

"Pish," she said.

I looked for a fresh glass of water to offer her, but the tray beside us was filled with odds and ends from the end of the night. A half-empty wine glass, a steak knife, a bobby pin, a button, even a steel tack from the bottom of a dining chair that must have come loose. Whatever was on that tray was eclipsed, however, by a napkin streaked in blood. I knew it was Charlie Archibald's blood and that Regina had used it to wipe her hands.

A man in a dark suit along with two policemen arrived at the entrance to the garden room.

Bill appeared beside him, as well as Phil.

"Ladies and gentlemen," the new arrival said to the room. "I'm Detective Thorne with the NYPD. I'm responding to a call regarding the suspicious death of a white, middle-aged man found on these premises tonight. This is a procedural visit at this point in time, but I will need to ask for your full cooperation."

As one officer began to string tape around the space where Archibald had fallen, Thorne led us all back to the ballroom and had us sit at separate tables. I counted seven other people: Mrs. Archibald, the Toppers, the Headrams, the waiter, and Elizabeth Everly, who looked as if her career was as doomed as mine going forward. Regina was noticeably absent. It seemed she had been moved somewhere else for her interrogation.

Thorne made the rounds, asking for contact information and jotting down details volunteered to him about the night. We were all too far from each other for me to hear the particulars, but I could see from everyone's body language that each person tried to impress upon Detective Thorne how much they'd admired Charlie Archibald and how devastated they were by his death. The detective politely thanked each, dismissed them, and then moved on. He stopped briefly to take a call which must have been from his wife. I heard him grumble about the inconvenience of a murder right before a holiday. When he finally approached me, I was the last person in the room.

"I appreciate your help," said Thorne. He sat at my table and after taking my basic info, he got down to business. "How long have you worked this circuit?"

"This was my first night on the job." And my last, I thought. "I met Regina this morning. She needed an extra photographer and liked my work."

"So, you're the newbie here and you found the dead body," he said. "How did you get the job?"

"Regina came by my photography studio," I said. "She lives nearby me."

"Was she behaving oddly when you met her?"

"No."

"What did she say?"

"That she liked my portfolio and that I could work the ball tonight. One of her photographers had quit unexpectedly. That's all. After that, an alarm to my grandparents' house upstairs went off so we were interrupted."

"Was there a break-in at your grandparents' house?"

"It was a false alarm," I said, shaking my head.

"What was the last thing she said to you this morning?"

I thought. "She was in good spirits. She made a joke that she didn't do well with sirens and then she told me not to screw things up tonight."

"Which brings us to tonight. Did you see Regina Montague kill Charlie Archibald?"

"No," I said, adamantly. "That was an assumption the waiter made."

"An assumption based on the fact that you and he found

Regina Montague standing over the body of Charlie Archibald with his blood all over her hands and saying that she had to get away from the scene, followed by her raising a champagne bucket threateningly as others arrived on the scene," said the detective. "Did you see a murder weapon?"

"No."

"Did you see her toss or try to hide anything as you approached her?"

"No!" I said. "Why would she have planned to kill Charlie Archibald, especially at a huge ball?"

"This appears to be a crime of passion," said Thorne. "Not pre-meditated. Therefore, something happened at this shindig to trigger so much rage that someone, perhaps Regina Montague, felt compelled to kill in a public space."

"Even before his death, Charlie Archibald had had a hell of a night," I said, hoping to help Regina's defense. "His wife's affections were erratic. Bill Topper picked a fight with him during the dance. Miranda Headram also had strong words with him on the dance floor. Before Regina discovered the body, everyone at the Archibalds' table left the room and came back again. Couldn't they have had time to kill him? Also, I heard Archibald speak in a creepy tone to someone behind the ballroom door earlier in the night."

"Who was it?" said Thorne.

"I don't know," I said, realizing that my observations might seem less convincing compared to finding someone standing over the body with blood on them. I had one other piece of ammo in my small arsenal, however. My photos never lied. I didn't have a photograph of Bill or Miranda fighting with Archibald, but I did have my portrait of their table. "Look at my work from tonight. I think my photos will speak volumes about the Archibalds' group. They didn't seem happy. Any of them."

"I hope those photos are good because the security cameras

were turned off tonight. Hoity crowd likes their security without cameras. The hotel's security team has at least assured us that no one arrived or departed from the party during the time that Mr. Archibald left his table."

"I'm telling you, there's a list of suspects who were on the scene at the time of Archibald's death, aside from Regina Montague," I said.

"Let's get back to Miss Montague. Did she seem upset with Mr. Archibald or any member of their party during the night?"

"No. But as I said, others did."

"What was her condition when you found her in the room by the deceased body?"

"Shock. She was leaning on the bar, as if she might fall. And she was retching. I know you are questioning her, but she couldn't have done it. She has a serious fear of blood."

Thorne nodded as I spoke, but I could tell my blood theory vis-a-vis her innocence didn't carry much weight with him. Maybe it was because his wife was angry about his case coinciding with a holiday, but I had the feeling that Thorne's investigation was starting and ending with Regina. He was looking for reasons that Regina was guilty, not for how or why anyone else might have killed Charlie Archibald

"As I told the others," Thorne said while he replaced his notebook into his jacket pocket, "I'll ask you for the sake of a smooth investigation not to post any information online about the case or to speak to members of the press at this time. We're waiting for an autopsy before we officially call this a murder. Once we make that announcement, you should not be afraid for yourself. From the looks of the scene, the incident was directed specifically toward Mr. Archibald and no one else."

"Thanks," I said, although I hadn't even considered I might be in danger.

"It's a holiday tomorrow. I'm sure you'd like to get a little rest," he said, rising. "I won't keep you any longer, but we might need to contact you with more questions, so please be available to us. And here's my card if you think of anything."

I rose and gathered my belongings in an indignant manner for Regina's sake. I was not so incensed, however, that the gorgeous flower arrangement in the middle of our table missed my eye.

In my family, it's a point of pride to bring home table décor, extra goody bags, or anything else up for grabs at the end of the night. Even Jinx had mentioned about finding perks at these events. If ever anyone had earned a vase full of gardenias and roses, it was me.

"May I?" I asked Thorne.

"Sure," he said, barely looking in my direction as he left the room.

I scooped up the arrangement and stubbornly juggled it along with my belongings during the train ride home. When I reached my street, the sidewalk was empty, but I was sensitive to my surroundings and felt vulnerable with my hands full instead of free to fight. The streetlights were on, but all that did was illuminate a rat that scurried into the gutter. Rodents are a typical sighting at night, no matter the neighborhood, but bumping into one now did not ease my nerves.

My discomfort worsened about half a block away from my stoop, where I noticed a man was sitting on my grandparents' steps. I stopped. I was ready to scream if I needed to call for help.

He hadn't seemed to notice me, so I crossed the street for a better look. I put my flowers down to retrieve my phone and dial the police.

"Liv?" the man called to me.

To my surprise, the man was Harry Fellowes, still in his evening attire and with my long-lost camera bag sitting right beside him. I don't think I'd ever been so pleased to see any two things.

"What are you doing scaring a girl in the middle of the night?" I said.

"I sent you a text," he said, standing to greet me.

"Oh my God." I broke into a smile as I crossed the street. "I felt my phone buzz on the subway, but I had all this stuff I was carrying."

Harry took off his coat, a dark gray wool that looked like it could melt like butter if you touched it.

"Are you OK?" he said, putting his coat over my shoulders. "News travels fast with this crowd. Aunt Bernie told me about Archibald and how you found Regina all bloody and standing over him. She said they're questioning her. You must be in shock."

"I was in shock but now I'm mostly tired," I said, impressed with the speed of gossip in high society. "I've got to help cook a Thanksgiving turkey in the morning. And my parents and baby sister are coming in for the day."

"You have a baby sister?" Harry smiled.

"Well, she's four," I said. "When I left for college my parents' rekindled their love life. When I came back home from college, it was quite cozy set up at our house. Try coming home late when you share a room with a toddler. I had to move out."

The soft wool hung loosely around me, but I could feel the warmth from Harry's body bounce onto mine, even over my puffy coat. I sat on the stoop. Harry sat back down next to me. I didn't stop him.

"You know, my grandmother always says, *l'abito no fa il Monaco*," I said. "It's Italian for *the robe doesn't make you a monk*. And she's right. All these successful people seemed so happy and secure tonight, but behind the glitter of diamonds was a guest with one very dark heart."

"I thought Regina was the one under suspicion."

"She's the one who had the blood on her hands and Detective Thorne seems certain that she did it, but there were people who had hostile encounters with Archibald tonight. As far as I know, Regina did not have any words with him."

"I'm sure the police will look at everything," he said.

"They'll look for facts, but I spent the night studying their faces, their behaviors."

I pointed to my eyes.

"My secret weapons," I said.

"Speaking of which," he said, and handed me my camera bag, which I gingerly took from him. "I figured after what you'd gone through, getting this back would cheer you up."

"I can't tell you how much I appreciate it," I said. "Photography is more than a business to me. I've had a camera in my hands since the day my dad gave me a used Nikon for my tenth birthday."

"You're lucky to have such a passion," he said.

"Why? What do you do when you're not at these soirees?"

"Me?" He looked hesitant. "I appraise art for insurance policies."

"You're an insurance guy?"

I didn't know anyone in insurance, but I never imagined a policy manager to be a high-flying society man. Harry nodded, as if knowing what was going through my head.

"I spend my days looking at art and deciding how much it's worth," he said. "More or less."

"Are you at least artistically inclined?" I said.

"Nope," he said. "In fourth grade art class, I questioned why a painting of a soup can was worth millions. I doodled one in my notebook and told the class it was for sale. I went to a private school and a kid in my class had a real-deal soup can painting in his house. He told his parents about me. They called mine. After that, my creative expressions were not encouraged but my education on the business of art was."

"You were robbed," I said. "I bet you doodled a great soup can. I challenge you to create another one."

"Deal," he said, reaching his hand to me to shake on it.

I did and he held it to help me to my feet. I could see he was cold and gave his coat back to him.

"So . . . are you on Instagram?"

"No, I don't like any of that. It's never as fun as seeing someone in person," he said. "But I have your number. You have mine. When I complete my art project, can I come show it to you?"

"I hope you will," I said, amazed to meet someone my age who didn't at least have one social media account.

"Good," he said. "And I'm glad you're OK."

"Crazy day."

"Crazy," he said and gave me a smile before heading down the street.

My first big job in New York had ended with one of the most horrific images I'd ever seen, but strangely, all in all, the night had had a bright spot. I took a breath of the City's late night air, that wonderful mixture of sea breeze and soot, and opened my gate. I wasn't feeling scared anymore, just tired. I pushed my mountain of clothes off my single-sized bed and promised myself I'd clean up tomorrow.

I climbed into bed and scrolled through the early news. Sure enough, the story of Charlie Archibald's death was big. Not only was he a co-founder in a successful venture capital company with success in the fintech space, but he was also a philanthropic supporter of many New York institutions and even had his own foundation. I usually love the *Post*'s headlines, but I'd never felt connected to one. When I read *Snapped* across their top story, I knew it included news that the prestigious Regina Montague had been found with blood on her hands. My fear that Detective Thorne was focused only on Regina seemed to be coming true.

I leaned over to the lamp on my nightstand and turned it off. Ten minutes later, I turned it on again. I had not sent the photos of the night to RMS as I had been instructed to do. I grabbed my camera and downloaded the photos onto my laptop.

"Oh, no," I said aloud.

The first thumbnail was of Charlie Archibald's dead body. I realized my finger must have hit the shutter before I'd passed out. Grabbing my phone, I found Detective Thorne's card and emailed the photo to him.

I'd told Harry I could see things others could not. Challenging myself, I flipped through the photos I'd taken of the Archibalds. I looked at the images where my lens had been focused on their party directly, and others where I could see the Archibalds, Toppers and Headrams in the background. There was nothing among them that the police would find interesting enough to switch their focus from Regina. I had to believe, however, that I had clues to the story of how Charlie Archibald had gone from being the most celebrated attendee of the Holiday Ball to being stabbed in the eye and left to die. I would look at those photos every day until I saw something I hadn't seen before. Meanwhile, I sent a copy of my files to RMS. A job was a job.

I turned the light out.

As I drifted to sleep, I heard my grandmother enter the kitchen right above me. Early as it was, I knew she had gotten lucky on her turkey hunt in Yonkers and was starting in on her roast. I also realized in my haze that something didn't look right in the image of Charlie Archibald I'd sent to Detective Thorne. I couldn't think what it was.

"Antony," I heard my grandmother shout. "What did you do with the turkey baster?"

I buried my head under my pillow. My last thoughts as I drifted to sleep were of Regina in her wonderful emerald-green dress.

Chapter 6

After what felt like five minutes, the sound of my baby sister blessed my ears. I was too beat to move, except for my lips, which involuntarily smiled. I knew the clock was no later than maybe eight, but Eliza's small feet thundered like one hundred thousand elephants across my ceiling.

"Poo-*py*," she cried from above me, bursting into laughter over her funny interpretation of my grandfather's nickname.

I lay still, the events of the ball drifting back to me. It was hard to believe that last night had existed at all. I could easily have dreamt it if it were not for my aching feet. Fortunately, the continued giggles of the munchkin, and the scents beginning to waft into my apartment from the kitchen above, conquered both my fatigue and anxieties about my life. I rolled any part of me that was willing to move off the bed and managed in that way to get up.

I checked my phone and swallowed hard when I saw an email from RMS. I was sure it was a note to say that I would no longer be welcome to work at Regina Montague Studios. I was therefore surprised when I realized it was a company-wide memo. It stated that staff should pick up outstanding paychecks due to us as early as Friday. The note made no mention that Regina was a prime suspect in a murder. I wondered if Detective Thorne had come to his senses.

Following the unwritten rule of a day-two blow out, I showered with my head hanging through the curtain. I then threw on the Spyers-Carrera holiday uniform, which consists of bottoms that have an elasticized waist, and an age-appropriate hoodie or cardigan, which remains open while eating, so that food stains are easily covered once the meal is over. When we stand around the table for grace at any holiday, we look like Olympians in a rainbow of track suits, favored to win the all-around gold for eating.

By the time I'd dressed, I felt the color returning to my cheeks and decided not to let Charlie Archibald ruin my holiday. Humming the Olympics Anthem, I jogged out of my apartment—my flower arrangement held triumphantly—took a sharp right, took another sharp right, sun shining, and jogged up the stairs and into my grandparents' home.

"Gobble, gobble, where's Eliza?" I said, popping into the kitchen and placing the flowers onto the crowded kitchen counter. Eliza ran toward me from a hiding place in the pantry. As my young sister jumped into my arms, I smelled cinnamon and nutmeg in her hair.

"*Mia carina*," said my granny, rushing to the counter. "Sweet Liv. These are beautiful."

"Honey," my dad cried out to me. His greeting was followed by the echo of my mom. Their chorus warmed my heart. I knew in that moment that I would not share with my family what had happened last night. They were aware that I'd had a big job, but not the who, what, or where. Under normal circumstances, I'd be regaling them with every detail, but in this case, if they knew the whole story, Thanksgiving would be over before it started.

As we shared the duties of peeling, roasting, mashing and baking, Eliza ran circles around us in a pink sweatsuit decorated with turkeys down each side of the zipper. I dodged her playfully as I began to set the table.

"Honey, look how fancy our daughter has become in the big City," my dad said.

I looked at my parents, who were clearly sharing a laugh at my expense. Without noticing, I had begun to fold the napkins into a fan, as I had seen them do at the Pierre. Since I couldn't fight them, I raised the last napkin into the air and threw it over my shoulder like a fur stole.

"I declare," I said. "How *do* you all *do.*"

I strutted around the kitchen, swishing my imaginary stole, and vamping it up as my family cheered me on with whistles and raspberries. The water for the mashed potatoes boiled over, the front door rang, and Eliza began to follow behind me, copying my every move.

"Hello, dahling," I said to her over my shoulder.

"Hello, hot shot," Eliza answered.

"Pip pip," my mother said, joining the parade.

My grandmother cleared her voice at the entrance to the kitchen.

"Livia," she said.

We all stopped. She'd used my given name. That meant business.

"*Ma che cosa fa?*" She looked to her right with an expression of bewilderment. "What are you doing? We don't bite. Come here."

Harry stepped beside her. He was dressed in a suit and tie and wore that nice warm coat. All to say, his outfit was sacrilege in our kitchen on a holiday. He also carried a white paper bag.

"This man wants to see you, Liv," she said in a suspicious yet amused tone. "He says he knows you."

"I didn't mean to interrupt this family occasion. I was leaving this for you, Liv, by your door downstairs," said Harry. He raised the bag. "As I was closing the gate to leave, your grandmother heard me. When I explained I knew you, she insisted I come up rather than, what was it you said? Slink around."

"Of course, she did," said my mother. "Come and sit."

She dusted off a spot at the table and pulled out the chair. Granny innocently focused on the gravy.

I watched as Harry, a good foot taller than the tallest of us, obeyed my mother and crossed the room. I was aware that I still hadn't had a chance to get a word in to my visitor, and I was prepared to rescue him momentarily, but I was also enjoying the scene after having survived his world last night.

"So, how do you know each other?" she said in a sing-song voice before Harry had made contact with the seat.

"Long story," I said coming to his aid. "I lost my camera. He found it. And then we danced at a ball last night."

"It's like friggin' Cinderella and the glass shoe," said my grandmother over her steaming pot.

Eliza appeared at Harry's knee, her eyes keenly honed on his mysterious bag. "Is there candy in there?" she said.

"If I'd known I was going to see you, I'd have made sure there was. But can you help me deliver this present to your sister?" he said. He handed his parcel to Eliza.

I opened the small package she handed to me. It was an actual Campbell's soup can, emptied out. Harry had glued a doodle of a turkey over the company's logo. And as the pièce de résistance, a small succulent, the kind available in every other deli these days, was planted into the empty can. A simple trip to the deli had produced a respectable piece of work.

"Not bad," I said with an approving grin.

"And it's practical, too," Harry said proudly. "It will last longer than flowers." My mother slipped a napkin into Harry's coat collar.

"Mom, leave him alone," I said.

"Let's get you away from these clinchpoops," Poppy said.

Harry rose with a bewildered smile but followed Poppy as he hobbled down the hall. I joined them. When we reached the key shop, Poppy opened the door. He'd been leaving the store door open lately, which I didn't think was the best idea.

"Wow, look at that," Harry said about the old safe which sat under the window and still hadn't been picked up. "These safes were expensive in their day."

"You know your stuff," said my grandfather.

"Well, this is basically a work of art. Sort of my business, you could say. This looks like it was made in the 1920s," said Harry. He kneeled to the safe and leaned his ear against its combination lock. His hand reached for the worn brass handle beside it where the paint had been rubbed away from use in the last hundred years.

"Wasn't an easy one to open, but I did it," said Poppy.

"Congratulations. What was inside?"

"Ah, it was empty," said my grandfather.

"I guess people hold out hope for unexpected treasures," said Harry.

"Let me get a photo of you guys," I said and raised my camera.

The two of them complied and put their arms over each other's shoulders. Eliza then flew into the room. Without pausing to acknowledge any of us, she spit up on Harry's shoe as only a four-year-old can do, and then burst into tears. My mom ran in and picked up her baby, apologizing profusely all the way back to the kitchen with my dad following behind her. My grandmother lured my grandfather back to the kitchen as well.

"Alone at last," I said when the party had all left. "Want to sit outside?"

"Sure," Harry said.

I handed him the dish towel from my shoulder, and he wiped it over the top of his shoe. I opened the front door to the sunny sidewalk. We took a couple of steps down and sat on the stoop together once more.

"I found out some more information about last night's murder. Stop me if I'm wrong, but I thought you might be interested," he said.

"How?" I said. "Yeah, I'm definitely interested, but I didn't think with the holiday there would be any new announcements about the case today."

"My uncle, Aunt Bernie's husband, was in the FBI in his day. Bernie still has her way of getting information when she wants it."

"What kind of crazy people are you?" I said, interrupting the casual way he dropped the FBI into conversation. "Don't get me wrong. My family has their stories. But they're more along the line of how my Uncle Jimmy stuck a fishing hook in his thumb and index finger last year. It's a good story, but things like the FBI aren't in our repertoire."

"They've confirmed he was murdered. Regina is still the prime suspect," Harry said, while acknowledging the FBI angle with a simple *I know, right?* kind of nod of the head and what I could tell was genuine interest in hearing more about Uncle Jimmy when we'd finished with Archibald.

"Damn," I said. "I was hoping Thorne had decided to investigate other suspects. I still can't believe I found a murdered man. Did your Aunt Bernie hear anything that we won't see in the news?"

"You didn't think I was good for just a soup can, did you?" he said. "The news is gross though."

"Spill it."

"His eye was punctured by a long, thin, pointed metal object of some sort. It's not clear what the murder weapon was exactly, but it went deep enough to reach through to the brain. The coroner said the weapon would have had to be at least four inches long. Archibald would have lost the power to speak immediately, and quickly thereafter his brain squeezed the blood from reaching his heart. Murdered this way, there was relatively little blood loss, I guess compared to your usual stabbings. As these crimes go, it was a very unusual way to kill someone."

"And that was a very raw description before a big holiday meal." I shivered, already Googling long, thin, metal, and pointed murder weapons.

"Regina was questioned, and the police haven't given up on her being the killer, but they had to let her go for lack of evidence."

"Wikipedia says that when hats pins were in fashion, they were long enough that women sometimes used them to stab men who came on to them," I said. "There weren't any hats at the ball, but there were a lot of decorative hairpieces that could easily have had four-inch combs. I wonder if a woman with an updo was defending herself."

"Like Regina?" said Harry. "Maybe Archibald hit on her."

He had a point. She'd had an updo. I hadn't noticed her hair accessories. I wish I had.

"Liv," my father said at the door. "We're waiting at the table."

"I'm sorry about them," I said, nodding toward my house. "If you don't make your escape now, you'll be eating and burping and watching football with us all night. It's not pretty."

"Are you kidding? It sounds great," he said and straightened his tie. He stepped down a couple of stairs.

Oh, men. They come so far to woo you with succulents and chat about murder, and then forget to close the deal.

"Are you leaving without asking me out?" I said to help him along.

"No," he said, turning around, and looking at my dad behind me, who was watching the two of us. "How's tomorrow? Are you free?"

"I might be," I said.

"Great." He tripped a little down the last step.

"She's coming," my dad said in answer to a question posed to him from deep within the house.

While Harry headed down the block looking as if a carefully planned strategy had somehow gone awry, I turned to my father with a cool stare of filial wrath, and slow-burned my way past the figurine of St. Catherine on the front table, and back to the kitchen. We dragged Eliza from the television where she was re-watching the Macy's Thanksgiving Day Parade. My father said grace. We said *amen*, and then the eating began. Pants were loosened, rules were honored, and to my parents' relief, Eliza was fast asleep by the time we'd washed all the dishes, finished our wine, and said our goodbyes. I made sure my grandparents were both in their jammies before I went down to my place.

Before turning out the light, I posted the photo of Harry and my grandfather by the safe on @livspyersphotography and ended it with my plug about my services. I had no messages for a job from either my account or OneShot.com, but it was a holiday. Things were slow.

Instead of worrying about my future, I looked at the photos from last night, this time searching for long, pointy, metal items, at least four inches long, that could be used as a murder weapon. I focused on hair pieces, remembering how Angela Archibald had bled after she'd pricked herself with her own. All the women had something decorative in their hair. As for the men, they all wore boutonnieres, which were fastened with long pins to the lapels, but Google told me that boutonniere pins ran an average of two inches long. Too short.

I was about to turn off the light when something else hit me. I rebooted my laptop, realizing what had looked wrong to me in the picture of Archibald's dead body. I returned to the photo of the prone corpse, careful to avoid the sight of his battered eye. Instead, I zoomed in on Archibald's arm.

"Oh, Regina," I said.

Archibald's cufflinks had the same lion's head I had noticed on Regina's keychain. I also remembered that Archibald was the head of a company called Lion's Mane. I checked out their website. It didn't surprise me to see that the company's logo was the same lion's head. Despite my belief that Regina was innocent, she had a link to Charlie Archibald that was suspicious.

My first instinct was to tell Detective Thorne and hand over the key. I drafted a note to him, but I found myself unable to hit Send. Thorne didn't put much stock into the minute differences in someone's expression to understand what was going on inside their heads, but I did. It made the difference between a client picking one photo over another after a photography session, and I'd become highly attuned to picking up those clues before I presented work to my customers. In this case, I still believed the expressions and behaviors of the Archibalds' guests throughout the night were as suspicious as Regina's bloody hands

Regina was the first person to have given me a chance since I'd arrived in New York City. She'd taken a leap of faith on me. I decided to take that leap on her. I believed she was innocent. If I couldn't prove otherwise, and fast, I'd tell Detective Thorne about the key.

I needed something more than the abstract moments I'd witnessed last night to convince me to approach the police. I could easily locate the distinctive blue door of the building where I'd learned she lived. Tomorrow morning, I would visit her under the pretense of delivering her key and do some investigating myself.

I turned the light back off and fell asleep.

CHAPTER 7

Eight o'clock the next morning, I climbed the stairs up to the blue door of Regina's building. An older woman swept the sidewalk in front, but the streets were quiet after the holiday. Kids were still on break. Families were out of town or sleeping in. Even the traffic was lighter than usual for a Friday morning. Given my impending interview with Regina, I wouldn't have minded the comfort of the usual hustle and bustle.

I scanned the stainless-steel placket beside the door upon which a half dozen buttons to apartments were listed. Regina's name was not beside any of them.

"Excuse me," I said to the street sweeper. "Do you know a British woman who lives here?"

"She's out of town," the woman said, stopping her sweeping. "She left this morning carrying the big suitcase."

I looked up at the four-story building and considered the fact that Regina had apparently left town with a big suitcase. Her actions looked guilty. I'd come here in search of a sign, and this could surely be considered a significant one.

I'd never, ever used keys entrusted to me by a Carrera customer to trespass, but a murder accusation wasn't something I could ever take back. I promised myself that for the rest of my life, I'd never trespass unless homicide was involved. Then, I decided to cross the line.

"I was supposed to drop off something," I said to the street sweeper. "I have the key, but she forgot to tell me the apartment number."

"4A," the lady said. She brushed the debris into the gutter, climbed the stairs, and opened the front door, thank you very much. "We all heard the big suitcase on every step this morning."

I left the woman shaking her head as I climbed the stairs of a building that I immediately noticed lacked the pizzazz that Regina herself emanated. Aside from that shiny blue front door, the place was very average. There were two apartments on each landing. On the second floor, the paint was chipped along the wall and a cat mewed loudly from inside an apartment. On the third floor I noticed a moldy pumpkin, likely left over from Halloween.

When I got to the fourth floor, I found apartment A. The door was freshly painted. The doorknob was polished to a shine. And smack in the middle of the door was a familiar image: a bright gold knocker in the shape of a lion's head. It was the exact design of Regina's key chain and Lion's Mane's logo.

"Regina, what have you been up to?" I said and slipped the key into the lock.

"Hello?" I said to the empty apartment.

I immediately noticed signs of Regina. There was a smell of the sweet tobacco and in an ashtray beside the sofa was a Gitanes cigarette stub, the French brand she'd been smoking at my studio. A glass of water in the sink was stained on the rim with what looked like Regina's shade of lipstick. There were even a couple of pock marks on the rug from her stiletto heels.

There were no framed photos, or anything personal for that matter, but there were fresh flowers on the coffee table, the fridge was stocked with two small wedges of cheese, and a bottle of wine. Tacked to the fridge was a small scrap of paper with a single heart scribbled onto it. There was also a catalog on the kitchen counter for upscale, imported cigars and cigarettes. I looked at the mailing label: *Archibald Residence or Other Occupant.*

Hanging on the door to the bedroom was a shopping bag from Maison Margiela, a nearby store where T-shirts can run a couple hundred dollars. There was a note stapled to the side of the bag: *Pick up: Archibald.* I could not see what was inside because of the layers of tissue paper, but I knew their men's line was just the kind of polished look Charlie Archibald might sport on weekends.

I hated to admit it, but everything pointed to the fact that this was the love pad of Regina Montague and Charlie Archibald. As I'd feared deep down when I saw the picture of Archibald's cufflinks, Regina had come to me for a copy of her lover's key.

Entering the apartment's one bedroom, I opened the dresser drawers. They were empty. Regina had thoroughly cleared out when she'd packed her blue suitcase. In a corner of the room, however, I saw a small pink duffel bag. A delicate piece of floral-patterned fabric stuck out from one side, as if the bag had been packed quickly.

I peeked inside the bag. The clothing was smaller in size and more casual in style than Regina's wardrobe would be. I wondered if the owner of these clothes was coming into or going out of Charlie Archibald's life. As they say, hell hath no fury like a woman scorned. I didn't have to read Shakespeare to understand that line. I'd worked Friday night shifts at the food court in our mall and had seen a lot of dates end in that kind of rage.

I opened the living room window to escape the scent of tobacco and looked down at the quiet street to think. Between the suitcase and the apartment, I wondered if Thorne was right to focus on Regina. It was an easy conclusion to make.

Given the small duffel bag I'd found, maybe there was another woman in the story who could be equally culpable of murder. I thought of the icy behaviors of two other women I'd seen with Archibald: Miranda Headram and Elizabeth Everly.

I don't know how long I stood there, but suddenly I heard a door open. Immediately, I jumped, my breath quickening. It took me a moment to realize that the sound had come from the hall outside of the apartment. Archibald's neighbor was leaving for the day. The heavy sound of a man's feet hurried down the stairs.

"Keep it together, Liv," I whispered to myself, forcing my breath to slow down.

I'd come to talk to Regina, only to find myself hiding in Archibald's love pad. Enough was enough. I decided to visit Regina Montague Studios to collect my paycheck and perhaps learn more about her life from a visit to her workplace. As I walked down the street, I had an eerie feeling that someone was watching me, but when I turned around it was only the old street sweeper who was now putting out the garbage.

Twenty-five minutes later, I was among the towering office buildings and heavy traffic of Seventh Avenue in Midtown. Tourists visiting for the holidays, many of them disembarking from the luxury-liner bus that had taken them into town for the day, mixed with a parade of professional men and women who entered and exited the skyscrapers, all looking as if they were late for important engagements.

As I pushed through a revolving door in the lobby of RMS's building, I noticed the three other photographers from the ball, exiting through another door beside mine. I waved but they picked up their speed and shot daggers at me. Clearly, they'd heard I was the one who'd directed all eyes to Regina as she stood over Archibald. I walked to the security desk and asked a woman in a burgundy uniform to let Manjeet know I was there.

"He says you have five minutes," she said as she handed me a pass after she'd called up to announce me.

When the elevator door opened onto the twentieth floor, a sign told me that I had arrived at Regina Montague Studios, and that I should take a right to get to the front desk. I did so, but before I made it to the end of the long hall, filled with floor-to-ceiling images of Regina's most iconic work, I could tell that the Manjeet I'd spoken to on the phone yesterday was a changed man. The phones were ringing, but he did no more than put each caller on hold. The lights blinked all the way down his switchboard.

I stood in front of his grand reception desk and cleared my voice. He looked at me blankly, but I tried not to take it personally. I was also a bit distracted myself. I couldn't help but notice a partially closed nook behind Manjeet that looked as if it was used to store packages. Today, it housed a large blue suitcase.

"Right. Paychecks," Manjeet said, recovering himself. He was dressed in a fashion-forward suit of a beautiful dark green that was similar in its shade to Regina's ball dress.

"Thanks. How's it going?" I said to kick things off.

"The police and the press want our pictures from the Holiday Ball," he said, not so much to me as to the air around us. He clasped his hands on the desk in front of him as he spoke. "Meanwhile, our clients are all cancelling. All those years they loved her and now, when she needs their support, poof. She's on her own."

The phone rang. Manjeet put the caller on hold and returned his hands to their clasped position.

"She's inside with the police," he said, jutting his chin slightly in the direction of a door with Regina's name on it.

"She's here?" I said, feeling as if I'd hit the jackpot. "And she was with them all last night, too. What do you think they're still talking about?"

"I don't know," he said. "That's the real kicker. I usually know everything there is to know here."

He looked at me accusingly. I thought of my unfriendly encounter with the RMS team in the lobby and realized I'd started a chain of events that had thrown all of their jobs into jeopardy.

"You know, we get our fair share of drama at RMS, but we've never had someone take down the company," he said with a judgmental sniff. "Do you have any idea how hard Regina worked to make this studio what it is today? And in one night *you*."

Before I could respond, he opened a drawer and began to flip through his files.

At that moment, Regina's office door opened. Today she was wearing a long black chiffon dress. Her makeup was lighter, and her hair was a mess. She looked right at me and dropped her jaw.

"Thank you, and do give Detective Thorne my regards," she said, pivoting without a word to me to shake hands with two men in drabby suits. "I'll be happy to give you any other information you'd like."

"Please be available for us to contact you."

"Of course," she said. "As I said, I'm an open book."

The two men walked down the hall to the elevators, their flat shoes pounding the hard floor.

Rather than acknowledge me, Regina came around Manjeet's station and pulled out her suitcase.

"Are you going somewhere?" Manjeet said.

"You bet I am. And it's better for you if you don't know where," she said. She walked to a closet by the front door and retrieved a sheered mink coat.

"I'm sorry for your loss," I blurted out to the back of her head.

Regina inhaled as if I'd stabbed her. She turned and looked at me for a long moment with her coat in her hands. I noticed there was real pain in her eyes. Again, not guilty eyes, like *I murdered someone.* Just grief eyes. Also of interest, she didn't look defensive or confused with my statement about her loss.

"They're going to officially confirm it this afternoon. That he was murdered," she said. Manjeet's hand flew to his mouth and tears sprang to his eyes.

"There's a side to Charlie Archibald that will come out. God help his family," she said.

I put my hand into my pocket and pulled out her key.

"Here," I said. "I made you your copy. You'd better hold on to it."

Regina took the key and held it mid-air.

"I know you didn't kill Archibald," I said.

"Damn straight I didn't," she said. I knew she was keeping up her tough exterior, but her voice sounded sad. "It goes against my faith to kill anything."

"It's true. She's been studying Buddhism," Manjeet chimed in, but I knew Regina's inclinations toward faith would not play into Detective Thorne's investigation, especially in comparison to something as juicy as a potential lovers' squabble leading to murder.

"I'm so sorry again, about last night," I said. "You took a chance on me and in turn I've put you and RMS in a terrible spot. I'd do anything to change that."

"I wish you could," she said. She took a deep breath, eyes closed. When she opened them, she seemed softer. "Bollocks. I hate to say this, but your photos were the best of the night. But don't think I didn't see you on the dance floor. I see everything. Be careful of mingling with the clients."

She buttoned her coat and then rested her hand decisively on her suitcase.

"Screw the police," she said. "Where I grew up, if the coppers wanted someone, that was a signal to get out fast. If the NYPD decide I did it, they can deal with me then. Manjeet, I'm sure you can cover the fort while I'm gone."

"It will be my honor," said Manjeet, rising inches in his chair.

Regina turned and walked down the long hall from the office that led to an open elevator. I knew that Charlie Archibald's death would have many repercussions. Angela would carry the burden that her special night had been the scene of her father's death. The guests at his table, aside from the murderer, would regret that their last night together had been fraught with tension. Investors in Lion's Mane might move their investments now that the company's brilliant co-founder had died. But what people might not think much about was the quiet casualty of Regina Montague Studios, which had been built by someone who had once stood in discount shoes like mine.

On Manjeet's desk, I noticed a phone message from Bill Topper that read quite simply: *Need to cancel today's photo shoot.*

"Who exactly is Bill Topper?" I said to Manjeet. I thought about how Bill had passed me in the hall right before I'd found Archibald.

"He's one of the partners of Lion's Mane," said the eyes and ears of RMS. "Regina was supposed to do a reshoot of their holiday photo today."

Regina's last words to me were that she wished I could help her. I decided I would.

"Manjeet," I said, "we need to support Regina."

"I think you've done enough," he said. "And I'll ask you kindly to leave."

"I can't," I said. "At best, I've put Regina and her studio into a scandalous situation from which it might never recover. At worst, my discovery of her next to Archibald might end with her arrested for murder. When I make a mistake, I try to fix it. You can help me or let me go rogue. What's it going to be?"

He stared at me as if I had gone truly bananas.

"Don't you want to help Regina?" I said. "With your intel and my camera, we can see things the police can't."

Manjeet took off his headphones and pressed his lips together.

"As a matter of fact, I'd love to help, but because of you there are no events to photograph, and no way to connect with anyone who was at the ball. What would you suggest we do?"

"Can you pull up the photos I took of the Archibalds' table? The Toppers, the Headrams, and Donna Archibald all left the room and returned to it after Charlie Archibald disappeared. I don't know what they did while they were out of the room, but each of them had a window of opportunity to kill him."

"Wow. OK," he said, his fingers flying across his keyboard. "Got it."

He turned his monitor toward me. I pointed to the Headrams.

"Do you know their connection to the Archibalds?"

Manjeet shrugged. "Whoever they are, they're not big players," he said. "My notes just say Headram. Not even first names."

"No worries," I said. "We'll start with who we know. Call the Toppers and let me speak to them."

Manjeet picked up the company's phone with a bit of the gusto of his former self. A moment later, he handed it to me. I introduced myself to Anne Topper and, as I had hoped, she was more curious than angry to hear my voice. I suggested, before she could change her mind about talking to me, that I take Regina's place to help them with their holiday photograph. I assured her I could be there after her girls came home from school. It was that easy. She agreed to have me.

"Have you seen the news? The police confirmed it was murder," Anne said before we hung up. "It will be interesting to see you again."

I had no doubt it would be.

"Let me know if you find out anything," Manjeet said to me

as I passed the receiver back to him. His initial reticence had now been replaced with sheer exhuberance, which I appreciated.

"As you said, the RMS team needs each other to succeed."

I lifted my fist to him for a mutual bump and received a light knock in return. We had work to do, but I felt sure we could be a good team.

"Don't forget this," Manjeet said, pushing my envelope toward me. As if I'd forget a paycheck.

When I stepped out of the office building, my day got even more interesting. My phone buzzed with a text from Harry.

Busy tonight?

I smiled and typed, **I've got work.**

Three dots, three dots. Dots stopping. More dots.

What time are you done? popped onto my screen.

I smiled and sent him my schedule and the Topper's' address. Then I opened my paycheck. I'd never received such a healthy sum for one night's work.

CHAPTER 8

Celebrating my financial windfall over a Shake Shack burger near Grand Central, I built my dossier on Bill Topper and his family. Most of my Google searches featured information about Bill and his job as co-founder of Lion's Mane. Several stories recapped Bill and Charlie's friendship. Legend had it, they had met while travelling the world after college in sailboats they'd each rented in the South of France crashed into each other. Apparently, after their "death-defying" adventure, they got drunk together and became lifelong friends. According to a *Wall Street Journal* article from about a year earlier, it was Charlie's "knack for numbers and his wizardry at using technology to enhance financial services" combined with Bill's "access to liquidity" that made them the "dynamos who blazed trails in the burgeoning fintech field." With another search, I learned that fintech refers to companies that use technology to make financial services, like digital payments, banking, insurance, and money management, more efficient. With Charlie Archibald's broad smile and Bill Topper's old-world ease, they'd skyrocketed to success.

There were several photos of the rest of the Topper family as well. Many were of Anne, at benefits, mostly to do with the arts. There was also a picture of the Toppers' twin daughters in which they looked like they had each just sucked a lemon.

When I finally arrived at the Toppers' residence in the late afternoon, I knew the basics about my clients. I wasn't entirely prepared, however, for the whole package when I reached their formidable green awning on Fifth Avenue in the 70s. Small fir trees, covered in white lights in early anticipation of the holidays, guarded each side of the building's heavy double doors like sentries. I'd changed into my photographer's uniform of my black leggings and white button down, but knowing I was seeing Harry after, I'd swapped out my boots for a pair of heels. I wished I was wearing my usual combat protection as I walked through the door, however. They would have given me a confidence I suspected I'd need.

"I'm Liv Spyers, for the Toppers," I said to a doorman in uniform.

"Ah," he said, with an efficient air about him. "I'll tell Estelle, the housekeeper, you're coming up."

When the elevator doors closed across the polished, wood-paneled cab, I took a breath and ran through my agenda. Of course, I would take some great photos of the Toppers, but I also wanted to learn more about Bill's fabled relationship with his partner, and hopefully connect that to why he looked so angry with Charlie Archibald at the ball.

Ten floors later, I stepped onto the Toppers' elevator landing where a single, front door was wide-open. As a member of a family that handles keys and locks for a living, I found their confidence in the security of their doorman way too trusting, but I stepped inside. The Toppers' large foyer, with polished, dark wood floors, was lit by a gold chandelier. Cream-colored walls shimmered, subtly, as if laid with delicate enamel. Their purpose, less subtly, was to show off an exquisitely curated collection of modern art.

"Hellooo," I sang out. "Anyone here?"

I heard three sets of doors open from a long corridor off the foyer, but only one set of footsteps marched toward me.

They brought with them Anne Topper. Her outfit was a chic, champagne-colored dress in what looked like cashmere. I could tell she put in some serious hours at the gym, and it was absolutely paying off for her. Whereas her hair had been pulled up in a high chignon for the ball, it was now pulled down in a low one. Under normal circumstances I'd have been impressed with her hairdresser, but all I could think of was how women once used hat pins as weapons.

"Liv Spyers," I said, my hand extended.

"Thank you for coming on such short notice," said Anne, giving me a firm handshake in return. "Our holiday card's photo was a disaster this year. We were going to use one from our trip to Saint Kitts but it's no good. I don't know what I was thinking. Bill thought we should cancel, given what's happened with Charlie, but when you called, I thought it might take our minds off things."

As she spoke, two girls, about thirteen years old, materialized behind her. They were the spitting image of each other, save for the gothic, dyed-black hair of one. Bill, I noticed, was absent.

"Peridot, Jade," said Anne, indicating the blond and gothic apparitions, respectively. "This is Liv. Um, Liv Sparder, right? She's going to take our holiday photo."

"Boringe!" said Jade by way of a greeting.

"That's a word we invented," Peridot said to me, confidentially. "It's a combination of 'boring' and 'cringe.' Like when Mom makes us take our holiday card photos twice."

I nodded with a good-natured smile and decided the moment had passed for me to correct Anne's mispronunciation of my last name.

Jade shot her mother a defiant look. "I'm too tired to sit for a photo, and I have a zit."

This troublesome dynamic transpires every time I take a family photo as each generation lays down its ground rules until someone wins. I've learned that the best way to handle it is to move through it. I usually take charge and direct everyone to a place to set up the shoot, but I wasn't familiar with the Toppers' residence. Another tactic that also works is to divert attention to something that has nothing to do with the shoot itself. That usually gives the group enough time to take a collective breath and resign themselves to the fact that the shoot will happen, whether they want it or not.

Deciding on the latter plan, my eyes jumped to something that gave me comfort.

Photographs. A couple of photos lay loosely on a black, lacquered console with silver-tipped feet. They were glossy shots of a shining Eros, the god of love, his arm raised and holding a bow and arrow, his whole being sparkling in the light.

"These are beautiful," I said, motioning to the pile.

Before I got another word out, Anne stepped between me and the table.

"Mom, did you order another ice sculpture?" said Peridot, peeking behind her mother at the photos.

Anne adjusted her pearls.

"I know you love ice sculptures," said Peridot, "but I don't think Dad could survive another Nutcracker episode."

Peridot leaned in, as if to take me into her confidence.

"We had one last year at Christmas," she said. "It was a four-foot Nutcracker for the server in the dining room. It was a small pond when we got home from church. Our neighbor's ceiling was ruined. Dad said repainting it was a fortune."

Anne was politely smiling, but I noticed her nostrils flare. A palpable silence fell upon the room. Jade bit her nails, then left. Peridot followed.

"While the girls are collecting themselves, why don't we have a drink?" Anne said to me rather than address her girls' dramatics. "Bill's running late, so we have a few moments."

"Works for me," I said, taking off my coat, which instantly

disappeared into the hands of Estelle, who appeared from nowhere.

Anne opened two lacquered doors that revealed a stately room at least twenty-five feet long. The room greeted us with a navy velvet sofa and two club chairs on either side that faced a giant TV, mounted in a sliver of built-in bookshelves that ran across the entire wall and were matched on the opposite wall as well. The shelves were filled with tomes and awards and other objects, lit by pin lights.

Straight ahead of us, a large, single-paned window showcased a view of Central Park and a vibrant red sky as the sun sank behind the West Side buildings. It was the kind of scenic beauty I never try to capture in a photograph, because there's really no way to ever match its majesty.

In front of the window, from which hung elegant, navy-blue, silk draperies, was a large mahogany desk.

Also of note was a potted palm, not far from me, parked next to a fully stocked bar cart.

Anne walked directly to a shelf of framed photos and began to straighten them. She was on the other side of the room from the bar cart, with her back to me, so I took the liberty of gently lifting the small bucket of ice and dumping it ever so quietly into the potted plant.

"May I take some photos of your lovely view?" I said when I finished. Anne turned to me and approached to prepare our drinks.

"Of course," she said graciously. "You can slip around Bill's desk to get a better shot. You know, I make an unbeatable Moscow Mule."

"Sounds delicious," I said over the clicking of my camera's shutter.

"Damn. We're out of ice. Estelle?" Estelle did not answer.

"Estelle?" Anne tried again. "Just give me a sec."

"No problem," I said. "I'm getting some gorgeous photos of the city. I'll send you a print."

"Oh, Bill will love that," said Anne. "I can give it to him for Christmas. Do you like glossy or matte?"

Pleased with her stocking-stuffer idea, Anne's shoes click-clacked to the kitchen for ice. Alone, I could now focus on Bill's desk. Snooping around the belongings of a powerful financier, however, wasn't something I'd ever done before. I stood quietly for a moment, listening for sounds of the twins' return or Bill's arrival. I knew I did not have much time until Anne returned, so if I was going to take the plunge, it had to be now. I pulled open a file drawer. I don't know what I was expecting to find, but I was ready to photograph documents or anything else that struck me as a potential clue. Unfortunately, the drawer was locked, as were all the others.

The desktop was also empty of juicy files, or anything one would consider work-related. Bill was probably one to keep everything on his computer. There was a leather blotter and an onyx framed clock with a matching cup for pens. A pad of paper with the Lion's Mane logo sat by it, thick and beautiful, but also untouched. One particularly luxurious item among these desk accessories caught my eye. It was a dark blue enameled fountain pen, dipped in red ink. Its cap lay beside the inkwell. I lowered my camera and lifted the pen, which looked to be about six inches long. It was thin but solid and the tip of the point looked sharp.

I remembered Bill had been fiddling with something on the table when he and Archibald had words at the party. I realized now that it had been his pen. I held the instrument in one hand and lunged it forward toward an imaginary Charlie Archibald. Then I put it into an imaginary breast pocket of a tuxedo as Bill might have. The tip could have easily pierced Archibald's eye. A pen would have been easy to hide.

"Did you get good shots?" said Anne, returning to the room

while I quickly replaced the pen. "If you can get me som
next week, I'll take a twenty-by-twenty-four print. Wait, that's a bit show-offy. Let's do a twelve-by-eighteen. I'll be honest, I usually only make this drink at cocktail parties, but I was on the scene of a murder this week, so all bets are off. Come sit down."

I took an extra burst of sunset photos for good measure as I walked backwards and sank into one of the club chairs. The cushions made me feel as if I were in a soft, floating cloud. I took a sip of my Moscow Mule, which had an expert mixture of vodka, lime juice, and ginger beer. It was as good as Anne had promised it would be. When I put down my glass, she immediately topped it off.

I knew she was trying to loosen me up for some scoop about Regina. Each time she poured, she asked me for details about finding Archibald's body. I fancy myself as someone who can hold their liquor, so I went along with her game. I had my own agenda, and I liked the idea that Anne was drinking as much as I was. I answered her as I'd answered Detective Thorne, minus my accusations that someone from the Archibalds' table seemed more likely to me than Regina to have been the killer.

"Thank you," I said when Anne refilled our glasses once again.

As I raised my drink to my lips, feeling more relaxed than I had in days, I noticed a funny thing. In many of the photos of the family on the shelves surrounding us, Bill was holding the pen I had seen on his desk. Mostly they were photos of him with important-looking people in stiff poses. In each photo, he gripped the pen with a slightly raised fist, as if to signify victory over a newly signed deal. I honestly understood his grasp. I hold my camera like that sometimes when I'm in need of protection, like it's a baby blanket. In Bill's case, however, his binkie could have been used as a murder weapon.

"You'll have to forgive Bill's absence. This is a nightmare for him," Anne said, kicking off unscuffed shoes. "First, Charlie's murdered. Then, of course, everything at work has exploded. *Murdered* at the Holiday Ball. Of all the low places to kill someone. Where is this world going, I want to know?"

"It was low," I agreed, swirling my ice, and feeling a bit light-headed.

"Charlie could be a pain in the ass, but he could also be a good egg," Anne said. "I'd like to think we left on good terms. Last thing he did was approach me with an opportunity to invest in their new fund, LaunchTech."

LaunchTech. I'd heard that name before. I remembered the guests at the ball discussing it. The fund was an investment portfolio of the most innovative companies in the field. Some were sure-fire winners that were already somewhat known, but others were up-and-coming businesses that Archibald believed would change the future of financial services.

"The fund was Charlie's brainchild," Anne said, "and he was very territorial about how it was managed, even within the company. He could be like that. Even with Bill, who was annoyed by the secrecy but trusted him. I made some money when I was younger that I keep in savings, and Charlie gave me the heads-up about the fund. We decided to keep my investment quiet until I made a return since Bill had not been active in building out the portfolio. Of course, now that Charlie's dead, Bill's taking over. Bill now knows about my participation, and he's been grumpy with me, but I know it's because he's so sad about Charlie. They've been friends and partners since they were in their twenties."

I wondered if Bill's irritability during the ball was connected to Archibald's rising popularity. I didn't need an expert education on venture capital to realize Archibald was the star of the brightest new money-making investment portfolio, and everyone knew it. Perhaps Bill was jealous. Perhaps he already knew about Anne's investment in the fund and was angry that

Archibald had put a hard sell on his wife without consulting him first. I knew these possible motives were all conjecture, but together they could drive a certain type of person to murder.

Anne leaned toward me and gestured for me to meet her halfway.

"Mark my words," she said, wagging her finger in large strokes while I bobbed my head as if I'd already marked her words. "That fund is going to skyrocket."

Money is often considered a major motive for killing someone. But in this case, the last thing Archibald did for Anne Topper was give her a tip that would make her rich . . . er. I was tempted to strike off Anne as a possible suspect, and not because I was beginning to like her spunk.

"Given Mr. Archibald's success, who would want to murder him?" I said.

"Regina Montague. You were right there with us, at the bar where we found Charlie," she said. "I told the police she was a piece of work. That woman was always hanging around Donna Archibald, trying to ingratiate herself with the family. She was a homewrecker and a fool. Truth is, Charlie has a wandering eye. Regina Montague probably saw him flirting with someone new and lost it."

Anne shook her head with distaste about the entire matter. I wondered how many women Charlie Archibald had entertained during his marriage to Donna, and how many other women had spent time at his secret apartment.

"You left the ballroom about the time that Mr. Archibald was murdered," I said. "Did you see Regina or anyone suspicious?"

"Not at all," said Anne. "I went to the powder room and right back to the ballroom."

"Did you see Bill when you left?" I remembered how her husband had followed her out of the room.

"No," she said. "He must have gone to the little boys' room. Our bladders aren't what they once were, I guess. Neither of us saw a thing."

"Mrs. Archibald was also gone for a bit. They always say it's the spouse," I said. "Maybe it was Donna who noticed Mr. Archibald looking at Regina."

"If you want to work in this town again, I wouldn't go around saying that to people," Anne said with authority. "People genuinely like Donna. She's approachable, generous. She organized her girls' school's entire benefit last year when she could have written a check. And I'm friendly enough with Donna to say that there's no way she did it. She and Charlie always knew where they stood with each other. I'd say their friendship was even stronger than their romance. And that's the secret to a good marriage."

"My parents are like that," I said. "No lies."

"I'm not sure I'd go so far as to say they never lied to each other," said Anne. "But they had always had each other's backs."

"I wonder who else the police will investigate," I said, although I was beginning to doubt that anyone other than myself was looking beyond Regina as a suspect.

"Obviously Regina did it, although I hope they question Miranda Headram, just to make her squirm a bit. She's a horrible woman."

"How is she connected to the Archibalds?" I said, eager to talk more about Miranda.

"She's Charlie Archibald's first cousin," Anne said.

I crossed off Miranda as a possible love affair gone wrong. Anne finished her drink and poured another.

"Miranda once told me, all the way back, that Charlie promised her a huge chunk of cash when he died, but that wasn't enough. She said he should support her financially while he was alive. Out of nowhere! She said this to me. I'll always remember that about her. She and I make nice with each other at Archibald events, but I can't stand her."

After an entire pitcher of Moscow Mules, Anne Topper had handed me two motives. Bill Topper could have been jealous of his partner's big splash with their new fund and his manipulation of his wife to help seed it. Or Miranda Headram resented her cousin's success.

I was both elated by my discoveries and aware of how low the sun had set. Taking another sip of my cocktail, I splashed a little of the drink on myself, on purpose. My meeting was going better than I had planned, but Harry would be waiting downstairs for me in a few minutes. I wanted to text him, but I didn't want to be rude in front of my client.

"Do you mind if I spot clean this?" I said, waving a corner of my blouse as if to air it out.

"Of course. The kitchen door is by the Rothko. I'll check on Bill, too," she said, lifting her phone.

I knew she was referring to the artist Mark Rothko because my dad used to roll his eyes over his abstract work, along with Jackson Pollock's, whenever my mom took us to the Metropolitan Museum when I was a kid. Armed with this information, I handily spotted the painting, found the kitchen door, and opened it. In the center of the kitchen, the twins sat at a large marble counter, eating something that smelled delicious. Estelle, an older, heavyset woman, cleaned the stove at the other end. She placed the salt and pepper shakers onto a shelf like Anne had arranged the family photos in the family's study.

Behind me, I heard the apartment's elevator open. I turned to see Bill Topper pad into the foyer. His first stop was a pile of mail on the silver-tipped server where he flipped through the envelopes until he abruptly stopped.

"Anne," Bill said, loudly. "In the middle of everything else going on right now, you got another ice sculpture?"

Bill might be a member in the courts of power in this city, but Anne clearly ruled the roost at home. He looked like someone who had woken up in the wrong house but was not sure what to do about it. Instinctively, his hand went to his breast pocket, but his pen wasn't there today. I wondered why not.

I felt a tap on my arm and turned to find Estelle beside me.

"Come," she said. "You'd better go. They're not going to be needing your services but thank you for coming. I'll get your things."

Estelle pushed past me through the door, which closed behind her as negotiations over the ice sculpture began to kick into gear.

"They can be tough," said Peridot.

"Here," said Jade, handing me a glass of water. "Thank you," I said.

I took a few good gulps and put down my glass carefully. The girls giggled as I realized the table's edge seemed to be shifting. I then turned my head to see my coat and bag coming at me.

"OK, here you go," Estelle said, handing me all my belongings. "They are a wonderful family, but Christmas makes them crazy. And this business with poor Mr. Archibald, God bless him."

I was halfway out the door.

"They'll pay, don't worry," she said.

When I was about to step on the back elevator, she stuck her head out once more. "Don't be too mad at the girls," she said and closed the door.

It seemed a strange thing to say. I thought Estelle could use a couple of Anne's cocktails herself.

CHAPTER 9

I'd expected to leave the Toppers' thinking about murder and motive, but I didn't have time to because outside of their building I found Harry leaning against a car. I was relieved to see he was wearing jeans and a hoodie, which peeked out over a warm jacket, topped with a felt fedora. It was nice to see he didn't live in tuxedos and suits alone. His legs extended to the sidewalk and his feet crossed casually. I could see by the easy way he loitered in this neighborhood that I was the one on a field trip, not he.

I sidled up to the car, rested myself beside him, and hiccupped. The cold air felt great. "It looks like you got a head start on me tonight," said Harry with a laugh.

"You got me."

"Do you want to start off with some food?" he said and looked at me. "Do you know you have—"

I put my fingers over his lips

"I do," I said, although I didn't know what I had. I mean, I knew what I had, but how did he know what I had? And did I need to know what he knew I had? Not really. I had my girl power. And I had a small studio, a date, friends, my camera. If I could just help Regina Montague, I'd have peace of mind too.

"Whatever you say," said Harry from behind my finger. He

offered me his hand, and I reluctantly slid my fingers off his beautiful face. Despite how emboldened I was feeling, after a day of sleuthing I appreciated being led down Fifth Avenue by this lovely man. When we were across the street from the Metropolitan Museum of Art, I thought of all the other Rothkos that might be casually hanging on the walls of the homes surrounding me. Who knew?

"Look. They kept the fountains on," I said.

I snapped a few pictures as we crossed Fifth Avenue to the fountains outside of the museum, where flowing jets arranged in a large circle around the fountain's border were lit from below. Delighted by their festive influence, I put my camera safely aside, away from the water but in my line of sight. Then I took off my shoes and waded between two jets. Turns out, there is nothing like a pitcher of Moscow Mules to fend off the cold of winter.

To his credit, Harry joined me without a moment's hesitation, even leaving his sneakers on as he stepped through a break in the water jets.

"Your feet will be cold when you get out," I said.

"You sound like you have experience with fountains," said Harry. It was too late for his shoes, but taking my advice, he hopped away from the jets to the fountain's center where there was less of a shower.

"As a matter of fact, I do," I said. "My favorite thing during summers as a kid was to run around the fountain at the mall near us."

A spout in the middle of the fountain exploded. The water sprayed high into the air and then fell with a glorious crash onto Harry. Amidst a muffled and frozen scream from my date, I waded toward the fountain's center, fully prepared to join him in all fairness. Before I reached the fountain's heart, however, Harry emerged from the flood. Under the dome of shining water above us, he reached his hand toward me.

"Hey," a policeman said at that exact moment. "You can't be in there."

"Come on," said Harry. He took my hand and dodged the waterspouts, grabbing my camera bag and shoes while apologizing profusely to the cop and then running with me down the street. Two blocks down, now feeling the cold air, we stopped. I put on my shoes as Harry held my hand for balance.

"You need to be careful in this City. One wrong turn and you're in trouble," said Harry. He linked a shivering arm through mine and crossed the street.

"But funny enough, I'm the dry one."

"A very sober observation, thank you," he said.

"I think we both need to change," I said. "If you don't mind some old-man clothes, I have a bag for the Salvation Army at home. Some of Poppy's stuff is in there. We can both get dry and then get some pizza nearby?"

"I don't mind old-man pants," he said. "They say, *'I've seen and done everything, so now it's time to tell people stories they've already heard a thousand times.'*"

"Ah, now you're just buttering me up," I said.

"Taxi!" Harry shouted to a passing yellow cab.

We huddled in the back of the taxi, and Harry made small talk with the driver while I rested my head against his arm around me and listened to them talk about the prohibitive expenses of being a driver these days. When we reached my stop, Harry walked me to my front door. I leaned against my gate, but found it was lower than I remembered.

"Are you OK?" said Harry, catching my elbow.

"I'm always OK."

"OK."

An awkward pause followed. I hadn't really thought through the part where I invited a guy I'd only recently met into my home so we could both change clothes.

"Remember Bill from the murder scene?" I said.

"I do."

"You picked me up at his building tonight. I had a photo shoot there."

A deep crease stole across Harry's forehead.

"You know Bill Topper was Charlie Archibald's business partner at Lion's Mane," said Harry. "He might not like you hanging around his house. Or, hell, if Regina didn't do it, he might be a suspect. Did he recognize you?"

"Bill never even saw me," I said. "And if anything, his wife seemed very happy to have me there. But you might have a point about him being a suspect. He carries around a fountain pen like it's a rabbit's foot. It is pointy, long, and metal."

"A murder weapon," he said.

I was pleased he was following along, and I nodded. "I'm impressed," he said. "But what about motive?"

"Jealousy," I said. "That new fund, LaunchTech, made Archibald a star. I have a feeling those types of men don't take kindly to being one-upped."

Harry took off his hat and put it on my head. He dipped the brim over one of my eyes. I felt like a proper detective.

"I think this suits you better than me," he said, wrapping his arms around my waist, as much to keep us warm as show his affection. "Are you going to tell the police?"

"No," I said. "I'd never accuse someone of murder unless I knew they'd done it for sure. And anyway, Anne had some interesting things to say about Charlie Archibald's cousin that could reveal another motive."

Harry rested his forehead on the top of my head.

"I think we should go out again tomorrow night," he said.

"Assuming pizza goes well," I said.

"Of course. If it does, Giorgio Popolous, the guy who Bernie invited to our table, is hosting an impromptu party tomorrow night. He lives in Greece, but apparently, he has a swanky pad here in town."

"Maybe I'll find out more about my suspects." I smiled.

"I hope you're not using me for my access to murder suspects," he said as our heads began to draw closer. "Which would be disturbing on so many levels. On the other hand, I do insurance for a living. I need some adventure."

This was the sexiest conversation I'd ever had. Our lips were now only about an inch away. The mood was right, and I leaned into him. As I did, we were interrupted by a shattering noise from inside my studio.

"What was that?" I said. I squeezed Harry's arm and looked at my storefront where I'd closed the privacy curtain. I couldn't see a thing inside.

"It sounded like someone dropping something," he said. "Is anyone supposed to be in your studio tonight?"

I shook my head. Someone uninvited was in my apartment. Damn our useless alarm system.

"I can't get robbed," I said. "My entire career depends on every piece of equipment in there."

"If I wave to you, be ready to call for back up," Harry said and glided me behind the garbage on the stoop.

I was ready to fight, but I liked his thinking. Two plans of attack were better than one. I nodded and pulled out my phone while Harry went to the entrance of my studio and forcefully knocked on the door.

Before I could call the police, the door opened.

I saw Harry's shoulders relax in the silhouette. Mine, however, tightened to knots.

Facing Harry from my studio, my grandfather stood in the doorway.

"Whatcha doing, Poppy?" I said as gently as I could and approached the door. "You scared us."

"I was looking for my thingymabobber," he said. "Um. You know, you're wet. Were you two at the beach?"

"No, and I was just saying good night to Liv," Harry said.

He smiled at me with more than a hint of sympathy, and I nodded my appreciation.

"Let's get you back upstairs," I said to Poppy. "I have the front door key, so we don't have to wake up Granny. And guess what? I learned a funny word today that these two rascals I met made up. *Boringe.*"

"Ha. Like it's so boring you could cringe," he said. "Clever."

Miraculously, I got Poppy back to bed without waking up my granny. On the way out of the house, I was filled with misgivings about my grandfather's health. I jiggled the handle of Carrera's, and was pleased it was locked tonight. I got a pit in my stomach however when I noticed the owner of the safe had finally come to pick it up. I suddenly wondered if Poppy had taken something from it. Was the *thingymabobber* he was looking for an item he'd found in the safe? Carrera's used to be in my studio, so perhaps he'd gotten mixed up in the night. I felt there was another mystery brewing at home, and wished I understood better what was going on with my grandfather these days. I resolved to talk to my mother about it next time we spoke.

I entered my studio carefully, even though I knew nothing had been stolen. Thankfully none of my studio equipment had been damaged. After changing into my fluffiest pajamas and a pair of socks, I began to feel warmer and drier. I closed the kitchen drawers Poppy had opened, and picked up a sauce pot he had dropped, which had made the clatter. I hugged the pot as I sat at my kitchen counter. Then I called my best friend, Maria.

"What the hell?" she said. "I get missing my party for the biggest assignment of your life, but you've been MIA for like two days."

"Would you believe there was a murder at my event and I'm investigating it?" There was silence on the other end.

"Probably," she said.

"I also met a guy," I said. "He's taking me to a party tomorrow tonight where there may be suspects."

"You found a guy who wants to help you find murder suspects?" she said, sounding deeply suspicious.

"It sounds weird when you say it like that, but he's kinda great. He gave me a hat."

"What happened to giving a girl jewelry?"

"Can I borrow your dress coat for my date tomorrow night?" I said. "I can't go out in my parka in this crowd."

"Of course. I'll be there at five tomorrow," she said. "I want to hear everything. I'm watching *Stranger Things*. I can't believe I've never watched it."

"OK, go. I'll give you the details tomorrow," I said. "Thanks."

"Love you," Maria said.

Before turning out my light, I posted a photo of the fountains from the night and liked some comments from my followers. I was happy that @livspyersphotography was growing, but I wished it would also translate to more jobs.

I also looked at my photo of Bill Topper's pen and wondered again why he had not carried it with him to work today. But in talking to Anne, I'd learned that Miranda Headram wanted Charlie's money. I'd seen her fake jewels and affectations up close, and I could imagine how hard the extravagance of that night was for her. Perhaps seeing so many people fawn over her cousin was too much for her and, finally, after years of resentment, she had snapped. The Archibald family had its problems. Anne had given me reason to check up on Miranda Headram, and I would.

My pool of suspects was not huge, but it occurred to me that before I took another step in my investigation, I needed a ten-thousand-foot view of the high society New Yorkers I'd met. I would never be able to discern what was important unless I had a better understanding of the big picture.

Like me, the police had reviewed the photos of the Holiday

Ball, but those images were only one piece to putting the puzzle together. It was the comparison of these images against others that could help reveal the true story of Charlie Archibald's last moments alive.

Tomorrow was Saturday, but I messaged Manjeet to see if we could meet at RMS in the morning.

I stepped into my bathroom to wash up. There, I caught my reflection in the mirror. A black circle was stamped across my upper lip, like a pencil mustache. I remembered the glass of water the Topper twins had given me when I'd entered their kitchen. And their giggles. And Harry's comment about my face. Oh my God.

Estelle was loyal. I'd give her that.

CHAPTER 10

"Antony," I heard my grandmother cry from the kitchen above me.

I saw daylight through the shutters across my window and massaged my temples. The fluffy pajamas that had been so welcoming in the cold last night now stuck to my skin.

"I found your glasses," she said.

Practically crawling to the bathroom, I popped a couple of Tylenol and threw open a window. With the street sounds serenading me, I opened my laptop to the photos from the night of the ball, and searched, once again, for clues. I knew there was something in them that could solve the mystery of Archibald's murder, but I didn't know where to start.

My phone binged. Manjeet was at the studio, ready and waiting. My black leggings were under a pile of clothes that had taken root between my bed and bathroom door. In my closet, a somewhat ironed button-down looked presentable. And my boots promised me that my head would feel better once they were on my feet.

A half hour later, I was feeling able to face the day. The scent of Granny's famous cinnamon buns began to waft into my room, but I resisted the fresh baked goods above me. I had work to do before I treated myself to such luxuries. I rubbed my lips together, to make sure my lipstick was even, checked my image in the mirror once more, and then opened my front door. I left my studio's sign at CLOSED, but reluctantly. I never wanted to miss a potential customer who might stop in to book a shoot, and weekends could bring in people, but I knew that we were technically still in the middle of the long Thanksgiving weekend. The chances of someone stopping by were slim.

The holiday spirit was popping up on everyone's doorstep, as if overnight. I got to work taking photos of the growing winter wonderland. The air was now officially cold, and the metal of my camera froze my fingertips. A few buildings down the street, a huge Frosty the Snowman blow up filled a small entry. His corn cob pipe and button nose were a highlight of the street, and children crowded around the stoop with excitement. Three brownstones over, I captured one couple's struggle to untangle last year's outdoor lights. I posted a photo of their challenge, as love turned to chaos in one DIY home project.

A train ride later, I was heading up the elevator to RMS studios once again. Like my first trip, I was concerned about the studio, my future, and how to proceed with proving Regina's innocence. On the other hand, I now had an ally waiting for me above.

When the elevator door opened, I saw immediately that Manjeet's posture was straighter than the first time we'd met. Although the office was empty, he was dressed in a three-piece, burgundy velvet suit and wore a crisp, navy bowtie. His hair was cropped in what looked like a fresh haircut. The phone was not ringing, nor did there seem to be any work on his desk, but he was cleaning out files with the air of someone who was tackling projects that might otherwise never get done.

"Mrs. Topper emailed," he said to me by way of a greeting. "She says they will take both a twenty-by-twenty-four and a twelve-by-eighteen of a sunset photo."

"Seeing as you are now my manager," I said, excited by the unexpected financial bonus from my investigation into the Toppers, "I expect you will get me a paycheck sooner than later? It might be my last in a while."

"Payment upon delivery," he said, retrieving two mugs with the RMS logo on them from a server by the coat closet. "So, chop, chop!"

"Meanwhile, have you heard from Regina?"

"I have not," he said, pouring coffee for us. "And the police have called twice. I said she was in a meeting, but it's only a matter of time before they realize she's flown the coop. Milk or sugar? We have oat, almond, and soy milk, too."

"No, thanks," I said. "Has she ever done that before?"

"She's never been a murder suspect before," Manjeet said. "I have no precedent for how she might act. Usually, she's a fighter. She built this business from scratch. It's her baby, but this is all new territory, so give me some good news."

He handed me a steamy mug and pulled up a chair for me to sit on.

"What did you find out from your visit chez Topper?" he said. "Did Mr. T have a motive for murder?"

I told him what I'd scooped so far and felt a sense of accomplishment in what I'd done in such a short amount of time. Manjeet's expression, however, did not mirror my triumph.

"You found a pen?" he said. "The sky is falling, and all you've found is a pen?"

"The pen is not the point," I said. "A more optimistic way of looking at things is I made my way into a prime suspect's home, realized he might have a motive for murder, and, yes, found a pen. And what about Anne spilling tea about Miranda Headram? Now we know she's his cousin. We didn't even know that much yesterday."

"Could Miranda have physically done it?"

I remembered Archibald's dance with Miranda. She had

grabbed his wrist hard enough to make his skin turn white under his elegant tuxedo cuff.

"If she was really angry, maybe," I said. "She might have been able to. I'm not sure."

Manjeet pursed his lips.

"If you want to make headway, you're going to need more than this," he said. "I don't think the police are going to drop their focus on Regina because Mrs. Topper got buzzed and dished about her latest investments and her dislike for some lady."

"Great minds think alike," I said. "Which is why we're here on a weekend. I live in a world where a plate of fresh pasta with some truffle oil and Parmigiano Reggiano is the height of luxury. Homes with Rothkos and Warhol's soup cans are not on the agenda. I need to learn more about this pocket of town. I'm sure RMS has decades worth of photos from all sorts of events. I want to see them."

Manjeet smoothed his fingers across his empty desk and then pressed his hands against the fine grain of the wood.

"You want access to the vault," he said.

He wasn't looking at me so much as an imaginary spot on the desk.

"If that's what you call it," I said.

I waited.

He kept staring.

I kept waiting, feeling as if extra dialogue might be gratuitous.

"You were only a temp. I think you're the bee's knees, but giving you access to the vault is a violation of our policy," he said. "We do put photos of all the events online for individuals to buy. You can look through those. I'll give you a password."

His fingers tapped the keyboard, but I shook my head.

"Photos on the website have already been vetted as customer-friendly," I said. "But I need to see everything. The funny faces, odd looks, background people. That's where the real stories lie in pictures. Not the glossy, social media–friendly images."

Manjeet stared at his screen. I could see he was thinking.

"Fine," he said at last.

"That's the spirit. Was that so hard?" I said. "OK, lead me to this vault."

"It's not an actual vault," he said, back to his keyboard. "Give me the names of everyone you think might be a suspect. Every photo we log is tagged with the person's name. All I do is type in names and voilà, you have every photo we have of that person. Even the bad ones, as you say, that don't make it to the public website."

"Let's take a different approach," I said. "Can you send me all the photos of Mr. Archibald? I could spend days looking at my suspects, but what I need to understand better is how they relate to him."

Manjeet smiled at me as if I were very clever, and I confess it felt gratifying compared to his tough love about my trip to the Toppers. After pulling up the log and handing me a password, he sent me to an empty cubicle in the middle of what I imagined was usually a busy studio. It was a dream to have a seat at RMS, although I'd certainly never imagined my place would be as an investigator rather than a photographer. But I knew if I combined these two roles, I could pull it off.

"Let me know if I can help," Manjeet called to me.

"See if you can find any dirt about Miranda or Phil Headram."

"On it!" Manjeet said, sounding increasingly pleased.

Nestled behind the divider of my cubicle, I tightened my ponytail. The file for *Charlie Archibald* had over eighty folders inside of it. Each was named for the event at which he was spotted, including the Holiday Ball. All in all, there were twenty-five hundred and seventeen photos.

"Do you have any snacks?" I said, immediately regretting I hadn't snagged one of Granny's muffins.

"Sunflower seeds," he called to me.

An hour later, still having had nothing to eat, I'd made it through twenty-seven of the folders which I'd organized into categories including Archibald's social appearances, his company events, and family festivities. I paid special attention to the photos that had remained in the vault, rather than those with checks on them, which I surmised had made it to the RMS website.

The largest group of photos was from social events such as benefits for institutions around the city, including the New York Public Library, East Harlem Tutorial Program, the Citizens' Committee for Children. They were all upstanding organizations, some of the top in the city.

One folder among these caught my eye. It was labelled the *Archibald Foundation*, which I remembered was mentioned in the news the morning after Archibald was murdered. I Googled the name and learned the goal of the foundation was to promote education about financial services to underprivileged city youth. As I scrolled through the site, I considered how complicated Charlie Archibald was. On the one hand, his cousin, Miranda, had voiced her bitterness that her cousin did not financially support her. On the other, he was helping the City's youth.

Donna Archibald was pictured beside her husband at every one of these social events. As for signs of his roving eye, there was not one photo of Archibald and Regina. The closest I could find was one of Charlie and Donna Archibald where Regina was in the background. She seemed to study the scene with a thoughtful but unhappy expression.

Meanwhile, there was no lack of pictures of Archibald and other women. He often had his hand on a woman's shoulder or waist while sharing a smile. The women varied in type. Some were older, others younger. Some were blondes and others brunettes. Some pretty, others not so much. Chic, not chic. When all was said and done, however, his affectionate smiles and warm embraces with his wife stood out above all else. I wondered if he used his charm on women to drum up business, or if his reputation was legit.

Archibald's cousin, Miranda, was at a handful of these events as well. I noticed the same resentful pose and heavy drinking she had displayed at the ball, but I did not notice any escalating resentment. Her attitude was always the same. Smiling for the camera when she knew it was pointed at her and dropping the pretense when she thought she was alone. Her husband, Phil, was almost always by his wife's side, and was usually pulling out her chair, pouring her a glass of wine, or holding her purse. I decided the only difference between these photos and those from the Holiday Ball was that Miranda had not been willing to muster a smile the night Archibald was killed.

As I scrolled through the Archibald Foundation photos next, I suddenly recognized an unexpected face.

"Whoa," I said aloud.

"What?" I heard Manjeet from across the room.

Returning to the website for the foundation, I clicked on the Leadership tab. At the top of the page was none other than Miss Felicity Cromwell, the woman I'd seen trying to crash the Holiday Ball. She was listed as the executive director of the Archibald Group.

I remembered that Felicity Cromwell had been trying to speak with a man, and I was now pretty sure the man had been Charlie Archibald. She'd been asked by Elizabeth Everly to leave the party, so she was not on the premises when Archibald was killed. Although Felicity could not have been the killer, she was certainly mad about something. I wondered what it was and if others shared her rage about it, too.

In the photos from the foundation's events, Felicity Cromwell wore chic pant suits and was perfectly groomed. Unlike the tormented, red-faced woman I'd witnessed at the ball, Felicity reflected someone who was poised, stood tall, and displayed an effortless cool. Her eyes were sharp. Her smile engaging. The combination reminded me of the expert salesmanship I'd recognized in Charlie Archibald. I could imagine why he had chosen her to lead his organization.

"What?" Manjeet said again.

"Nothing, yet," I said, but I tucked away the idea that a chat with Felicity Cromwell might be of some value.

Moving on from Archibald's social life, I opened the folders related to events for Lion's Mane. I noticed that the dynamic between Bill Topper and Charlie Archibald was wildly different than their mutual agitation at the Holiday Ball. In these pictures, Bill and Charlie were laughing together, engaged in affable conversations, and all-around enjoying each other's company. In keeping with the press about them, they seemed to have a great bromance that had resulted in their becoming tremendously wealthy.

The last group of photos, that of the Archibalds' personal life, was the smallest folder. In addition to portraits likely meant for Christmas cards, they also included years of parties. There were also more intimate events, which counted the Toppers and Headrams. As guests.

Regina and her photographers were certainly a regular and trusted presence in the Archibald's' lives, but so was Elizabeth Everly Productions. Elizabeth herself was at most of these events. Although almost always in the background, her red hair made her easy to find. In piecing together my photos from the ball, I had been focusing on the people at the Archibalds' table, but Elizabeth Everly had remained until the party's end, too.

"What do you know about Elizabeth Everly?" I called out to Manjeet.

"She's still young but she's at the top of the game. Hard

worker. Gave us a lot of business in the past. She's now cancelled everything we had booked with her."

I thought about the suitcase of women's clothing in Regina and Charlie's apartment, and of Elizabeth's cold exchange with Charlie Archibald as he led me to the restroom. I wondered if she was a jilted lover. If so, perhaps she had figured out that Regina and Archibald were now seeing each other. That seemed to me to be a motive for a crime of passion.

I logged out of the RMS vault and left my cubicle to download with Manjeet.

"Did you find anything out about the Headrams?" I said.

"Indeed, I did. They are not an RMS client, *but* . . ." he said, very excited, "Miranda Headram called us recently. It was right before the ball. Not sure why she called. She left no details. Regina hadn't had a chance to get back to her before all this mess."

"Given what Anne told me about Miranda's financial worries, doesn't it seem odd that she would call RMS, one of the most expensive photography firms in the City, for a job?"

"Yes," said Manjeet. "It does."

"Do you have her number?" Manjeet gave it to me.

"Time to meet with another suspect," I said.

CHAPTER 11

I dialed the Headrams' home number. While the phone rang, I Googled the couple. Unlike the Toppers, there wasn't much to learn.

"Hello," Miranda said after four rings. There was a chorus of yapping dogs in the background.

"Mrs. Headram?" I said.

"Yes?" she said as the yapping continued. "Oh, Mr. Binders, here you go. Yes, here you go. I see you, Lady. Yes, I see you, too, Sugar."

"Hello, Mrs. Headram?" I said in case she had forgotten we were on the phone. "This is Liv Spyers from Regina Montague Studios. We met the other night."

I heard her move what sounded like a kitchen stool across the floor, and a moment later the sounds of the dogs became more muffled.

"I remember you," Miranda said, sounding wary of my call.

"First, I wanted to say how sorry I am for your loss," I said. "I can't stop thinking about how hard this must be for you and your family. It isn't our usual practice at Regina Montague Studios, but I wondered if you would like copies of the happier moments of the night. I thought you might want them."

Manjeet gave me a thumbs-up approval for my plan to connect with our suspect.

"Thank you, but no thank you," Miranda said primly.

"On the house, of course," I said, not ready to give up. Manjeet squinted disapprovingly at my offer of a freebie, but he'd have to let me off the hook this one time.

"That's very kind of you," she said. "Yes, I think I would like them."

"It's the least I can do. I'm on the Upper East Side today. If you live in the area, I'd be happy to drop them off," I said. As I'd hoped he would, Manjeet re-joined the cause and began to pull the file so I could make prints.

A couple of hours later, I was in front of Miranda's white brick building on a side street in the mid-70s, holding a thick, creamy envelope embossed with the RMS logo.

Technically, Miranda lived in a chic, Upper East Side neighborhood, but her building was nothing compared to the Toppers'.

When I stepped off Miranda's elevator, I followed the sound of yapping dogs down a long hallway dotted with doors to several other apartments. I rang the bell, and the barking escalated to a frenzy.

"All right, all right," I heard Miranda say from inside.

She opened the door to meet me in a purple suit. I could see it was probably smart as hell twenty years ago. In keeping with her flair for big jewelry, today she wore a choker of oversized pearls. The same perfume she had worn the night of the ball hit my nostrils like a shot in the head.

"Come in," she said, ushering me into a small foyer that opened into a modest-sized living room and dining alcove by the kitchen. A door on the other side of the foyer hinted that there were a couple of bedrooms off a short hallway. "Heidi is off today, but if you'd like some tea, I have the kettle on."

She corralled at least six bow-tied and barrette-clad Pekingese dogs into the kitchen and closed the doors before I could answer. I gently pushed aside one of a dozen pet toys that littered her floor while I waited.

"Why don't we have a seat?" said Miranda when she finally came back to the room carrying tea service and snacks on a silver tray.

"Thank you," I said.

I followed her across an ornate Oriental carpet that was fraying in spots. We each settled into wingback armchairs with hard backs and English flowered upholstery. A blanket was folded over the arm of the chair she chose to sit on, and she didn't fool me. The Carreras have long observed the blanket-over-stains aesthetic. I also noticed a dust bunny in the corner of the room. I decided that Miranda had been making her own tea for a long time, since Heidi hadn't been around to clean in a while.

"Here you go," I said, handing the photos to her.

She opened the envelope and dabbed a tissue to her eye as she flipped through the prints while I poured. She indulged in an extra eye dab at the one I'd taken of the Archibalds' table when she would not crack a smile. I tried very hard not to roll my eyes. I'd photographed this woman. That meant I'd studied how the face of this otherwise wholly affected woman was unable to fake a smile around her cousin when he was alive.

"I can't believe that woman killed him," she said, looking up from the photo. "He was so loved by everyone."

"Who is this?" I said, motioning to a frame on the table between us that featured a formal portrait of a young girl with a horse.

To be polite, I took a biscuit from the tray. I'd never been to a tea party before. If this was the standard menu, I planned to never go to one again. The small confection was hard enough to take a tooth out.

"This is Bethany," Miranda said. She took the photo from me and rubbed it with her sleeve as she held it lovingly. "The photo is from years and years ago. She's out of college already.

She recently became engaged to a very successful young man in finance."

"Fintech." I nodded, knowingly. I noticed Miranda hadn't taken a biscuit, and found her increasingly untrustworthy.

"No, he's old-school, dear. He's from the Beston family from Rhode Island," Miranda said with the first hint of a real smile I'd seen on her. "We're planning to throw her a big, big wedding this summer. They'll all be expecting the best, as will we."

Miranda had handed me the best motive I could imagine for killing Archibald: wedding expenses. She'd already called RMS to book the nuptials, so the Headrams were clearly going for it. Otherwise, Miranda would have called someplace more affordable like, for example, Liv Spyers Photography.

"I'm sure you will miss Mr. Archibald at the wedding," I said.

"We will. We will," said Miranda. She was still looking at the photo of her daughter.

"I feel so badly for your niece, Angela," I said. "What a horrible night for all of you. Mr. Archibald seemed like a very special man."

Miranda put down the photo and sipped her tea. I could see she was not happy about something I had said.

"Lion's Mane is a very special company. I'll give you that," she said. "As for my cousin? You want to know something? I wanted to invest in the LaunchTech Fund Charlie was boasting about at the ball. Everyone was congratulating him and fawning all over him. But I had asked Charlie about it before the ball and at the ball again, and he brushed me off. He always did, you know. He always said I didn't have enough money to play with the big boys."

"I hate when people write you off," I said in solidarity. "I get it."

"He toted me around, so he looked like a good family man,

but he never took care of us. It was all business with him. Angela knew it, too."

"Angela?" I said.

"When Angela was a child," said Miranda, putting the photo back onto the table and speaking as if to Bethany's image rather than to me, "Angela was enamored with Bethany's horseback riding career. Angela couldn't ride because she has weak ankles, but she's a love and wished her cousin well. She begged her father to buy Bethany a horse, and he said no. Not that Charlie couldn't have afforded it. If Angela had wanted a horse, that would have been another story, but Bethany had to quit. Angela saw it all."

"Well, hopefully he left enough behind so you can make up for it now and throw an unforgettable wedding for Bethany," I said. "With flat shoes for Angela's wobbly feet, assuming she's a bridesmaid."

"He did remember me. We haven't read the will yet, but I know. Charlie showed me his will once and then told me to stop asking him for help while he was alive."

Out of nowhere, Miranda began to cry real tears. Her nose even began to run and her one tissue quickly became too soggy to use. The tears seemed to reflect genuine grief, but I wondered if it was more like remorse. By now my napkin had half-eaten biscuits stuffed inside, so I had nothing to offer to wipe her tears, but a door opened from the other side of the small foyer and Phil Headram raced out to comfort his wife. I was startled by his appearance since I'd heard nothing beyond the sounds of the pups. In contrast to his wife's attempt at a ladies-who-lunch ensemble, he wore wrinkly twill pants and a polo shirt. His eyes were also watery and red as if he, too, had been having a good cry.

"There, there," Phil said, his arm around Miranda's shoulders.

"I'm sorry, Phil," said Miranda. "I'm trying my best, but it's just all so much."

"She's been very shaken by her cousin's death," Phil said to me.

"I understand," I said. "It's sad and frightening. For all you know, when you left the ballroom at the end of the night, you might have walked right by his killer without even realizing it."

It wasn't the kindest thing to say to a shaken woman, but it seemed as good a time as any to get to the heart of my visit.

"I didn't leave the ballroom," she said, her tears stopping abruptly, anger replacing them. "Nor did Phillip. Although I believe the Toppers left at one point or other."

Instead of calling foul, I rested my cup on the silver tray and stood. If she or Phil were a murderer, I wanted out of there.

"Thank you for the photos," she said and joined me. "Phil, I'm OK now."

We walked into the kitchen—a long, narrow room—which was filled with her dogs, who had been quiet during our conversation but now jumped with glee at seeing their mistress. As the dogs' enthusiasm grew to a ridiculously loud pitch, Miranda stuck her hand in her pocket and then lifted it to her mouth. In one second, the dogs quieted and stood at attention.

Miranda turned to me and waved a small whistle.

"This is a lifesaver. I trained them to stop barking and sit still when they hear the whistle. In return for their obedience, they each get a cookie. Don't you, my sweethearts?"

While Miranda rewarded her dogs' impressive obedience, I looked around the old linoleum-tiled kitchen. By the sink, I noticed a row of jewelry that Miranda must have been cleaning. The treasures consisted of the pieces I'd seen her wear at the ball, including a brooch at least four inches wide. When opened, the fastening pin would be long, pointy, and metal. When she'd left the ballroom after Archibald's disappearance, she could have confronted her cousin at the bar and used the pin to kill him. Then, she could have replaced it on her dress without anyone being the wiser. Phil might even have helped.

Miranda pushed the jewelry to the side and put our tray in their place.

Phil sneezed.

"Poor Philip is allergic to dogs, but he loves our little ones to bits as well," she said.

"I do love them," he said. "But you'll have to excuse me."

Between the brooch, the dogs' barks, and the strong scent of Miranda's floral perfume in the small kitchen, I was tempted to follow Phil.

"I hope you'll keep the photos I gave you between us," I said. "Regina Montague would be furious with me for sharing them with you for free. I didn't offer them to the Toppers or Mrs. Archibald because I thought they might tell Regina. They seem to have a familiar relationship with her."

"You're right about Regina and the Archibalds," she said, leading me to the door. "They certainly mingle outside of working hours. But I'm no gossip."

"Of course not," I said, biting the inside of my check.

"Regina did it," Miranda said firmly when we reached the door. "She was the one with blood on her hands. I'd think twice about working for RMS, assuming it's still around in another month. The police will have Regina arrested in no time."

I didn't put too much stock in Miranda's opinions. She was bitter toward the deceased, had a pressing financial burden that Archibald's death would solve, and had worn a piece of jewelry that could transform into a murder weapon.

I kept my ear trained on the Headrams' apartment, hoping to hear some unguarded conversation. Phil was the first to speak.

"Look at this, my dear," he said before sneezing.

After a pause, I heard a shout from inside the Headrams' apartment.

"Ha!" Miranda cried out with great emphasis on the word.

She wasn't laughing, however. There was a bitterness in her

voice. It was mixed with something else. I realized it was glee. Bitter glee. Like the sound of someone dancing on someone else's grave. And it didn't stop. She said *Ha!* to Mr. Binders, and again to Lady, and then Sugar and the rest of her small and loyal army.

Then, the sounds of joy shifted to those I could only describe as panic. She started cursing, and the dogs began to wail with her. I had not left the Headrams with a ring of ink around my face as I had at the Toppers, but my visit to Miranda had left me equally, if not more, turned around.

The elevator opened and as it descended, I saw that Harry had sent me a text.

Did you see the news? Check out story on Charlie Archibald.

I looked to see what had interested him. It was bigger than I could have imagined.

Archibald's murder was old news. A breaking story suddenly made the victim look like the villain.

> *Charles Archibald, co-founder and managing partner of Lion's Mane Capital, who was murdered last week at his daughter's social debut at the exclusive Holiday Ball, is now being investigated by officials regarding corporate financial irregularities. Last month, Archibald introduced a new investment fund, LaunchTech, through Lion's Mane, which focuses on fintech investment. The fund has been one of the most talked about of the fourth quarter, and Archibald privately secured most of the financing himself.*
>
> *Federal authorities along with the SEC now report that that the fund began to tank immediately after launch. To keep up the appearance of*

> *success, Archibald skimmed revenues from the Archibald Foundation, which he founded to support fintech opportunities and education in New York City schools. It appears that Archibald hoped the fund would recover, and in the interim used funds from his not-for-profit group to cover his losses. Authorities are now investigating whether he used the foundation for other schemes in the past.*
>
> *No arrests have been made of the partners at Lion's Mane. At present, authorities believe that Archibald acted on his own accord. However, Lion's Mane assets have been frozen, and the Archibald Foundation has been closed indefinitely.*
>
> *It is not clear if Archibald's murder was related to his financial crimes.*

When I finished the article, I stared in disbelief at a photo of Charlie Archibald in his office, an American flag hanging behind him. I studied his eyes for a clue to his devilry, but I found, instead, his terrifyingly affable look. Charlie Archibald had started from humble beginnings, like Regina. Like me. But he had cut corners following his dreams and his bad karma had caught up with him.

I understood the outbursts I'd heard from Miranda. Her first reaction was probably relief that she had not invested in Archibald's illicit fund. She'd probably felt she had had the last laugh.

When the news sank in, however, she must have realized that her cousin's assets would be frozen for the foreseeable future. The inheritance she'd been banking on was likely gone, as were her plans to throw a lavish wedding for her daughter.

I thought about Felicity Cromwell, too. I'd been wondering what was behind her outburst in the reception hall outside of the ball. Now I suspected she had uncovered the fraud. And if she had discovered Archibald's scheme, Bill Topper might have as well.

Unbelievable, I responded to Harry. **Much to discuss tonight.**

I wondered how the Toppers were reacting to the news. I was thrilled that Anne had supplied me with the small job of her husband's gift. I had an excuse to visit the Toppers again. I headed home to get to work.

On the subway, I thought about Miranda Headram's pile of jewelry, particularly her brooch. The truth was, I remembered that Regina had also been wearing a brooch about the same size at the ball. I felt my chest tighten as I considered the fact that Regina, as Archibald's lover, might have been an investor in his fund. If so, and she had found out about his scam, his betrayal might have driven her to desperation. I wished I knew exactly who had invested in LaunchTech.

CHAPTER 12

Back at my studio, I was struggling to make the best of my skyline shots from the Toppers' window look like something more than an image from a real estate brochure when there was a knock on my studio door. I hadn't realized the day had flown by so quickly, but sure enough, Maria was outside, waving at me through my storefront's window. I ran to greet her, and we hugged each other as if we hadn't seen each other in years instead of days. Maria dropped her oversized handbag on the floor and laid the coat she had brought for me on my desk chair.

Maria was a full-time paralegal at a law firm in Midtown while studying to take the LSATs at night, and I knew she'd come straight from work by her attire. She was dressed in a brown suit decorated with a strand of pearls. They were more tasteful than the statement pearl choker Miranda Headram wore, but Maria's current look was the opposite of everything I associated with her love of bright colors and bedazzled clothing. The only remnant of the friend I knew was her five-inch heels. How she could run around on those every day was beyond me, but I took great comfort in the fact that she hadn't given them up. I was very proud of her.

"I'm so glad to take a break from studying for this test. You have no idea," she said, heading to my fridge, which she opened. "I brought nail polish. Beauty night. Let's get you looking your most gorgeous for date night."

"You are my hero," I said.

She closed the fridge and turned to me, holding the last of my leftover pork and fennel stuffing from Thanksgiving. Granny's classic. I handed her a fork.

"Seriously, though." She took a bite of stuffing. "What's with this guy and murder?"

I handed her a glass of water and gave her the run down. When I finished, she washed up her empty plate.

"I know you'll do anything to get a foothold into this world," she said, "but you don't have to find a killer to prove yourself."

"I'm not trying to prove myself," I said, surprising myself by my defensive tone. "I'm trying to help someone who helped me."

"OK. Keep your pants on," she said with a smile that reminded me how lucky I was to have a friend who knew me so well. "Wash your hair. Let's do a blowout."

I gave Maria another hug, and we got to work. About two hours later, I was waving my freshly polished nails from the mountain of clothes on my bed to make sure they were fully dry. Since I wasn't going to be the help at Popolous's party tonight, I'd decided on my strapless red. Maria also convinced me to put on my highest heels after I told her how tall Harry was.

"You don't want to have to stand on your stoop for a goodnight kiss," she said to convince me.

As we were finishing up, there was a knock at my door.

"He's early," said Maria. "Good. I get to check him out."

Maria skipped out of my room and peered around the partition between my room and the studio. I followed.

Rather than finding Harry outside my studio window, we saw a delicate blonde, lit from the streetlamps, peering in at us.

It took me a moment to realize it was Angela Archibald. Without her professional makeup and white ballgown, she looked much younger. She also looked fragile, and I knew that must be from the shock of having lost her father so violently. Although she was much changed, her perfect haircut and highlights, dewy skin, and clothes that seemed to have been custom cut were still a knockout.

"Just watch yourself," Maria said as she lifted her bag. "These people can be crazy. And before you know it, you will be, too."

"But I have you," I said. "No need to be crazy when I've already got the perfect kind of crazy."

"I want to hear everything when you get home," she said as I opened the door. She gave Angela a smile that I knew was judgmental and walked down the street.

"I'm so sorry for your loss," I said to Angela.

I wasn't sure if I should hug Angela, or what, but I let her into the studio.

"Thanks," she said. She squeezed my hand. "I love your dress. Am I intruding? You look like you're about to leave."

"Are you kidding?" I said. "If my date's worth dating, he'll wait. You've had the worst week of your life."

"Thank you," said Angela, fighting tears. "Your place is amazing."

When Regina had entered my studio a couple of days ago, I'd suddenly felt small. Watching Angela take in my space now, I remembered how fortunate I was. Angela had the weight of the world on her shoulders, and here I was with a studio and my work hanging on the walls.

"I know that view. It's from Bill Topper's home office," she said, looking at my photo of the Toppers' skyline.

I nodded.

"I saw that desk in a lot of Zoom calls during Covid," she said with a sad, nostalgic smile. "Dad always said Bill's desk was a little too 'oval office' for him."

"I get what he meant. And how about Bill's fountain pen?" I said.

She looked confused, so I figured she wouldn't have anything to add on that subject.

"Come and sit down," I said, leading her to the guest chair at my desk.

"You must think I'm crazy to come here like this. In the middle of everything. My poor dad. They haven't released his body yet. Who would want to kill my father?"

She looked at me as if she wanted an answer, but I had no idea what to say.

"I was going to message you, but then I realized this is something I wanted to talk about in person," she said. "I heard you saw my father's body."

"I did."

"I was hoping you could tell me what you think happened that night. Why do you think Regina did it?" Angela said.

"You saw how she was when your hand was bleeding before the ball," I said. "Do you think she could have stabbed someone?"

"The police think she did it," said Angela.

She shifted her eyes away from me to focus aimlessly on one of my photographs. I got the feeling she knew something, but not about Archibald and Regina. I wondered what she might be hiding.

"I know people are saying my father and Regina were having an affair, but it's not true. My family has known her for years," she said. "It's actually my mom who has the closer relationship to her."

"Maybe Regina invested in his fund? I heard about the situation with LaunchTech," I said, opting to not be the one to tell her about her father's affair.

Angela's pale cheeks flushed a deep red and left her perfect skin mottled with shame.

"I don't know who invested, to be honest. I probably know

a lot of people who were clients. I guess hundreds of people wouldn't mind seeing my father dead now," she said.

"How was he these last few days?" I said.

"He did look anxious," she said. "Of course, now I know why. He bought some little gifts for me and Mom that week. I'm thinking now, maybe he knew things might fall apart and he wanted to be a hero for a bit longer. Can I look at the table photo of us during dinner?"

"Sure," I said.

I opened my laptop to the photos from the ball. Before turning my screen toward her, I moved the photo of her father's dead body to another file. I also hit Send on the photo I'd taken of Angela and her father on the dance floor. My printer started to hum as it made a copy. Angela didn't notice. She stared at the photos for a good long while.

"Do you see anything unusual?" I said.

"No. The thing that makes me so sad is that I didn't even care that much about coming out."

"So, why did you?" I said. "It's kind of an old-fashioned thing to do."

"Honestly," she said, "it sounded like fun to get dressed up, but mostly I knew it would make my dad happy. He didn't grow up with much. He's a self-made man. He got a scholarship to Yale and from there, many doors opened for him. He walked through every one of them. He knew how important it is to take advantage of every opportunity in life. It made him happy to think he'd given me a leg up, too. I'm not sure, these days, how much my debutante will matter, but for me, it was special for that reason. Now I keep thinking that if I had said no, he might be alive."

"You can't think like that," I said.

Angela pushed my laptop back toward me so we could both see the screen. I wondered what she had been looking for.

Then, I noticed something I had not seen before. In one

photo of their dinner table, Regina was watching the group from a quiet corner of the room, her expression serious and sad. It reminded me of a similar photo I'd seen of her in the vault at RMS. In it, Regina was also in the background, watching the Archibalds from afar.

"May I?" I said.

Angela nodded. I flipped backward, to the photo I'd taken right before this one, when the group had been assembling. I'd noticed that night that Charlie Archibald had been momentarily distracted. Now it seemed to me that he had noticed Regina looking at their group. Skipping a couple of thumbnails ahead, I also noticed Regina had eventually turned away, her hand on her heart.

"Do you see something?" Angela said.

"Only that your aunt doesn't look particularly happy in these photos," I said.

Angela laughed sadly.

"She never looks happy," she said. "Dad always said family is important, but sometimes I thought his invitations to posh events and parties only made Aunt Miranda bitter."

"I agree with him on family," I said. "A little smile wouldn't have hurt her. What's her husband like?"

"Phil? He's all right. He bought me a stuffed zebra from the zoo when I was little," she said. "Miranda was angry because he spent too much money on me that day, but Phil is a sweet guy. He works in accounting, seems to like his job. He does anything Miranda says, which I guess is sweet."

I wondered if he'd help Miranda with murder.

"Thanks for talking," she said. "I don't know who to trust these days and my mom's disappeared."

"What do you mean?" I said, warning bells going off in my head as loudly as if Carrera's alarm had been triggered upstairs.

"My mom is a wonderful person, but my father's death has been an unbearable shock," said Angela. "She told me she needed some time alone to plan the funeral. We've texted, but I am worried about her, mostly because I don't even know where she is. Our country house is being renovated for next summer, so that's not habitable. First Dad, now her. All because Regina Montague is a psychopath."

I come from a family where a flat tire merits a battalion of visitors, all with an opinion to share. The idea that Donna would disappear to plan the funeral alone seemed particularly suspicious to me, especially if she was usually a doting mother. I wondered what would drive a mother away from her daughter at such a tragic time. Guilt seemed like a fair reason.

"I'll be honest with you," I said. "I keep looking through these photos as well, for an answer. I didn't know Regina for long, but it doesn't add up for me."

"I'm sorry you feel badly about Regina, but you shouldn't," she said, fighting tears. "My father was murdered. Everyone's saying she did it. If you find something, or if you remember anything, you need to tell the police right away."

"I will," I said. "And I'm sorry about your mom."

"I'll be fine. She'll be home after the funeral. She promised and I trust her."

"Here, take this," I said.

I reached over to my printer and put the photo of Angela and her father dancing into an envelope.

"Don't look at it now or my mascara will be running all down my cheeks and I want to look good tonight."

"Thank you," she said. She took the envelope and gave me a quick hug.

When I closed the door behind Angela, I headed into my bedroom for one last look at myself. I'd forgotten earrings. As I fastened in my hanging crystally ones, I thought about Angela and realized something.

I flipped through my photos until I found one that would never make it to RMS's public website. It was of a group of debutantes and their friends on their way out. Angela was among the crowd. I hadn't focused much on the photo, but now I noticed that the sharp comb that had caused her to prick her hand earlier that night was gone. Her hair hung loosely as she headed out for a more relaxed after-party. I wondered if Donna Archibald had taken the comb from her daughter. I also wondered if a prong on her comb could have been bent in such a way that it could have been used to poke Archibald's eye out. If it could stab through someone's skin, it could have penetrated an eye.

A car honked outside my studio, and I saw Harry approach my gate.

Chapter 13

"You look nice," he said as we stepped over some garbage.

"Thanks. You too," I said.

Our car took us to Hudson Yards on the West Side, near the Hudson River. I was familiar with the Yard's mall, and Vessel, which is a honey-combed, multistory attraction, but I was amazed when we pulled up to one of the luxury residential towers nearby.

"Here?" I said as Harry opened the door in front of a soaring shaft of glass that changed from a typical, rectangular-shaped building at its base to connected, circular towers at the top.

"That's what the invite says." Harry looked as excited to check out the building as I did. I assumed he'd seen a lot of amazing real estate in his time, but it was nice that he could appreciate something special.

In the lobby of the building, a woman in a bright pink boa and matching slip dress, which was optimistic for the cold weather, checked in a growing line of guests arriving to the party. An actor I'd seen in a reality TV series I'd binged on for a full week after I'd dropped out of college entered ahead of us with two young women.

"Welcome," she said when it was our turn. "You'll be heading up to the Skytop tonight, New York City's highest outdoor residential roof deck."

When we got on the elevator, I started to feel pressure in my ears at about the fortieth floor.

"This is basically an open house," said a guy with slicked-back hair and a pin-striped suit behind me. He struck me as the kind of guy my lost OneShot client was hoping to become. "This building has a pool, a spa, private dining suites, and screening rooms, all that kind of stuff. They even have a golf club on-site. I bet he'll get a lot of offers after tonight. I heard the last sale in this building was for fifty million dollars."

I looked at Harry and dropped my jaw to silently express my awe. He nodded and mouthed "I know" back to me. Access to a dozen amenities didn't come cheap. When we stepped off the elevator and walked out to the roof deck, I almost thought fifty million dollars was a good deal. The skyline was magnificent. The view of New Jersey, I might add, never looked so good. If the sun were shining, I'd be able to see my parents' home, sixty miles away.

I thought of Popolous, the man with the gentlemanly cane from the Holiday Ball in comparison to the scene of B-list celebrities, rising financiers and a general cadre of beautiful people on his roof. I'd have wagered good money that Popolous knew fewer than half the people on his roof. In fact, as far as I could tell, the host for the evening wasn't even at his own party.

Harry checked our coats while I took two glasses from a passing waiter's tray. "Have something pink," I said about our brightly colored cocktails.

"Assume these are a lot stronger than they taste," said Harry. "I think that guy in the elevator was serious when he said this is an open house. Check out the people being trailed by real estate agents with bright pink roses in their lapels. I'll bet you this party is ultimately for these people; to let them see the luxurious life they would lead here. And to see the competition they face to call this place home. Super wealthy guys like Popolous sometimes dabble in real estate. They buy something and turn it for a profit."

"Our host is not as wealthy as he pretends to be."

"How do you know?" Harry said with a smile I took as a challenge.

"His fingers are manicured, and his cane and shoes are polished," I said, "but he stayed until most of the guests at the Holiday Ball had left. Then, when he felt no one would notice, he asked for leftovers to take home with him."

"Interesting," he said. "As you said, your eyes are your secret weapon. Aunt Bernie invited him at the last minute because she knew his late wife and heard he was in town."

"I guess to sell this place. Shall we?" I said.

"Lead the way."

Harry and I spent the next half hour or so exploring the party. The weather was cold, but the roof was toasty warm because, in addition to several heat lamps, the designers had had the good sense to enclose the space with a several-story-high glass wall. We headed into a couple of indoor areas and wove our way back outside where a DJ at the far end of the roof was surrounded by women dressed as very sexy Statues of Liberty.

"This *is* a very different crowd than the other night," Harry said as if reading my mind. "I'm not sure we'll be finding any suspects here."

"Actually, I'm not so sure about that," I said. "Check it out. That's Elizabeth Everly. She was the party planner for the ball."

Elizabeth Everly was indeed talking to the DJ and holding her trusty clip board. "A suspect?" said Harry.

I shrugged.

"She was there when we discovered Archibald," I said.

We were blatantly staring at Elizabeth Everly at this point, and she noticed us. I decided she recognized me because she furrowed her brow and made no effort to return my greeting. She purposefully turned and joined the crowd, which was now too thick for us to weave through before we lost her.

"Damn," I said. "Where did she go?"

"OK, OK, partyers!" said the DJ. "Who wants to get crazy?"

The crowd cheered. The Statues of Liberty gathered around the DJ and extracted bags of inflated, pink balloons, each about the size of a grapefruit.

"My girls here are looking for some fun," said the DJ as the women tossed the balloons into the crowd. "Grab a balloon and a partner."

Harry grabbed a balloon as it flew over his head.

"Listen up. Everyone, look at these lovely ladies," said the DJ. "They're going to show you how it's done."

The Lady Liberties paired up in front of the DJ's table.

"OK, girls," he said, turning up a rhythmic beat. "Show 'em how it's done. You put a balloon between your back and your partner's, and you've gotta pop this baby with only your bodies. Only one rule, you can't use your hands."

"What's the winner get?" said a man in the crowd. The DJ laughed.

"What do these guys get?" he said to the dancers. "I don't know, dude, you get to live here."

The crowd laughed and cheered.

"You get a membership to the Classic Car Club," Elizabeth yelled over the crowd from a spot across the roof from us. She sounded muffled, which made the announcement of her prize sound not that exciting.

"And you get to part-tay," said the DJ raucously into his microphone to keep the partyers energized.

The cheers rose again as the dancers threw balloons into the crowd. "Let's do this thing," said the DJ.

"There's one way to get Elizabeth Everly's attention," said

Harry, swinging the tied end of his balloon between his fingers. "Let's do this thing."

"Even if it's just a fancy rental car, I love a good party favor."

"I see that," said Harry as he watched me put my clutch beside us and adjust my dress.

Happy that my highest heels now brought me to a halfway decent height to Harry, I turned my back to him and soon felt the supple balloon between my bare shoulders and Harry's jacket. The music picked up and about a dozen couples began to push against each other. One couple immediately lost their balloon. I moved gently against Harry and the balloon rolled up my back. Harry rocked his shoulders to keep them balanced as we turned around to face each other.

"Hello," he said.

"Hello."

Picking up the rhythm of the music, I leaned my shoulder into his. "So, Elizabeth Everly?" Harry said.

"We can't leave a stone unturned."

"Spoken like a true detective."

I rolled my hip up the balloon, which had fallen to Harry's thigh. "Just like Regina, Elizabeth Everly was in and out of the dining room. No one was really focused on her. It's why she's considered one of the best in the business. She's there when you need her . . ."

". . . And she knows how to disappear in plain sight while getting work done." Harry nodded in agreement.

A balloon from a couple next to us flew into the air, and the pair left the dance floor.

"Now all you need to do is figure out why she'd kill one of her best clients," he said. I stopped moving.

"I think it's time we talk to her," I said as the balloon rolled into my cleavage. I lowered my head and popped the balloon with my teeth, determined to get my moment with my suspect.

Harry took my hand and raised it in the air. I turned under his arm and twirled across the floor in a victory spin. Before I turned back, I saw Elizabeth make her way through the crowd to award us our prize.

"Hang on," I called out to her, spinning back into the crowd toward Harry.

"I think you're a hit," he said.

"Well, we've got her attention."

"I see you're here as a guest tonight," Elizabeth said to me as the crowd dispersed.

She handed me my prize, a small envelope. It had been secured onto her clipboard and when she removed it, I noticed a thin pair of scissors was attached to the board and lived artfully inside the clasp. It wasn't odd that a party planner might need a pair of scissors handy during an event. Jinx had her emergency items tucked away. We all had these sorts of essentials on hand in our profession; except one of Elizabeth's tools was a long, thin, metal, pointy blade.

I stepped on Harry's toe with excitement. Murder weapon? Check.

"I can put the envelope in my—" Harry began to say, and then stopped as I tucked my party favor into my purse.

"Last time I saw you it was quite a different night," I said to Elizabeth. "Are you doing OK after Archibald's death?"

"Better than your boss," she said.

Elizabeth looked at Harry and smiled. Then she glanced at me and tilted her head. I could see she was wondering how I'd gotten myself on the guest list. I smiled back.

"Can I leave you two together for a moment?" Harry said tactfully. "I've got to use the restroom."

I knew that Elizabeth had no interest in hanging around with me. If I hadn't been with Harry, she would have turned on her heels. My date, however, was a different story. She did not want to look bad in front of a potential client. I nodded to

Harry that we'd be fine. After a few minutes of awkward chit chat, I jumped right into it.

"Wild night, the other night. Huh?" I said. "At first, I couldn't believe someone would kill Charlie Archibald, but now that the scandal about Lion's Mane has been reported, it makes a lot more sense. Don't you think?"

"I guess. I would have killed him myself if Regina hadn't beaten me to it," said Elizabeth in what I thought was a bold statement to make while Archibald's murder was under investigation.

"Why's that?" I said.

"Charlie—Mr. Archibald—was going to invest in my business. We'd had many meetings about his investing in my firm so I could grow nationally. And then, last week, he pulled out of the deal. Left me high and dry. And I'd already invested some of my own money in development, so I'm now worse off than before."

"Sorry about your business," I said, appreciating her predicament. "Your parties are amazing, though. I'm sure you'll bounce back."

"Regina is an idiot," said Elizabeth. "She threw away her reputation and her business all because she was afraid that Charlie was going to leave her. Of course, he was going to leave her. I don't know how she could have thought it would be otherwise between them in the long run."

"Did you ever go out with him?" It was a bold question, but she seemed to be too familiar with how he worked.

"Honey, never date the clients. That's rule number one. Keep it in mind," she said, reminding me of Regina's same advice. Except Regina had not followed her own rule. I wondered if Elizabeth had.

"I saw your encounter with Felicity Cromwell, when she tried to crash the party," I said. "Thinking back now, she must have known something was up with the foundation's accounting. She clearly wanted to confront Archibald."

Elizabeth clenched her jaw. I wondered if I was on to something.

"Felicity Cromwell has always been a very trustworthy, level-headed woman," said Elizabeth. "What Charlie Archibald did to her and the foundation was awful, but she would never have killed the man."

"Did she leave the party as you asked her to?" I said.

"I led Felicity into the room where you took the portraits of the debutantes before the ball began. She promised she'd leave after she composed herself, and I trust she did just that."

It was clear to me that Elizabeth had not checked to confirm that Felicity had left. I appreciated Elizabeth's confidence in Felicity, whom she'd clearly met before the night of the ball, but I wasn't ready to blindly trust anyone at this point. The fact was, Felicity Cromwell could have still been around at the end of the ball, despite what Detective Thorne had told me about no one coming or going from the party after Archibald disappeared. She had had the benefit of not being seen by anyone. And she had a grudge against Charlie Archibald.

"Sorry about that," said Harry, who returned to my side.

"Excuse me," said Elizabeth. She took advantage of his return to disappear back into the crowd.

"So?" he said.

"Archibald screwed her financially," I said. "Not through the LaunchTech fund, but he was going to invest in her business and then dropped out at the last minute."

"Interesting. Do you think they were having an affair?"

"Not clear," I said. "I wish I had paid more attention when I visited Charlie and Regina's love pad. When I was there, I was looking for a reason to clear Regina. I should have been focused on learning more about Archibald."

"Charlie Archibald had a love pad, which you broke into?" said Harry, looking more than a little surprised. "I didn't realize how deep your investigations have gone."

"It's not that bad. I had the key," I said. "Regina gave it to me to copy. That's how I first met her. I didn't know at the time they were keys to the two's apartment, but it's how I found out where it was. Long story. Although, point of pride, I've been a skilled lockpick since I was four."

"You're so out of my league," Harry said with a laugh. "Do you want to get out of here?"

"On one condition."

"Name it," he said.

CHAPTER 14

"Tell me this isn't the best pizza you've ever had," I said as we sat at a table on Bleeker Street at my favorite pizza joint.

"This was worth it," said Harry.

He reached for a second slice from the large pie we'd ordered. The mozzarella stretched from the tray to his paper plate. I handed him a jar of red pepper flakes.

"OK," he said, tossing a healthy amount of the herbs onto his slice. "Who are your suspects at this point, and what do we have on them?"

"Excellent question," I said, wiping my mouth with my third napkin. "Detective Thorne said that the murder of Charlie Archibald was a crime of passion. That deduction was based on the violence of the act itself. I guess stabbing someone in the eye isn't the sort of thing you plot."

"Unless the murderer was going for a symbolic 'eye for an eye' statement."

"True," I said. "But when balanced against the fact that the murder itself was so public, and therefore risky, it still reads 'crime of passion.' I'd like to take credit for that deduction, but it came from Detective Thorne."

"The crust is amazing," said Harry.

"I've tried to replicate it at home," I said, agreeing with his appraisal. "I've come close, but I've concluded that it's the oven here that provides the magic touch."

"I see investigating things isn't entirely new to you," he said with a wink.

"I honestly think it would be easier to find a killer than discover the secret to this pie crust."

It was weird to laugh over murder, but that's what a great pizza can do for you.

"So, a crime of passion," he said. "Basing the investigation on this assumption, who are the suspects?"

"There were nine of us remaining at the Pierre, at the time Archibald was murdered: Donna Archibald, the Toppers, the Headrams, a waiter, Regina, Elizabeth Everly, and me. Thorne said that security was watching points of egress, and no one exited between the time that Archibald left the ballroom and when Regina and I found him."

"Assuming you and Regina were not the killers, that leaves seven suspects?" said Harry. "Maybe eight," I said. "I am not sure, but I think Felicity Cromwell might have been there, too."

"I'm overwhelmed already."

"Me too," I admitted.

We each focused on our pizza for a moment.

"We know at least seven suspects left the room and returned at some point after Archibald stormed out," I said.

"Who had motive?"

"Between love and money, arguably everyone had a motive," I said. "Detective Thorne has focused on the love angle from the get-go. Given the behaviors and dynamics I observed in my suspects the night of the ball, however, I keep coming back to money."

"Since Archibald was skimming off of the foundation to prop up LaunchTech, it feels like money's a solid motive," said Harry.

"Except the news of Archibald's financial crimes was released after his death," I said. "It seems certain that Felicity Cromwell had figured it out. Bill Topper or Donna Archibald might have, too. I haven't spoken to Bill Topper, yet, but I know he was furious with Charlie that night, and tried several times to talk to him. But even with the fraud, would he want Archibald dead? Wouldn't it be easier to deal with the fall out if Charlie Archibald were around to take the blame?"

"You're assuming Bill Topper had nothing to do with the scandal," said Harry. "If he was involved, too, Archibald's death could be convenient. He could lay the blame entirely on his partner."

"I hadn't thought of that," I said.

"I'm glad I've got something to add to the mix," he said with a little flirt thrown in for good measure. It worked. My cheeks grew a bit warm, so I forged ahead.

"Anne Topper had also invested in the fund. I had crossed her off my list, but if she'd overheard the men talking during the ball, she might have become distraught."

"Which fits with the spontaneity of a crime of passion," Harry agreed.

"I'll follow up on that when I next visit the Toppers," I said. "Honestly, Anne didn't look as if she knew about the scandal when I talked to her. In fact, she made a point of telling me she was expecting a windfall through the fund."

"Seems like Bill is the likelier suspect of the Toppers," said Harry, now truly hooked, his elbows on the table and his fingers pressed against his lips, as we delved deeper into the list.

"There were others whom Archibald financially screwed over, outside of the fund," I said.

"This guy was on fire," said Harry.

"Right? Miranda Headram wanted to invest in the fund, but Charlie wouldn't let her. I'd like to think it was the one decent thing he did, keeping his cousin from losing money he knew she couldn't afford to play around with. Miranda went to the party that night thinking her cousin was keeping her out of the fund when he knew she needed money for her daughter's wedding. Meanwhile, Charlie's daughter was in a designer dress. Miranda could have snapped. There was a lot of resentment building up over the years. I've heard those weddings cost hundreds of thousands of dollars."

"Sometimes millions. But just wondering, how do you know all that?" he said.

"I visited Miranda and Phil Headram, too."

"I guess that was a silly question."

"I get focused when I have a goal," I said. "On to Elizabeth Everly. She also wanted him dead. She told me as much. Archibald's changing finances caused him to cancel the investment in her company that he'd promised to make."

Harry pulled a sip of his root beer from a straw. "What about Miranda Headram's husband?" he said.

"Phil? From what I've heard about him, he probably doesn't share his wife's ambition to throw a big wedding. On the other hand, he adores his wife. I've seen it in many photos RMS has taken of them, and I witnessed it firsthand at their apartment. He would do a lot for her. If Miranda wanted Charlie dead so she could get some inheritance, would Phil do it?"

"You think he'd murder Charlie Archibald to make his wife happy?"

"Honestly? Not really," I said. "It's only my opinion, but it doesn't seem like a guy who has spent decades listening to his wife complain about Archibald would suddenly kill the man in the middle of a party."

"I agree," he said. "But guys can do crazy things when they're in love. Which leads us to the love motive?"

I smiled, folded my paper plate in half and shoved my used napkin in between the folds. "Which leads to Donna Archibald," I said. "She might have killed her husband because she had discovered he was involved with Regina. And, get this, she's been MIA this week. Her daughter said she's been in touch with her mom but doesn't know where she is. She's left her daughter alone right after the murder of her father? What the hell?"

"The jilted spouse is a classic motive for a murder and would seem to fall into the crime-of-passion category," said Harry.

"She also might have discovered that her wealthy life was in jeopardy with Charlie's shady dealings."

"She's the only suspect we know of who had both love and money as motive to kill," said Harry.

He tossed his plate into the trash bin.

"You broke into Regina and Charlie's apartment. You've visited the Headrams and the Toppers. And you interviewed Elizabeth Everly tonight," he said. "Are you ready for your next move?"

"Are you going to join me?" I said.

"You are breaking into Archibald's love pad again, right?" he said. "Or am I reading this wrong?"

I smiled confidently.

"And you're going to go with or without me, I assume?" he said.

I continued to smile.

"OK," he said, sighing resignedly. "Let's do this?"

"I know how this looks," I said. "I take photographs. This is murder. Those two things don't usually go hand in hand."

"I mean, yeah, it's kinda nuts, but somehow here we are. That eye of yours saw that Regina avoids blood at any cost, that Elizabeth Everly and Archibald had friction between them, that Miranda Headram's affectations are brutal, and the list goes on. Those are important nuances that the police probably haven't had time to think about. At least not yet. They're probably negotiating with the FBI and the SEC about who's in charge and dealing with a bunch of other red tape. Plus, you've got me."

"When you put it that way," I said.

I crumpled my last napkin and tossed it at his head.

We thanked the pizza makers, and I pushed the door open. The sky was dark, but the streetlights blazed and car horns honked. When we breathed, we could see our breath. I kept Maria's coat open, despite the chill in the air. My silky dress felt good.

"It's over there," I said a few blocks later.

I pointed to the building with the blue door, a block away.

"What's the apartment number?" said Harry when we reached the building's stoop.

"4A," I said. I looked up at the apartment's window. All the lights were out.

We climbed the steps to the front door. I pressed the button to make sure no one was home. I pressed again. There was no answer.

"We're in luck, I guess," I said.

I looked at the lock on the front door. "Damn. This is a Bowley lock."

"You've lost me," said Harry as he raised his coat collar to stay warm.

"Bowley locks are designed with a unique shape so that lock-picks can't reach the pins. Only specially designed keys can reach the angle to the shielded pin system inside. Someone was interested in their privacy here."

"I have a much less sophisticated technique for breaking in," he said, and proceeded to press the buttons for all six residences.

We waited for someone to ring us in. No one did. I pressed again and a window opened above us. A man from 3A stuck his head out and cursed at us. We waved and apologized. He slammed the window.

I walked back down to the stairs and looked up at the apartments from the sidewalk. Harry joined me. "Don't even think about it," said Harry as he, too, saw the fire escape in front of the A-line apartments that had caught my attention.

"Obviously no one is home," I said, taking off my high heels, which felt great. "And I left the window unlocked the other day. I can shimmy up there in no time, and ring you in. We'll take a brief look around and go."

"It just occurred to me," he said. "I've never been on a date where there's a possibility it might end with one or both of us needing to be bailed out of jail."

"You've just been dating the wrong kind of girls," I said, and handed Harry my shoes. "Give me a boost."

Harry looked both ways. There were people on the street, for sure, but no police or cop cars, so he stuck a shoe into each of his coat pockets and cupped his hands. I stepped into them.

"I can't reach," I said, raising my hands to the rusty iron ladder that dangled from the building. Unlike the beautifully painted front door, this baby hadn't been touched in decades. "Can you hike me up a little?"

I felt myself rise a couple more inches. Harry was strong for a guy who processed insurance claims at a desk all day. I felt him straddle his legs for extra balance, and I stepped on his shoulder with one foot. I was careful, because of the dress, but thankfully my fingers reached the bottom rung of the ladder. I was able to lower it enough that I knew I'd be able to hoist myself up on my own.

"What do you think you are doing?" said a woman walking her dog.

"It's OK," I said from above her, one foot still on Harry's shoulder. "I left my keys inside. I've done this before. I just need to climb up to my window and open it up."

"What are you thinking?" she said, not budging. "You could fall and kill yourself. Call a locksmith."

"I did," I said. "They're closed. Can't come until tomorrow. But I've done this before. I'm not worried."

The woman's dog began to poop.

"Carrera's keys?" she said, opening her poop baggy. "I saw the old man who runs it talking to himself on the street the other day."

My hands were beginning to freeze on the iron, which was the only reason I didn't pause to defend my family.

"She has a point," said Harry. "We can spend the night at my place and come back in the morning."

"I bet you'd like that, wouldn't you?" I said to Harry.

"I mean. Yeah," he said.

I took time out from breaking-and-entering to smile at this man who was holding me up on his shoulder while a woman yelled at us. The good news was that the lady seemed to be more comfortable knowing that I'd at least reached out for help before risking my life.

"I like your outfit," she said, bending down to her pup's mess.

"Thanks," I said.

Sensing she wasn't going to stop me, I reached my free hand below me and wiggled my fingers.

"Shoes," I said.

"What?" said Harry. His perfectly combed hair was all over the place and I thought it suited him very well.

I looked at the woman with an expression of pity about my date's ignorance about women's shoes, hoping for some female bonding to move things along.

"I can't climb up without shoes on," I said. "I'd need a tetanus shot by the time I reached the first floor."

"Give her the shoes," the woman said to Harry.

"But they're heels," he said.

"A woman knows how to do anything in heels," the woman said.

Harry handed me my highest heels without further argument.

"Not that I don't agree with him," the woman said. "You're taking a terrible risk."

To prove to her otherwise, I balanced my shod foot on the bottom rung of the ladder and hoisted myself up.

"See?" I said, showing off with another wave. "I'm fine."

A couple of boys walked by and cheered me, but the woman drove them away with a few sharp words.

Although I had successfully overridden her objections, she now seemed quite content to watch me climb. I heard Harry try to distract her by playing with her pooch and asking her about the dog's breed. She answered, but her attention to me did not waver.

Fortunately, the building's residents had not noticed the commotion below, but I wasted no time climbing that ladder. I knew from my own visit to 4A that to reach to the fourth floor, I would have to pass the living room windows of each of the A-line apartments.

At the first floor, there were no lights on. My only challenge was to navigate my spiky heels across the gaps between the metal bars of the landing. And yes, it was as acrobatic a feat as it sounds.

The next floor up was a bit trickier. The light was on. I gathered up my dress and dipped down low, beneath the window's sash, and proceeded to squat-walk between each metal bar.

The rush of adrenaline at my success in reaching that ladder was extraordinary, until the woman's dog below began to bark up at me.

"Are you OK?" the lady called to me.

I should have been freezing. I was in a strapless silk dress under my coat, my breath rising in cold clouds above me. Instead, I was sweating buckets. Afraid of attracting the attention of the third-floor tenants, I gave her an all-good wave.

"Are—you—O—K?" she said again, more loudly.

I saw Harry trying to distract her, but as he did the window opened not two feet away from me and the occupant of 3A stuck his head out the window.

I pressed myself against the cold brick wall. I could see the dog lady was about to give me away, probably thinking 3A was my alleged neighbor and could rescue me. Fortunately, her dog began to bark even more wildly at two large Labradors heading toward them from the other end of the block. I said a prayer, which was answered. The woman's love for her dog matched that of Miranda Headram's love for her own furry friends. She lost all interest in me and started to scold the large dogs, while their owner began to defend them.

"Do you have a cigarette?" said the guy whose head still hung out the window.

For one horrible moment, I thought the guy was speaking to me, but then I heard a muffled answer from inside 3A. He must have gotten the response he wanted, because I could hear him step away from the window. Taking advantage of his retreat, I leapt onto the last ladder and scurried up its rungs. Once there, I didn't have a moment to spare. I could see straight across the street and into another building. Whether I imagined it or not, I was sure I'd made eye contact with the occupant there, so I turned to the window and looked inside.

I was in front of the living room of apartment 4A. Although the lights in the apartment were out, I saw that there was someone inside. To my complete shock and surprise, I realized that I was looking at none other than Donna Archibald. I knew this because she was standing at the front door of the apartment, which was ajar. The light from the hallway outside cast a glow on her. She was wearing a long-sleeved T-shirt I could have bought at Target and pajama bottoms with little sheep on them. Unlike the night I'd seen her at the ball, her hair hung messily down her shoulders. She wore no makeup.

I had solved one mystery: Donna Archibald's undisclosed location. It was certainly an unexpected twist, however, to see her in her husband's lair. Upon further study, I also realized she was in trouble. Donna had the chain hooked across the door, but a man's shoe was rammed over the threshold and his hand gripped the side of the entry to block her from shutting him out.

Chapter 15

Donna looked small, her shoulders sagged, and she held herself close to the door, somewhat behind it. The two were speaking, but I could not make out their words. After a moment, Donna began to push against the door to no avail. Her visitor wasn't going anywhere.

I'd assumed with Charlie dead and Regina MIA that no one would be in the apartment. I had no idea why Charlie Archibald's wife was there, or whether she was guilty or innocent of his murder, but I wasn't going to leave her. I pulled at the sash.

"Damn," I said. The window was locked.

The struggle inside was growing and Donna had not heard me, so I banged on the glass pane, as loudly and as strongly as I could without risking the window shattering. Donna suddenly froze. The foot and hand disappeared. She took advantage of the unwanted visitor's retreat and slammed the door.

The apartment was now completely dark, but my eyes were becoming adjusted. I watched as Donna's shadow scurried to the kitchen. Then, I saw a glint of light bounce off what I realized was a knife. She raised the blade in my direction. I raised my hands in surrender, hoping she could see I meant no harm, and turned to head back down the fire escape. I'm all for taking risks and kicking ass, but I also know when to call it a night. In this case, a potential murderer wielding a knife at me was as good a sign as any to hightail it to the safety of the street below. I'd done my job. Saved her from harm. No guilty conscience. Good night's work.

"Heel, toe. Heel, toe. Heel, toe," I chanted to myself.

As I stumbled to the ladder, I looked through the metal slats to the street below, to see if I could spy Donna's visitor, but no one had yet left. Then, I heard Donna open the window.

"Oh my God, look," I heard the woman say from the sidewalk. "Her roommate was home the whole time."

Donna stretched her torso out the window and looked at me. She held her knife and her eyes flashed, but her fierce stare could not hide her trembling chin or the pained curve of her upper lip.

"Will you people ever leave us alone?" Donna said.

"I don't mean to cause you harm or distress," I said. "I'm going."

"No, you're not," she said. "Who do you work for?"

I grabbed the ladder, confused. She raised her phone and took a picture of me. "I'll find out who you are," she said. "And I'll call your editor."

She began to close the window again.

"I work for Regina Montague," I said. OK. Sometimes I don't know when to call it a night.

Donna stopped closing the window. She didn't speak for a moment. I stood there while she studied me.

"Oh God," she finally said. "You're the one who found Charlie."

She looked at me as if I were a wicked child, but her fear that I was with the press had at least diminished.

"How the hell do you know about this place?" she said.

I wanted to ask Donna the same question. She looked as confused as I did, and I now wanted to leave for a whole new set of reasons. I didn't want to tell her how I knew about Regina and Charlie.

"I made a duplicate key for the apartment on the day of the

Holiday Ball," I said, looking at my feet and noticing how high up I was through the open metal grate. "I work part-time at my grandparents' key store. Carreras."

When I looked up, I noticed her eyes widen.

"You're the key girl?" she said. "That's how Regina met you. I remember."

"She told you about the key?" I said. I had accepted that Regina was a home wrecker, but I hadn't realized how cruel she was. Personally, I'd have wanted to stick a long, pointy, metal item into Regina's eye if she had done that to me. I'd climbed a ladder up a building to protect Regina, and now I felt like the ultimate fool.

I realized that Donna was looking at me. Studying me. Her head was tilted to the side. All the anger and sadness and indignation that had consumed her was melting away. Replacing it was a bemused smile. She lowered the knife. A good sign.

"You don't know much about Regina," she said. "Or me."

She sat on the sill. Not like someone who was camping out at her dead husband's love pad, but as someone who had sat on that sill many times before. That's when it hit me.

"Oh," I said, thinking of the small suitcase I'd seen in the bedroom with women's clothes that would not have fit Regina.

"Oh," she said, nodding.

"I thought . . ." I gave a sheepish laugh.

"No," she said. "Charlie wasn't involved with Regina. I was."

"You were," I said. "Regina is in love with you. How presumptuous of me."

"Not entirely misguided though," she said, which I thought was generous on her part, especially given the circumstances of our conversation. "Charlie had a reputation. Easy mistake. You'd better come in."

She disappeared inside.

The cold night was beginning to hit me, and I was grateful for the invitation. I looked down below me to see Harry looking up desperately. His hand was on the bottom rung of the ladder, and he looked ready to climb up after me. I motioned for him to remain below. He shook his head, but I shook mine. We went back and forth for a moment, but he eventually calmed down. I took a delicate step toward the window where I saw her sit on her sofa, still in the dark. I climbed over the windowsill and stepped inside.

The warmth felt good, but I remembered I was still in the presence of a murder suspect, even if some of my facts had changed. Safe to say, now that I was inside, the tables had turned.

Donna Archibald was in charge, and I was trying to count how many steps there were to the door. I turned on a light, and sat in a club chair, but chose one farthest away from her. The bag from Maison Margiela still hung on the bedroom door. I now realized the note for an Archibald pick up was for Donna, not Charlie.

"What are you here for? I mean, if you didn't know about me and Regina, that means you're not here for money," said Donna.

"You thought I came here to blackmail you?" I said.

"It would have been a waste of your time. Not only am I broke, but the police know all about me and Regina," she said. A look of worry crossed her face. "Did you tell Detective Thorne about the key?"

"No. I believe Regina is innocent," I said. "And I would never waste Detective Thorne's time with something that would distract him from finding the real killer."

"Thank you," she said. "But then why did you come?"

"I'm a photographer," I said, not knowing how else to proceed. "I see images and I add them up so I can make some sense of the world. When I walk down the street, I make up stories in my head about who someone is and where they are going by how they're dressed or the pace at which they walk.

Usually, it's fun. But when I found your husband, and I saw Regina over him, the pictures didn't add up. In fact, none of the pictures I took that night add up. I've gone over and over them, knowing there's a clue in there somewhere, but I haven't been able to find it. I thought if I came here, I might learn something about your husband. Of course, I see now, this isn't the place to come for any insights into him."

"Do you really think you can see something the police can't?" she said. Her question wasn't judgy, but she didn't sound like she had any faith in me either.

"Regina hates blood. If she wanted to kill your husband, she'd have poisoned him or something. Right?"

"She can't even shave her legs for fear of a nick," Donna said.

"Do you know where she disappeared to that night?" I asked.

"Waving off advances from one of the top politicos in the City in a side alley where she had a cigarette break. And how do you think that went over when she told the police? He denied it all."

I thought about Popolous, who'd squeezed my hand that night, and I believed her.

"Regina was found with blood on her hands. Ergo, she killed Charlie in a jealous rage. Of course, they don't have proof. As a result, they're circling around me, like hawks after prey, waiting for me to break instead of looking for the real killer."

"Of course, that was Detective Thorne at the door," I said. "I should have recognized the scuffed, leather shoe."

"I guess you do have a good eye," she said. "He calls, shows up, hangs around my building at all hours of the day and night. The questions are neverending and always the same. It's as if he thinks I'm going to give him an entirely different story one day."

"Is he allowed to do that? Isn't that harassment?"

Donna picked up a throw pillow at the end of the sofa and hugged it. I stepped into the tiny kitchen off the living room to make her some tea.

"In the last few days, my access to liquidity has all but disappeared, and whatever remains is going toward Charlie's funeral and the mess he left behind," she said. "I'm not able to pursue a police harassment case. That's why I'm here and not at home. I don't want them going after Angela. If I'm here, they're not looking her way."

"I spoke to Angela this morning," I said, turning on the stove and placing the kettle on the burner. "She came by my studio to look at my photos from the night of the ball. She's worried about you."

"You showed her pictures?" she said. Her eyes welled with tears. "Was she OK?"

"She's a strong person," I said, nodding. "Like you. But she's also grieving for her father and worried about her mother."

"You probably won't believe this but I'm a real family person. I haven't run away from Angela. I'm fixing up this place before I bring her over. This is where we'll be living. I'll sell off everything if it means that I can help make restitution to Charlie's investors. And you also probably won't believe that I loved Charlie. I did. Once. But when I met Regina, everything changed. It was as if I suddenly became alive. To be loved so wholly and be free to return my love entirely. She makes me laugh and cry. She has those crazy get-ups and that sassy British way. Even the cigarettes don't bother me. She painted the front door to our building blue, in the middle of the night, to give our building some character. Charlie and I? We were best friends. We were a family. We just weren't meant to last forever. It's probably why his roving eye never bothered me."

"I'm sorry," I said. "For all of you." I handed Donna the tea.

"I don't drink tea," she said. "But thank you."

I put the drink on the table. I would have appreciated it if she'd mentioned that while I was in her kitchen, but she was in another world.

"The thing is," she said, "I really was going to leave Charlie for Regina. We started moving in here a few days before Thanksgiving. I had planned to tell Charlie about us the day before the Holiday Ball, but when the time came, all I could think of was Angela. I didn't want our tension to ruin her big night. I know I fussed over Charlie that night. It was dumb. I could tell that Regina was impatient and confused, but not to the point that she'd murder anyone."

I remembered how forced Donna's affections toward her husband had seemed that night.

I also remembered the photo where Regina had been focusing on their table from across the room. For the first time, the moments of the party and my photos were starting to piece together into a story.

"Are you sure he didn't know about you two?" I said.

"When you've been married to someone for many years, you know them. You know their moods and triggers and everything. I'm pretty sure he knew I was having an affair," she said.

I nodded.

"People can't believe Charlie would destroy Lion's Mane and the foundation," she said. "But I think I understand what he was trying to do, however misguided he was. His company was his pride and joy, and he was desperate to save it any way he could. He probably hoped he'd be able to buoy the fund and repay the foundation before anyone was the wiser. Poor Felicity. He's brought us all down with him."

"There was tension that night," I said. "I noticed it was like a stand-off when I took the photo at your table."

"Everyone we'd invited had a bone to pick with Charlie, but he wouldn't tell me why," she said. "If you can believe it, I was even feeling badly for him. He'd been so excited about the night. Seeing Angela come out meant a lot to him. The idea that his daughter was cemented into a society that he'd had to claw his way into gave him so much pride. I know he sounds silly. The whole thing probably looks dumb to you. For Charlie, however, it was like he finally got some approval he'd always wanted. All week, he was buying Angela and me gifts, sending us flowers. The day of the ball, he seemed manic with happy energy."

"I guess it makes sense, then, that he got sick and tired of everyone giving him a hard time during the ball. That must have been why he stormed out of the ball room at the end of the night."

"I guess," she said. "Although I remembered something this morning that was sort of odd. Frankly, I'm too afraid to tell Detective Thorne for fear that he'll begin a whole new line of questioning, or he won't believe me."

"What is it?" I said.

"Charlie's iPhone was in his breast pocket, like it always was. Before he stormed out of the dining room, I heard it faintly rumble. You know how it does that if you set a reminder?"

"The little buzz," I said, nodding.

"I'm sure it was a coincidence," she said. "But right after it buzzed, he left."

I'd thought that Archibald had left because he needed to get away from his disgruntled guests, but perhaps he was actually going to meet someone.

Donna suddenly looked as if she could sleep for two weeks. She had shared details about her relationship with Regina, and her desire to leave her husband, and her commitment to liquidating their estate to help pay back whatever she could to investors. Plus, she'd explained without my having to ask why she had behaved so effusively toward Archibald at the ball.

I suspected Angela knew something, if not everything,

about her parents' marriage. I had sensed from her, after her mother's toast, that the act was transparent to her. And at my studio, Angela was probably able to confirm her mother and Regina's friendship was more than that.

"I apologize for climbing my way into your apartment," I said.

"Do it again and I'll call the police," she said. "Regina will be furious I spoke to you. She can have a temper."

Donna gulped, as if she realized she was incriminating her girlfriend. I rose.

"If there's anything I can do for you, please let me know," I said.

"Maybe you can," she said as she walked to her front door. "They released Charlie's body today, and the funeral is in two days. Angela and I talked last night and decided that we'll have a small service at the Frank E. Campbell Funeral Chapel. Charlie always used to say that's where he wanted his funeral because they've handled so many important people. Even in death, these things were important to him. Will you come? As a friend? Angela might like that."

"Of course," I said.

"If you don't mind my asking, why are you all dressed up?" she said. "I was at a party," I said. "My date's downstairs."

"You're on a date?" she said incredulously.

"You'd better get back downstairs."

I took her advice and headed down the stairway, feeling like a real sleuth. For one thing, Donna had confirmed that Regina's phobia with blood made stabbing an impossible choice for murder, even if she did want to kill Archibald. Most interesting: her comment about the phone's buzzer, like an alarm going off. I'd been operating under an assumption that a crime of passion meant a spontaneous attack, but there might have been some premeditation in Archibald's murder after all. At least to lure Archibald to the bar.

At the bottom of the stairs, I had a view through the front door's small glass window. The woman with the dog had left, but Harry was not alone. To my great dismay, however, I saw that he was speaking to none other than Detective Thorne who had not left after all

I was going to hide in the small lobby until Harry got rid of him, but the body language between the two men was not what I expected. I've always noticed that when people who have just met say goodbye, they maybe shake hands. In contrast, when people who know each other well say goodbye, they might pat each other on the back.

I was surprised, then, when I noticed Harry and Detective Thorne slap each other on the shoulders before Thorne headed down the street.

CHAPTER 16

I opened the building's door but slowly, not sure what I had just seen. Harry rushed toward me, looking sincerely concerned.

"What happened? Are you OK? You were up there for so long I almost called the police," said Harry.

He'd *almost* called the police?

"Nothing happened," I said. "I mean, obviously something happened. Donna Archibald was upstairs. She and Regina are lovers. We had it all wrong."

"Oh, *shi—*"

I cut him off. "Regina has an alibi, but it's complicated. If Detective Thorne had a brain, he'd accept it."

I began to walk home. Harry followed.

"What's wrong?" he said. "Are you OK?"

"I'm fine," I answered.

"You don't seem fine," he said.

I was fine-*ish*. Of course, I wasn't *fine* fine. I was thinking about Harry and Detective Thorne. It was inexcusable, given Harry's enthusiasm for my investigation, that he hadn't told me he had a connection with the detective in charge of the case.

I stopped and turned to him.

"Why have you been so interested in helping me prove Regina's innocence?"

"Because you're smart. And good at it. As you said, you're smarter than that Detective Thorne," he said. "Trust me. I've seen a lot of fakes in my day. You're the real deal."

I continued walking, quickly. He followed shortly behind me.

"What exactly do you do at the office all day?" I said.

"I only have to go in twice a week," he said. "The rest of the time I work from home."

"I never asked you," I said. "Where is home?"

I'd imagined him in a bachelor pad. In a building with amenities like a doorman and a gym.

"Greenpoint," he said. The area in Brooklyn was a hipster spot, but still rough around the edges.

"Are you like Popolous? Buying and flipping places?" I said.

"No. I like my place, but nobody's going to be that excited to buy it."

I kept walking. I was two steps ahead of him, but I needed the distance between us. "Does that disappoint you?" he said. I picked up a wounded pride in his voice.

"Not at all," I said. "In fact, that makes you a little more human to me."

"You don't think I'm human?"

"I'm not sure who you are," I said and stopped walking.

"What is that supposed to mean?"

"I don't know. Who are you? Why can't I find you anywhere on social media? Even my mom and dad are at least on Facebook."

Harry shrugged.

"Is that what this is about? Social media?" he said.

"Who are you?"

"I'm Harry Fellowes. I work in insurance, appraising art for wealthy people. It's boring but I've found a niche and I make a good living. And I'm not in the rat race of the finance world, which I prefer. My parents passed away. My mom when I was young and my dad a couple of years ago. Aunt Bernie has stepped in as mother and father to me. I've been in love twice. Neither worked out, obviously. I hate pickles. I watch anime and my friends make fun of me for it. I don't care. I care a little."

If Harry had made that speech two hours earlier, he'd have passed all marks for boyfriend material. Now I knew I couldn't trust him. I'd given him a chance to mention something, anything, about a connection to Detective Thorne. He'd failed miserably.

I turned back toward my apartment and continued to walk. I listened to Harry follow me.

The next thing I did might not seem all that impressive. I'd like to think that I was trying one more test to see who he really was, but I might also have been exercising some growing anger.

I turned around with a tight fist and, expecting to take him by surprise, I swung at him.

Without flinching, Harry intercepted. He grabbed my fist and hooked his leg around my knee like he was a major league pitcher catching a fast ball. To a passerby we might have looked as it if we were ready to tango. That, of course, was the last thing on my mind. Intertwined as we were, we both looked at his hand grasping mine. Harry's eyes shifted to me. I stared right back into them.

"I saw you with Detective Thorne," I said. He let go of me, gently.

"It's not what you think," he said.

"I don't think anything," I said. "It was a great party. And thanks for the pizza. I've got it from here. Good night."

"Let me walk you home," he said, trying to catch up as I began to beeline home. I was now only half a block away. I picked up my speed and took out my keys. "I'm not trying to trick you or anything," he said from behind.

I puffed a cloud of cold air into the night to convey my skepticism. I was now only three buildings away from home. I had no idea who Harry really was, but I didn't care. Maria had been right. A date who is interested in murder was bad news. Period.

The gate in front of Liv Spyers Photography never looked so good. I opened and closed it firmly behind me and headed straight to my front door, stuck my key in the lock, but then stopped. The door was not locked. I knew I had locked it when I left. I thought of my grandfather's recent behaviors, but after the night I'd had I felt vulnerable.

I'd interviewed every suspect but Bill Topper and Felicity Cromwell about the murder.

Had I put the killer on guard? Worse, was I in danger of being next on the list?

I turned back to Harry.

"I need you to check out my studio," I said. "For intruders. My door is unlocked. I locked it. And I now know you have a masterful skill in self-defense."

Harry sulked at my tone, but he opened the gate and passed me to enter without looking at me. I thought he had a lot of nerve to take any type of attitude, but I waited outside for him to confirm that my place was safe to enter. He turned on lights and went so far as to peek in my bedroom. When he returned, he looked relieved.

"No one's inside," he said. "And nothing seems out of order although it's hard to tell in your bedroom."

He tried a weak smile at his joke, but I wasn't having it.

"Listen," he said. "I want to tell you something, but it's delicate."

I opened the gate and Harry stepped on to the sidewalk. I closed it behind him, but I waited. It would be interesting to hear what he had to say. It would give me that much more to discuss with Maria when I called her in five minutes' time. I folded my arms and said nothing. Harry looked up to the sky and took a deep breath.

"I'm really not allowed to talk about this, but I want you to know the truth," he said. "I know I can trust you won't abuse the information I'm about to give you. First? I'm not really in insurance."

"Tell me something I don't know," I said. I wished I'd come up with a bit more of a zinger, but I never can think of them fast enough.

"I'm with the ACU," he said. "The Art Crime Unit."

"What is that? The FBI or something?"

"Something like that," he said. "Most people don't realize this, but art crimes are big business. We have offices around the globe. Our headquarters are in London."

"Let me see your badge," I said.

Harry slipped his hand into the inside pocket of his coat and pulled out his wallet. He opened it and removed a laminated card with his name, photo, Art Crime Unit across the top, and some other official-looking stuff. I was happy to see he'd at least given me his real name.

"I don't get it," I said, handing his wallet back to him. "Why all the secrecy?"

Harry rubbed his head and paced in front of my gate. He looked as if he were a caged animal, and I felt a little sorry for him but not enough to let him off the hook.

"Art crime is a seven-billion-dollar industry, and whether it's a thief or a buyer, the players are often very wealthy. That's where I come in. I can move in and out of that world with ease. No one suspects me. They never do. Even after they've been caught."

"You're like a spy?"

"More like an undercover cop," he said. "Except I happen to be undercover in my own community."

"And you know Detective Thorne because of these cases?"

I was considering easing up a bit, but Harry still looked anxious, like there was something more.

"I'm on a case," he finally said. "Which included, at first, protecting those who might be at risk."

"Who were you protecting?" I said. Harry stopped pacing and sighed. "Your grandparents."

I wanted to punch him all over again.

"Are you telling me my grandparents might be in danger and you didn't warn me?" I said. "How are they in danger?"

"The safe," he said.

"What safe?"

"The one your grandfather showed me the other day," he said.

"I thought you were hitting it off with Poppy," I said. "That was an act?"

"Not at all, but, yes, I was on the job."

"I'm such an idiot," I said. I smacked my forehead, thinking of his appearance at my family's holiday, one where he knew we'd all be home. "Did you even make the soup can art yourself?"

"I did. But the safe is linked to a cold case, if you can call it that," said Harry. "It has been rumored for almost a century that the safe was hiding a stolen jewel. One from the English royal family. For various reasons of provenance and restitution and other red tape, law enforcement has never been able to open the safe to confirm the story. The only way we would be able to prove its existence was if someone else found it and could attest to it. When the safe arrived in the US and the owner dropped it at Carrera's to crack, we hoped your grandfather could help, but he said the safe was empty. Our suspect was much cleverer than we expected."

Usually, I consider my talent at seeing and remembering images a blessing, rather than a curse. At that moment, however,

I wished I could unsee all the images that were rushing back to me and rearranging themselves.

"Poppy said he found the safe empty, but what if he didn't?" I said. "You've seen how forgetful and proud he is. And he's been snooping all around the house lately. If that's the case, my grandparents could be in danger."

Harry shook his head.

"Your grandfather's job to open the safe was a set up. In fact, it's possible he was chosen because he is a bit scatter-brained; he wouldn't ask questions. The safe was empty already when our suspect dropped it off. When your grandfather cracked the lock, he would be able to vouch that the safe was empty inside. We'd be forced to bury the case once more, while the owner is now free to sell its contents."

The first wave of fear for my grandparents receded. In its place came a new emotion. I couldn't describe it, but I didn't like it.

"When did you start working on this case?" I said.

Harry didn't answer but he could see I wasn't going to let up.

"The morning I encountered you on the subway," he finally said. "I'd been out on another case the night before. When I got the call, I went right to your house."

"You were outside my house all night?"

"As I said, we suspected the safe would be empty, but I had to be sure."

I felt a stabbing pain in my heart; something like a long, thin, metal weapon had struck me.

"You didn't just happen to be on the same train car as me," I said. "And I didn't happen to drop my camera in the scuffle, did I? I knew it. I would never do that."

"I got a call from headquarters that I should go home to rest and get ready for the Holiday Ball where our suspect was going. It was about the time you left, too. I saw you take photos of everything along the way," he said. "I decided to see if you had taken photos of people in your neighborhood who could be of interest."

"Did I?"

"No."

I cringed inside, remembering the photo I'd taken of him on the train that morning. He must have seen it when he'd look through my photos. He had been cool enough not to bring it up, which I appreciated, but oh my God.

"And the ball?" I said, still dying. "I thought it was such a coincidence to see you there."

"It really was a coincidence," he said. "Except for the fact that I was still on the job. That's the other thing I should tell you. Bernie isn't just my aunt. She's my boss."

I raised my hands in utter defeat. "And who was the waiter? A sniper?" I said. "Or the band, for that matter?"

"No," he said, sadly. "I understand if you don't believe me, but everything else you know about me is true. Even down to my date at the ball, who really is Bernie's niece. But when Bernie's husband died, she decided to continue where he left off. She'd already been in the agency's world forever, so it wasn't a huge leap. It's worked well, until now."

"Just tell me one thing," I said, trying not to lose my cool in front of him. "Is any of this tied to Archibald's murder?"

"No. Truly, it's not. I met with Thorne after Archibald was killed to compare notes. There's no connection we can find between the two cases, aside from the fact that we are both focused on a very small community of people who were gathered at the same event that night."

"Do you have a list of investors to LaunchTech?"

"I can't share that information with you," he said. "But nothing you told me tonight was different from what I know."

"And tonight," I said. "Why did Thorne think you were at Donna's?"

"When Thorne came out of the building, I was shocked, but

that lady with the dog came in handy," he said. "I pretended I had stopped to pat the dog."

"OK," I said. "I guess that's it."

"What do you mean?"

"You don't honestly think I can go out with you again?" I said. "You followed me, stole my camera, and pretended to be interested in me so you could keep an eye on your precious safe."

"That's not at all what I did. I mean I did do the first two things. But the last one, you got totally wrong. The ACU has been waiting for our guy to make a mistake, yes. But the safe and Carrera's? That's all a moot point. I've been seeing you because I like you. I've never met anyone who decides to investigate a murder because they've screwed up at work. But now that we're being honest, if I'm not working on the case with you, I don't think you should continue. You can't interview suspects and break into places without expecting to be in real danger. This is murder, Liv."

"Did you just mansplain the danger of my investigation?"

"I guess I did," he said. I could see he felt busted, but he wasn't backing down. "This is a dangerous business. And if you plan on kicking me to the curb, I think you should tell Detective Thorne everything you know."

I had never wanted to catch Charlie Archibald's killer more than I did at that moment. "Are you going to tell Detective Thorne about me?" I said, fighting my tears.

"No. You could get into some real trouble. If he heard it from me, he would probably arrest you," he said. "But I hope you tell him yourself."

"Good night," I said.

"Night," he answered.

"Merry friggin' Christmas."

We both turned and walked away. I entered my apartment, closed the door firmly, locked it tightly, and turned out the lights. I disagreed with Harry entirely.

In one night, I'd learned that Elizabeth Everly had a weapon and a motive; that Felicity Cromwell might have been at the Pierre when Archibald was killed; that Charlie might have been lured to his death in a pre-arranged plan with one of my suspects; and that despite his reputation, Archibald had not been cheating on his wife with Regina.

I'd also learned tonight that I could climb a fire escape in heels, face a woman with a knife, and hear things that suspects would not otherwise tell the police. Harry had a lot of nerve to say that I couldn't handle the danger.

Donna had invited me to Archibald's funeral. Harry could work on his case. I'd work on mine.

CHAPTER 17

Why was my door unlocked last night?

Assuming I could believe Harry, my grandparents were no longer involved in the case he was working on. Their involvement in the underbelly of the criminal world had ended swiftly and without incident. Striking any connection between my break-in and his case, that left those closer to me as suspects.

Watching Poppy open the store the next morning, I struggled over whether to ask him if he'd had anything to do with my unlocked door. He seemed to be having a good day and was even humming as he stood over the key duplicator. I couldn't decide if I'd been reading too much into Poppy's erratic behavior over the last weeks—maybe months, now that I thought about it. Every time my radar went up, he seemed to be his old self the next day. As betrayed as I felt by Harry, I was grateful he hadn't interviewed my grandparents. He had done his best to protect them from needless worry.

"Poppy," I finally ventured, "I was thinking. For decades, the key shop's been where my studio is now. I could understand how, if you wake up at night and want to putter around the store, you might forget that you moved it upstairs. Speaking of which, did you ever find the thingamabob you were looking for in my apartment the other night?"

"Hmm?" he said. He looked up at me with a reassuring smile that made my heart melt. "Yes, I found it. I had a moment where I forgot where it was."

"What was it?" I said.

He scratched his head.

"Old age can make the best of us a little fusty," he said in answer.

I decided not to be too hard on my grandfather. Instead, I called Maria and we met for brunch. I told her an abbreviated version of my botched-up romance, leaving out the more confidential details of Harry's job at the ACU. I was grateful she didn't say *"I told you so."* Maria is good like that. Instead, when we were all talked out, she gave me the last piece of bacon.

"Men. Who needs them?" she said.

"Not me," I said, but we both knew we like men like a stiletto likes the color red. It was hard to let go of the ones you thought were special.

"You're in corporate law, maybe you can help me" I said, when I was ready to change the subject. "There's been something bothering me about the Archibald murder."

"Not this again," Maria said.

"Do you know if it's possible to find out who invested in Lion's Mane's last fund, LaunchTech?"

Harry had mentioned that he and Detective Thorne had compared notes about Archibald's LaunchTech investors. I wished I had asked him if Regina had been on it, not that he would have told me. If I was going to follow the money as the motive for murder, I wanted to know as much as I could about Archibald's investors.

"I don't want to encourage you," Maria said, waving to the waiter for our check. Even on the weekends she had LSAT class. "But it's safe to say the investors were all super rich. From what I've read, Lion's Mane is a hedge fund. Hedge funds are usually only open to wealthy people who can take on risk.

They pay higher fees for higher returns. It's like a high-stakes card game."

"Like how much?" I said.

"For something like LaunchTech? Definitely mid-six figures."

"Also," Maria said, "venture capital firms are not required to register with the SEC, which is probably how Archibald got away with his bullshit for as long as he did. If he hadn't died, and he'd been able to reconcile the books, he might have gotten away with his scheme."

"So, is that a no to getting my hands on the list of investors?"

"Not unless you have permission. The investor list does not need to be public information," she said. "And probably only people cooperating with the SEC and FBI right now will be in the news. I bet a lot of those folks don't want to look like idiots, so that information will be slow to come. If you want to know who invested, it's probably easier to ask around. People talk."

I nodded, and tried to narrow down the list myself.

Of my seven suspects, Anne and Bill Topper were probably the only ones with an extra six figures to play with. Felicity, Elizabeth, and Regina were all very successful women, at the top of their game, but even if they were pulling in six figures a year, that would be an incredibly risky allocation of funds to make. And after my visit to the Headrams' apartment, it felt safe to assume they weren't in the game either. Miranda had practically told me as much.

"I don't like that look," she said to me. "I didn't mean you *should* ask around. Harry had one thing right. You've done your bit. You found out the foundation lady was at the Pierre, and she had a motive for murder. And the dog lady needed to throw a wedding. Also a good motive. That's great work. Call Detective Thorne. Tell him you heard it through the grapevine and move along. Meanwhile, how's your business?"

"Great," I said, lying through my teeth.

"Atta girl," she said. "You're going to make it big. I know it. You don't need Regina Montague."

I decided Maria was right to have faith in me. My ratings on OneShot.com were not good, but I'd never let something like that stop me before. If I had, I'd still be making a seasonal eggnog latte at Starbucks right now. When I returned to my studio, I added a new promotion on my OneShot.com page for a discounted holiday photo session.

I reloaded the page about half a dozen times, hoping each time I did that I'd see a new message. I knew it was an unhealthy way to pass the time, so I opened the Archibald Fund's website. Across their web page was a legal statement which communicated the foundation's dismay upon learning of the misappropriation of funds from Lion's Mane, and further assured its supporters that they would be contacted regarding next steps. I could only imagine the number of donors who felt betrayed that their well-intentioned contributions had been stolen.

When Monday arrived, I called Manjeet.

"What have you learned?" he said by way of greeting.

"After Felicity Cromwell tried to storm the party to confront Charlie Archibald, Elizabeth Everly let her calm down in the event space before leaving," I said, dropping a piece of bread into my toaster. "Did she stay, or did she go? I'd like to know. Can you find out if Felicity is going to be at any upcoming events?"

"The foundation was supposed to have a benefit in February, but of course that's been cancelled. No foundation, no party."

"I thought you might say that," I said.

"I wish Regina would be a little more deferential with the police," Manjeet said. "They haven't come up with enough to arrest her, but they keep calling. Her continued absence has absolutely ticked them off and has clearly kept her at the top of their list of suspects. She's done herself no favors."

Time was ticking for Regina, and I knew it. If I didn't discover something soon, I doubted I'd be able to help. After we hung up, I checked OneShot.com again. No one had responded to my offer, yet.

Instead of dwelling on this fact, I buttered my toast and looked up the address for the Archibald Foundation. It wasn't far from Hudson Yards. The foundation was now closed, but I wondered if that meant the office was, too. I couldn't imagine it had become a ghost town so quickly. The legal notice across their homepage proved that there were many loose ends to tie up.

I decided to see for myself. As I left my studio, I grabbed the hat Harry had given to me the night of our trip to the Met's fountains. Some days you need to dress the part to make it happen.

When I opened the iron gate to my sidewalk, I walked along wet pavement and appreciated the scent of fires warming the homes on the street. The day was cold but still nice, so I unlocked a Citi Bike and cycled up to the foundation's office. Their headquarters was on Tenth Avenue, in a red brick building that had once likely been a warehouse and had been converted to open-plan offices for startup companies.

A small group of protestors loitered outside the building. They carried signs that dumped on the rich and decried the abuse of the poor. If absolute strangers could feel this passionately, I could only imagine how Felicity felt. If I were her, I know I would have wanted to kill Archibald. I returned my bike to a dock nearby and headed to the office.

In contrast to the grand lobby and high security of RMS's Midtown office, I found a panel of buzzers, not unsimilar to that of Regina and Donna's small apartment building. I pressed the button for the Archibald Foundation. There was no answer. I pressed again. No answer. I noticed the crowd across the street quieted down a bit and I sensed their eyes on me. Pressing the button for a third time, I was greeted with the sound of static.

"Hello?" said a voice without identifying the name of the company. I couldn't tell if the voice was Felicity's because the only time I'd heard her speak was when she was barking at Elizabeth Everly at the ball.

"Miss Cromwell?" I said.

I don't know how anyone could have heard me say Felicity's name from all the way across the street, but someone did. The crowd began to boo and hiss at me with tremendous passion.

Before I had a chance to introduce myself to whoever had picked up, I was disconnected. I turned to the madding crowd and wanted to chant my own retorts, but decided that wouldn't get any of us anywhere, and I wasn't about to give up on reaching Felicity.

"Join us or leave us!" a woman shouted to me.

For about a second, I toyed with joining the mob. If I did, I might be able to see Felicity coming or going, assuming she was even at the office. If I were Felicity, however, I'd have an Uber waiting for me when I left so as not to have to deal with anyone. Spending an afternoon in peaceful protest seemed like a waste of time.

Instead, I walked to a vendor on the corner who was roasting chestnuts from a cart.

"I'll take a bag of chestnuts if they're ready," I said as I approached him.

He nodded, shaking the pan on the side of his cart.

"What's going on here?" I said.

He seemed entirely indifferent to the excitement down the block.

"Crazy people," he said. "It's always something. Hopefully they will get hungry. I'm here all day, every day, and I've never seen anything like this."

I was happy to hear that he was a regular in the neighborhood.

"I think it has to do with one of the companies that's in that building," I said, popping a fresh, warm chestnut into my mouth.

"Six dollars," said the man. He rubbed his hands over the roasting pan to warm them up.

I'd made peace with the fact that the price of basic sidewalk food can rival a restaurant's, but my impulse buy had been too extravagant for my currently modest income. To justify the splurge, I rededicated myself to learning something new about the case.

Not sure how I'd achieve this goal, I lingered beside his cart while I ate. The vendor and I both looked at our phones for a bit, but then, as often happens in this big city filled with people who might never connect otherwise, he nodded to me, and I nodded back. We'd vetted each other and decided the other was all right.

"There was a rich guy who was murdered last week," he said. "He has one of his companies in there. He was a crook. These guys."

He shook his head. I did too.

"These people are just as bad," he said, motioning to the protestors. "What are they going to do? The guy is dead. He can't hear them. I don't care. At least they're buying waters and hot dogs."

"I heard the story," I said, my eye still on the building. "The lady who was running the company sounded so nice, too."

"She is," he said. "I know her. She comes here every day at noon. On the dot. That's the kind of lady she is. Predictable. She packs her own lunch and gets one of my bags of nuts for dessert. When the weather is good, she heads to the park for a break. And she hasn't stopped, even with all this craziness. In fact, she's been giving me nice tips this week because she feels badly about the noise."

Casually, I checked the time and noticed the weather. It was eleven thirty in the morning.

Although the sky was cloudy, even hinting at rain, it was not prohibitively cold out today. My street cart informant had said that Felicity Cromwell enjoyed her meals at the nearby park. I knew that park was likely Little Island, along the Hudson River, at the refurbished Port Fifty-Four, the famed port where the *Titanic* never set sail. In its new incarnation, the park combined engineering wonders with a nature and art excursion.

Rather than confront Felicity in front of the foundation's building, while crowds were protesting, I wondered if I might talk to her there.

"Have a good day," I said.

The vendor nodded and shook his chestnuts over his fire. I walked the few blocks to the park. Assuming my hunch was right, and that Felicity would stick to her lunch routine, my first challenge was knowing which of the two entrances to the park she'd take. Rather than commit to one, I hung out at the Hudson River Esplanade and paced back and forth to both stay warm and keep a lookout for Felicity. The park is a huge tourist attraction, and the crowds are even worse during the holidays. I did not have my camera, but I snapped a few Instagram-worthy photos of the visitors' delighted faces with my phone. The activity allowed me to keep my eyes peeled on the crowds discreetly so that I would not miss her.

At about ten minutes after twelve, as I was beginning to wonder if it was worth waiting around I finally saw a woman in a long wool coat and heeled boots head toward the park with a brown bag and a pretzel. I was glad I had the visual cues of Felicity's style of dress, her height, and her lunch routine, because she would have otherwise been difficult to spot. She was wearing a hat pulled across her forehead, but I knew it was her. She walked quickly but confidently through the underpass of one of the entries to the park.

I followed her. Felicity did not hesitate once she entered the park. She walked with purpose along the winding walkways, without pausing to admire the landscape, and headed straight to an amphitheater at the end of the park that had open seating and beautiful views of the Hudson River. The scene was a street-level view of the one I'd seen from Popolous's building, but this one was free.

Felicity sat about halfway down and center stage. I sat a few rows above her. She opened her lunch, what seemed to be a homemade salad, and which probably tasted great with her pretzel. I opened my bag of nuts. I had a few left and finished them up as I watched her open her lunch and then stare quietly across the river.

I took off my hat and tossed it lightly, so it hit her on the back of the head. As I hoped, she caught it for me.

"Sorry. This wind," I said, and hopped over the seats. "Not a good day for hats."

She handed it to me with a soft smile.

"Hey, are you Felicity Cromwell?" I said.

I'd clearly come on too strongly because Felicity immediately began to repack her lunch without a word.

"No, no," I said. "I was at the Holiday Ball. I found Charlie Archibald. You run the foundation, right?"

Felicity stopped packing her lunch and looked at me.

"I'm Liv Spyers. I worked for the photographer, Regina Montague," I said.

"I'm sorry you had to find him," she said. "I heard it was horrible."

"I basically lost my job at RMS over it," I said. I sat down next to her. "Nothing like what you're going through, I'm sure. But still."

"He screwed over a lot of people," she said with a sympathetic nod.

"I now have time to sightsee," I said, motioning to our surroundings. "How're you holding up?"

"I've lost the best job in the world, betrayed my donors, and let down the schools I was dedicated to helping."

She took a bite of her salad. I nodded.

"Were you also an investor in Archibald's fund?" I said.

"You need to be very wealthy to invest in those funds," she said.

I noticed she hadn't answered my question. I didn't know much about the foundation world, but I knew that Felicity must make a halfway decent living based on her wardrobe. Sample sales can only get you so far.

"I've gotten to know Elizabeth Everly a bit since this whole fiasco," I said.

"You should ask her to help you get a new job," Felicity said. "She knows everyone."

"I have to confess; I saw you at the Pierre that night. I saw Elizabeth call security to escort you out. Had you found out about Archibald's accounting games?"

"You're nosy," she said. "But yes. A couple of days before the ball, I'd gone to Bill with my suspicions about Archibald's scam. He assured me such a scheme would be impossible, but I could tell he sounded both shocked and agitated, so I spent the next couple of days going back over the books. There were too many clever, casual discrepancies over time. The night of the ball, I finally accepted that I'd been had. I went to the Pierre to confront him."

"And Elizabeth let you compose yourself before you left," I said. "But, did you ever leave?"

"Of course, I did," she said with a snap, but oh, snap, I knew she hadn't left.

"Did you see or hear anything after Archibald left the ballroom?" I said, but Felicity was already packing up her lunch again. "Were you able to talk to him?"

"No, I was not."

Felicity began to take two steps at a time back up the amphitheater's seating. I realized I'd ruined any chance of ever photographing an event she might host in the future, if she was ever able to manage a foundation again, but I'd learned for sure that Felicity had remained behind at the Pierre.

She was officially a suspect, and I followed her, but she was too fast for me. This was a woman who was a creature of habit, according to my hot dog vendor informant. She knew the paths of the park much better than I and she was able to weave her way through the crowd expertly. By the time I reached the esplanade, she was gone. I knew it was no use following her back to the office, if that's even where she'd gone.

My heart was racing from our encounter, so much so that it took me a moment to realize that my phone had pinged. I looked at my notifications and realized I had a message from OneShot.com. A new client wanted me to shoot her baby shower. I checked the details and noticed the request was for the same day as Charlie Archibald's funeral. It would be a tight squeeze to do both, but I knew I had to try. I hit Accept.

And with both murder and income on my mind, I dialed Anne Topper. Manjeet had been very clear that I wouldn't get paid until I delivered my photos. Now was as good a time as any.

Estelle answered. We both knew what we knew about my last visit there and how I'd been the butt of the twins' practical joke. I guess the fact that I had not called their parents to complain about them had earned me some street cred because Estelle told me I could come by any time. Mrs. Topper would be in and out of the house today, but I was welcome to wait.

Chapter 18

Waiting is hard when you are ready for action. It's even harder when you are in the library of a murder suspect's home. And harder still when a laptop with a Lion's Mane logo on its cover is on your suspect's desk. That laptop teased me mercilessly from across the room. I'd been wondering who LaunchTech's investors were, and I knew the computer, sitting safe and sound at his home, likely stored Bill Topper's work files.

Estelle must not have figured that out, however, because she had tucked me in the library with it, where I'd now remained for over an hour in one of the cloud-like armchairs by the door. Before being seduced by their cushions, I'd browsed the photos and tchotchkes on the bookshelves but nothing clue-worthy stood out. Since then, I'd checked my social media, looked three times at OneShot to see if I might have additional jobs (I didn't), and perused my Hinge app, hellbent on putting Harry in my past. I scrolled through a dozen or so pictures and prompts, but no one caught my eye.

Dropping my phone to my lap in dismay, I looked around the room for a way to pass the time. A shelf filled with old photo albums caught my eye. Wondering what Jade and Peridot might have looked like as babies, I pulled at one. I realized the row of books hadn't been touched in years because they stuck together as if they were glued to the shelf. I tugged harder until one came free.

Sure enough, there were baby photos, but not of the twins. Instead, I looked at a bouncing baby Bill Topper from what looked like the 1970s, based on the outfits. He was in a home with a rolling lawn and a wraparound porch with clean white rocking chairs. Turning the pages, many of the photos were of Bill's parents and siblings at private family events: opening gifts around the tree, blowing out candles for birthdays, Bill's graduation from high school, and a photo of him raised upon the shoulders of teammates after what looked like a basketball victory. He'd clearly had a comfortable upbringing even before his success with Lion's Mane. Paying for college had not been an issue for this guy.

I put the album back and pulled out another. This book contained photos of Bill's overseas travels after he'd graduated from college, around the time when he met Archibald. I remembered reading that Charlie Archibald had the brains and that Bill had access to liquidity. Charlie had probably been working Bill since the first day they'd met. I wondered if the infamous sailboat mishap which lead to their friendship was even an accident.

I sat back in my cozy chair and studied the photos. About halfway through the chunky book, the sound of the elevator opening jolted me back to my surroundings. Not wanting to be caught red-handed with a family treasure, I panicked. I threw the album into my bag. I listened for the click-clack of Anne's heels. Instead, I heard the squeak of rubber soles on the marble floor.

"Madame Florange hates us," I heard Jade say. "I'm going to tell Mom to call her."

"That's because you put holes in the paper drinking cups so the water would drip all over her," said Peridot.

"You did it, too."

"I have a snack for you," I heard Estelle say as she joined the girls. "Take off your sweaty clothes and I'll throw them in the wash."

I assumed the girls headed to their rooms by the echo of continued complaints about their day as they headed down the hall.

There were two ways to play it with the Topper twins: ignore their antics or join the game. Their mother chose the former, evidenced by her indulgence on their snarky behavior last time I'd visited. Listening to the sound of Jade and Peridot slam their bedroom doors, I decided on the latter course. When they passed back through the entry gallery, en route to the kitchen, I pressed my ear against the door.

"Coral said it's going to be amazing," Jade said to her sister. "She said there will be boys, and her parents are away for the weekend. We're going."

"No way will Mom and Dad let us go," said Peridot.

"No way will Mom and Dad know. We'll say we're going to Laura Schmeltzer's for the night, and we'll Facetime Mom from her place, in our pajamas, and tell her we're going to watch a movie and go to sleep. Then we'll head out. At eleven, we both text her good night, and that's that."

Peridot squealed.

"We're going to have so much fun," she said. At their height of excitement, I opened the door. "Hello," I said.

The girls, who had both been dancing with abandon over the thought of the fun they were going to have at Coral's boy party, froze. They did not speak, but their catlike eyes studied me carefully.

"I heard it all," I said, to be clear before we began our negotiations.

Jade and Peridot rolled their eyes in unison, but their eerily synced dismissal of me did nothing to dampen my spirit. I rolled mine back, so we all knew where we stood.

"What are you doing back here again?" Jade said.

"Waiting for your mother to come home."

"OK." Jade began to do ballet pliés and relevés while grasping a door handle for balance. Random. "What do you want?"

I leaned against the door frame to the library and folded my arms. "Some basic hospitality would be nice."

Jade lowered her heels to the floor and folded her arms to mirror mine. "Like what?" Peridot asked.

I stepped back into the library where I grabbed from my bag a flash drive I carry for emergencies. I heard the twins' footsteps behind me, as they whispered in half phrases and words that only women who know each other well can do.

Undeterred by their evident scheming, I headed to their father's laptop, and sat behind Bill's massive desk. I was well aware I was about to ask a man's children to hack his computer. However unpleasant they'd been to me, it was still a questionable move. But I needed to get into Bill Topper's laptop, and if they could get me in, I was ready to try. I raised the flash drive.

"I'm in a bind with work," I said, knowing full well these two would need a concrete reason to do what I was about to ask from them; even if it was only so that they'd have a story if they got caught. "I need to send photos on this drive, ASAP, to a client. The files are too big to send from my phone."

"What about using Dropbox?" said Peridot.

"Forget about Dropbox," I said.

"Upload them to a private page on your website."

"Or use Google Drive?" said Jade. "You just have to—"

"—All I want is a password, so that I can pop these out while I wait for your mom." Jade and Peridot looked at me skeptically.

"You should've brought your laptop with you," said Jade. "Our dad doesn't let us use his computer. And the battery on both of ours is dead. Sorry we can't help you."

My idea was seeming less brilliant.

Jade shook her head slowly, with victorious, saccharine-laced regret, but Peridot fussed with her hair and avoided making eye contact with me. It was a dead giveaway. They knew the password. These two made a life out of playing the system, whether for personal gain or just to pass the time. There was no way they hadn't hacked into their dad's laptop at some point or other.

"Coral's party sounds like it could be fun this weekend," I said, leaning back in the ergonomic, leather chair. "It would be a shame if you couldn't go."

I tipped my head and creased my brow to show my own concern for their well-being.

"Look, he changes the password," Jade said in a tactical shift. "We never know what it is."

Peridot flashed her eyes at her sister. There was no way she was going to miss Coral's party.

"He writes the new passwords down on a piece of paper he has taped under the ledge thing above the top drawer," Peridot said.

As the two girls scowled at each other, I looked for Bill's secret hiding place. Above the top drawer on the left-hand side of the desk was a small knob. I pulled it, and out came a shelf, maybe large enough to hold a cup of coffee. Removing it entirely from its frame, I turned it over. Peridot had been right. There was a password, just one, pasted to the underside of the small board.

"Are you happy?" said Jade.

"Yes," I said. "Go give your dirty clothes to Estelle. She's got a long night ahead of her with your dinner and laundry."

The girls turned and exited the room like soldiers who had been set back but not defeated.

Once they had stepped out of the room, Jade laughed.

"That was way too easy," I heard her say after they closed the doors. "I'd have asked for a lot more."

For a moment I wondered what else I should have asked for, especially when I heard them high-five each other.

I turned on the computer, my palms a bit sweaty. If I was going to do this, I wanted to get in and out, quickly. I typed in the password.

Mylovelyjade123 was the last password Bill had jotted down. Lovely Jade? I felt sorry for the guy.

I hit Enter.

Incorrect password flashed above the password box. I'd been played. Part of me respected the twins more than ever. "Well done, girls. Well done."

I closed my eyes and thought about passwords. Bill had to have started a new list. He probably hadn't had time to write it down with all the distractions of the week. If so, what would come after *Mylovelyjade123*?

I typed *Mylovelyperidot123.*

I was in! A home screen opened with a screensaver image of the Topper family on the beach in coordinating green sweaters. Probably last year's Christmas card.

I quickly scanned the file names on Bill's desktop: *Bills*, *Tuition*, *Apartment*, *Southampton*, *Girls*, *Anne*. If anything, they told a story of someone who was a dedicated family man. On the bottom of the screen, I saw the logo for Lion's Mane. I clicked on it.

"Oh, come on. You're kidding me," I said as another request for a password popped up.

I took a breath. Bill had used Jade- and Peridot-themed passwords. I knew from personal experience that once I was on to a formula I could remember, I stuck to it. I hoped Bill thought like me. I gingerly typed:

Mylovelyanne123

I smacked my hand across my mouth when I got through. My eyes flew furiously across the file names, but now that I was in, I realized I'd merely reached the next level of a much larger quest. Most of the files had alpha numeric names that made no sense to me. I could feel my knee start to nervously bob. I'd hit the motherlode but did not have time to go through all these files. I scrolled up and down, completely at a loss over which to open first.

I had to be strategic. After a few deep breaths, I had a thought. I clicked Date Modified above the file listings. Bill's focus this week had to be on Archibald's disastrous fund. He'd need to address the scandal quickly to keep his company afloat. If I was right, he would have been compiling documents about LaunchTech all week. He'd likely have downloaded some of Archibald's documents.

Sure enough, the first folder I opened had a list of names. I knew I'd found the list of investors of LaunchTech, organized alphabetically. I scanned it, finding Anne Topper's name among them, and confirmed that the Headrams, Donna Archibald, Elizabeth Everly, Felicity Cromwell, and Regina Montague were not on it. Of all my suspects, only Anne and Bill Topper had invested, each of them separately. Archibald had double dipped into the Topper's funds.

Closing the file, I saw two more folders below it with the names *Legal 1* and *Legal 2*. I clicked on *Legal 1*. True to its name, it contained documents with legal mumbo-jumbo about covering Lion's Mane's fiduciary responsibilities while the feds sorted out Archibald's trail of money laundering.

Below these two files was another. It had no name. I opened it and found only one document inside. It was a letter to the FBI from Robert Topper, founder and managing partner of Lion's Mane. "*Pursuant to our conversation today . . .*" I quietly read to myself.

"Blah, blah, blah. *I am prepared on behalf of Lion's Mane, its Board of Directors, and other constituents, to provide your department with all accounting, correspondence, prospectuses, etc. to investigate my concerns regarding the LaunchTech fund, my company's most recent fund, which has been developed and managed by my partner, Charles Archibald, my co-founder as well as a managing partner of Lion's Mane Capital."*

The letter was dated two days before Archibald's murder.

I had wondered if Bill Topper might have killed Archibald for a few reasons: he'd been jealous; he'd been irate that Archibald had used his wife's money to invest without consulting him; or that he, himself, was as guilty as his partner, and Charlie's death would focus any improprieties away from him. Now, I realized it was none of the above. Bill Topper had approached the FBI and invited them to investigate his company. It took a strong character to do that.

Suddenly I heard the elevator door open, followed by the familiar sound of Anne Topper's heels. I quickly logged out of the laptop and hopped back to the comfy armchair while I heard Estelle tell Anne that I was waiting for her. Anne sounded pleased, and I realized I was happy that Bill might enjoy them during this tough time for his business.

"Liv," Anne said, entering the room with a cheerful greeting.

I knew the week had been a devastating one for the Toppers, but you'd never have known it by the looks of Anne. Her wardrobe was more understated than the other times I'd met her.

She was wearing dark grays and burgundies, and her hair had a less coiffed styling, but everything about her was still impeccable. The statement she made was clear: She wasn't going to let Archibald have the last laugh.

"I thought you might like your Christmas gift to Bill, hand delivered in case it's not to your liking," I said.

Her eyes misted a bit as she sat down, no drinks today. Carefully, I removed the photographs I'd taken of the Topper's' skyline and put them on the coffee table for her approval.

"You're like Santa Claus," she said. "This is the only gift I can think of that would make Bill smile. He loves our home.

He loves his city. This is perfect. I have no idea which one he'll prefer, so I'll take both. And if we move, at some point, he'll have . . ."

"I heard about Mr. Archibald's scheme," I said as my client trailed off. Gently, I put the photos away while she collected herself.

"Charlie Archibald, life's all-time disappointment," she said, pulling herself together. It sounded a little rehearsed and I was sure she'd had to come up with a few lines to manage the not-so-subtle inquiries people had about her husband and his company.

Anne opened her purse and fished out her checkbook.

Manjeet had said payment upon delivery, but I hadn't expected such instant gratification. And when she handed me the check, I knew she'd given me a holiday bonus.

"Thank you," I said.

"It's my pleasure," she said. "How are you doing these days? As you can imagine, I'm much more supportive of Regina Montague's decision to stab Charlie in the eye, but I'm sure her recklessness hasn't been good for your business. What are you going to do?"

"Oh. I'm fine," I said. "I have my own studio, actually."

"Well, you're lucky. As someone who's married to the city's persona non grata right now, I went from serving on a dozen committees to one small project for the last debutante ball. If I wasn't footing the bill for my contribution, I'd probably be dismissed from that, too."

"Knock, knock," a man's voice called out from behind us.

Anne and I turned to face none other than Bill Topper, home uncharacteristically early.

Anne crossed the plush space between them to give her husband a hug.

"Bill, this is the photographer who found Regina," she said.

"I still can't believe she did it," said Bill, shaking his head. "I'm sorry you had to see all of that."

"I can't believe it either," I said. "But we were all so close to the violence that night. Actually, I noticed you both left the dining room before Archibald's body was found. If you think about it, the murderer might have been right there."

Anne shuddered.

"I hope for safety's sake that Thorne is interviewing everyone," I said. "I've heard that Felicity Cromwell might have been in the anteroom. Do you think she might have done it?"

"Where did you hear that?" said Bill. He distractedly pulled his pen out from his jacket's inner pocket, where it had been restored, and began to roll it through his fingers.

"Regina, I think," I lied.

"She'll say anything to save her butt," said Anne.

"Actually, Liv isn't wrong," said Bill. They seemed to either have forgotten I was there, or they didn't think I posed any kind of threat. Either worked for me. "I just didn't want you to get mad that I was working during a night out, Anne."

"Please. I knew you were working. You are always working," she said. "But I'll admit I'd had it with you for working at the ball. That's why I stormed off to the powder room at the end of the evening. I was so tired of you working all the time. And now, with Charlie dead, you'll be chained to that office."

"I couldn't help it. Felicity was steaming outside the ballroom," he said. "She'd figured out Charlie's scam and was about ready to kill him. But she didn't do it. I calmed her down, told her I knew and that I was working on it. Security joined us and I watched her leave."

"Did either of you hear anything in the garden room?" I said.

"I didn't hear Regina kill Charlie, if that's what you mean," said Anne. "I heard a waiter, or someone, say 'what *arrogance*' when I left the bathroom. Someone must have noticed that Felicity had camped out at the private affair. Showing up like that is in very poor taste."

"Anne," said Bill, "I won't be chained to the office anymore. See? I'm here."

"Duly noted," said Anne with a tender smile.

Bill looked at his desk where his equally gentle eyes immediately hardened. "Why is my laptop open?" he said.

My heart started to palpitate. Then, my breath became shallow as I saw Jade pass by the open door. She looked at me squarely, and I knew she was going to give me away.

"Someone, answer me," Bill said.

"I was trying to get on Google Docs for school," said Jade. "I'm doing extra work for French."

"Good for you," said Anne.

"You have your own laptop," said Bill.

"The battery was dead," she said. She then directed a triumphant nostril flare at me before heading back to her room. She really wanted to go to that party this weekend.

"Well, I see a big envelope there," said Bill, motioning to my package containing his holiday gift. "I'm sure you two are up to something fun. I'll leave you ladies to it."

Bill closed the door behind him, and Anne put her head in her hands to rub her temples.

"What a mess," she said. "I didn't grow up with all of this." She waved her hand to the room. "I made my money with a lot of sleepless nights and hard work. I don't know what's going to happen with Lion's Mane, but I'll be able to handle it. Bill? It will be harder. He grew up with the proverbial silver spoon in his mouth, but he's an honest man."

She looked at me earnestly while speaking her last few words. I could see she wanted me to acknowledge her husband's character. Given the letter I'd read on his laptop, I decided I could. Writing that letter, exposing his partner, opening his company to an investigation, that took a strong person.

Could I say the same about Anne? She was generous and had been kind to me, but she was also fiercely loyal to her husband, who placed the integrity of his company above all. Anne and Bill Topper liked the game of making money, certainly. But unlike Charlie Archibald, they knew that there was a line. As far as I was concerned, they were innocent of his murder.

"I think Mr. Topper's an amazing person," I said.

"He is," she answered. "I'll be by his side all the way. And who knows? Some things are better already for us. He's home by dinner. Speaking of which, I must talk to Estelle and then tell the girls they are not going to a party this weekend, however hard they try to pull one over on me."

"I remember those days when I was their age. It's probably some harmless fun and they'll feel like wonderful rebels," I said. After all, a deal was a deal.

"Maybe you're right," she said.

Chapter 19

The morning of Charlie Archibald's funeral, I dressed for work, and donned Maria's black dress coat out of respect for the dead.

After checking in on my grandparents, who seemed in good spirits, I packed my camera bag for my first Liv Spyers Photography location shoot since I'd met Harry on the subway that fateful morning. I promised myself I'd put aside all the mysteries in my life—who killed Charlie Archibald? Had Poppy been breaking into my apartment? Why did Harry Fellowes turn out to be a fake? —and focus on my goal, my dream, my no-guts-no-glory agenda of photographing people. Capturing a smile, a head tilt, or a shaft of light on a shoe was all I'd ever wanted to do. It was time to get back to it. And, of course, head to Charlie Archibald's funeral afterward.

The baby shower I was shooting was uptown, past the swanky buildings of Park Avenue, in West Harlem, not far from City College. I was so excited to work, I arrived early, like, really early. To kill some time, I walked around the campus. I'd never been before, and I was awestruck by the fact that in the middle of the metropolis I'd grown to love, I'd never known about the campus. It felt like something you might see in a movie. Trees and grand buildings screamed '*higher learning*' and I watched the day's early birds head out, wondering if they were going to class or to the library. I'd told the world that dropping out of school had not bothered me, but Maria was right. On some level I was always trying to prove myself. I had goals and dreams. Finding myself on such a magical campus, I realized that my education was one of those dreams.

"Met Gala, Met Gala, Met Gala," I said to myself and headed over to the morning's job.

I spent three hours celebrating the impending arrival of one Baby Delgado, enjoying the party attendees' excitement over the baby's unknown gender, the onesies the expectant mom opened, along with hearing details about childbirth that shocked and appalled me. With a piñata of a stork which, when broken, opened to a cascade of condoms, the party was the opposite of an Elizabeth Everly production. The living room in which I took my photos was sun-filled and the laughter that pealed from their party and out onto the sidewalk was infectious.

I could have stayed all day, but I had a funeral to go to, and so I said my goodbyes when the time came. On the subway downtown, I yelled out an involuntary *yes!* when I saw that my new client had given me a five-star review before I'd even delivered the photos to her.

The sun followed me to the Frank E. Campbell Funeral Chapel on Madison Avenue and Eighty-First Street. When I arrived, I noticed a group of protestors across the street, guarded by police. The crowd was larger and louder than the one at the Archibald Foundation had been, but they were not the main attraction. The press took center stage. Vans from all the major television networks were parked along the street, while reporters and cameramen stood ready to scoop the funeral of a man who had hit the news twice in one week: first for his murder, and then for pulling off one of the biggest financial cons of the century.

Despite the hubbub outside of Campbell's, I noticed very few people entering the funeral home to pay their respects. I'd never been to a funeral before, and I wondered if I was going to see Charlie Archibald in a casket. The idea of viewing his lifeless body was as terrifying as when I'd discovered him at the Pierre. At least in that case I hadn't had time to think about it. If I hadn't promised Angela I'd go, I might have easily turned on my heels for home. But I was here. I'd made a promise to Donna. I'd see it through.

When I entered the building, I was relieved to see the group of attendees was beginning to file into the funeral chapel on the first floor. At the door, a woman kindly asked me my name, which she checked against a list. I knew the circumstances around Archibald's funeral were unusual in that he was both a victim of murder and a crook, but the fact he had a guest list for even his final farewell was not lost on me.

Fortunately, Archibald's casket was closed. Perhaps because of the injury to his eye, Donna had decided that less was more. I knew she desperately wanted to protect her daughter and wondered if that might be part of it.

Angela was seated in a pew in the front of the room, surrounded by friends as well as her cousin Bethany, whom I recognized from Miranda Headram's photo. I headed toward her to pay my respects.

"Thanks for giving me the photo of me and my dad. I'll treasure it. And my mom told me you spoke," Angela said.

"We had a good talk. Hang in there today," I said.

The gathering was probably small for a man of Archibald's power, but the room was filling up. I noticed that the Toppers were in the good seats, if you could call them that, by the coffin. Anne noticed me, and I could see she was surprised I was there, but she wasn't snooty about it. After all, I'd found the man's corpse. Miranda Headram was seated on the other side of the room in a similar place of honor. Both she and Phil sat together with their heads hung low. Elizabeth Everly sat in a back pew, swathed in black that made her look even more beautiful.

Detective Thorne stood behind the back row of pews, watching the gathering like a hawk. I wondered if he was hoping Regina would show, or if he'd come around to realizing that it was worth looking beyond his first suspect.

I noticed someone waving me over to her. Of all people, it was Bernie Andrews, and she patted a spot beside her, which, it seemed, she had been saving for me. Leave it to Bernie to know the guest list. The last thing I wanted to do was hang out with Harry's undercover family, but Bernie was an octogenarian secret agent and the last thing I wanted to do was snub such a cool woman. I also noticed that Felicity Cromwell was conveniently seated to the right of her. I waved and headed over.

"I heard how badly Harry behaved," Bernie said before I even sat down. "These men. They botch it up every chance they get."

"It's so nice to see you," I said, hoping we could skip over the formalities.

"My husband was the same when I met him," she said, confiding in me. "You might have heard from Harry he was with the FBI. I didn't know he was with the organization until four months into dating him, when one night he excused himself to make an arrest, which I watched from a phone booth. This was way back before iPhones. Then he came back to the table and continued with the soup like nothing had happened."

I couldn't help it. I laughed.

"I don't think you need to defend Harry," I said. "He's a big boy. He can take care of himself."

As I spoke, I noticed that Felicity Cromwell had risen to move to another seat, presumably away from me.

"Harry's a good man. I hope it all works out," she said,

reaching her arm out to stop Felicity as she spoke. "Stay, Felicity. Liv, Harry told me you wanted to speak to my friend here."

"Oh, we've spoken," Felicity said.

"It doesn't sound like it was a good conversation from the tone of your voice," said Bernie. I thought she looked a bit surprised and even somewhat impressed that I'd found Felicity already, without their help.

"She suggested that maybe—" Felicity looked around the room. She leaned in to speak to Bernie more intimately. "She suggested that I *killed* Charlie Archibald."

"Nonsense," said Bernie. "Liv, dear. Felicity's not the murdering type. She has a head on her shoulders. I've given her a lot of money over the years for the foundation and other work she's done. I never did that for Charlie over there." She nodded toward the coffin without seeming to care who heard her. "I always had a red flag about him. Come on, Liv, get up."

She stood and pulled me up with her.

"Switch seats with me," she said. "Get it all out of your systems. You should be friends."

Before either Felicity or I could refuse, there was a burst of melody from a harpist to get everyone's attention.

"Ladies and gentlemen," the officiant said into the microphone from the dais by the coffin. "If we might all sit. We'd like to begin."

Bernie, Felicity, and I took our seats.

"You sound the opposite of your nephew," I said to Bernie. "He's not a fan of my talking to certain people about certain things."

"You strike me as someone who knows how to take care of herself," Bernie said.

"We're gathered here today," the officiant said, "to remember our son, Charles Hegimore Archibald."

The harpist began to play, we stood again, this time to sing

"Amazing Grace." Bernie nudged me in the ribs to address Felicity. I could see Harry had a tough boss in his aunt.

"I'm sorry if I upset you the other day," I said to Felicity as we flipped through our hymnals.

Felicity didn't answer me.

"I've spoken to Bill," I said. "He explained everything to me about the night of the ball."

"He shouldn't have," Felicity said. "We agreed to keep that between us and the police. Neither of us need to add to the gossip mill."

"My lips are sealed. I promise," I said. "I swear on Bernie."

Felicity's eyes remained on her hymnal, but I saw her smile. I'd said the right thing. Bernie had everyone's respect, even those who had no idea what she did behind the scenes.

"Anne also told me that she heard someone say something in the garden room," I said as the second verse began. "Something like, '*what arrogance.*' Did you hear that, too?"

"Nope," she said, closing her book.

The music ended, we all sat back down, and the officiant began his eulogy. I didn't think that Felicity and I had exactly become friends, but I was glad she knew that I didn't think she was a murderer.

I found the officiant's comments to be remarkably generic. He did skirt around the concept of redemption. Overall, I gave him good marks on his performance. This had to have been an awkward service to plan when half of the attendees had been profoundly betrayed by the deceased. When he finished, Donna rose and stood behind the dais.

"I know we're filled with mixed emotions today," she said, addressing the elephant in the room. "It's only natural. I'd ask, however, that while we're here, right now, we remember that Charles Archibald, husband, father, family man and friend, was murdered."

No one spoke, but you could feel every person tense at her words.

"Good for her," Bernie said into her program.

"Angela," Donna continued, now looking at her daughter. "I want you to remember the father who adored you, who danced with you on the last night of his life, and who was at peace knowing that you were better than he and I could ever be. I'm here for you and by your side at every step of the way."

She sat back down.

The harpist started up again, and we rose for one last hymn. The crowd started to disperse, and several people approached Bernie to say hello.

"Actually," Felicity said to me as we stood, "I did hear something. I'd forgotten it completely, but when I was leaving the Pierre, I think I heard someone say, *'You'll have to pay up first.'* I didn't give it any thought. I figured it was a waiter or someone like that looking for his paycheck."

Anne had thought she'd heard a waiter, too.

"You should probably tell Detective Thorne," I said. "Any information he has that could help is important."

"OK, I will," she said. "Good idea."

Felicity approached the detective, but he was making a quick escape behind the coffin which Bill and a small handful of friends carried through the back door to a waiting hearse, around the corner from the protestors.

When I stepped out onto the sidewalk, the sun gleamed into my eyes. I watched as Angela and Donna Archibald were ushered into a private car with tinted windows. The hearse pulled around Madison Avenue and their car followed it uptown. Another car, driven by Detective Thorne, joined the entourage. Even at her husband's funeral the detective was putting pressure on Donna to point a finger at Regina.

"You seem to be everywhere."

I turned to the speaker, Elizabeth Everly.

"You too," I said. "Saying goodbye to the man who put you in dire financial straits? You're a better person than I'd be. Honestly, you had a very good motive for murder."

Elizabeth raised her eyebrows. "Oh, I wanted to see Charlie Archibald dead," she said. "I'll tell anyone that. Unfortunately, I needed him alive. The Archibalds were my better clients. They throw at least two big bashes a year. One in the summer, in the Hamptons. One to celebrate Lion's Mane in the first quarter. I needed some way to make up the money I'd lost on my failed expansion plans."

Of course, with Lion's Mane's scandal, those parties were now a thing of the past, but Elizabeth Everly had not known that the night of the party.

"Some say people invest with Lion's Mane primarily so they can go to their party," she said. "It's an amazing bash. Archibald was smart. He knew how his investors liked to rub shoulders with each other. Lion's Mane was like a Who's Who club."

"I'm sorry for your lost business. I bet if he'd pulled off his money-laundering scheme, he would have kept his word and invested with you."

Elizabeth's eyes welled with tears. "Excuse me," she said.

She might have hated Archibald, as she freely admitted, but I could see why murder was not a way for her to solve any problems.

Elizabeth hadn't even made it to the street corner when I heard a voice rise above the crowd. I was surprised to see Phil Headram calling out to Miranda, who had taken off down the street. Bethany came to her father's side. I could see Phil was ready to follow his wife, but his daughter kept him from leaving.

Me? I followed her. Miranda's pace was remarkably fast, and I was fascinated by the emotions that had overtaken this woman.

"Miranda!" I cried out, but my voice was drowned by the blast of a delivery truck's horn and a jackhammer.

A couple of blocks away, Miranda turned right and continued east on a side street between Park and Lexington avenues. She slowed her step, and I watched her approach a man who was wrapping flowers outside a deli. Miranda took out her wallet. She handed the man some money but took no flowers. Instead, the worker opened a side door for her to a decrepit building. I wondered if the good times had ended for the Headrams, too. Was she looking to move into one of the apartments above the deli?

CHAPTER 20

"What apartment did that woman go to?" I asked the man tending the flowers when I arrived a moment later.

"*¿Qué?*" said the man.

I pointed to the door that Miranda had entered. "*La mujer,*" I said and did an impression of her holding her purse.

"Ah," said the man with a laugh. "*No apartamento. El techo.*" He pointed up. "The roof."

I dug into my coat pocket and pulled out a crumpled five-dollar bill. It was Maria's coat pocket, but I was good for it.

"Can you open up for me, too?" I said, handing the money to the man. "*Abre la puerta, por favor.*"

The man seemed happy with his easy money. He unlocked the door, and I ran up five flights of stairs to the roof. I was impressed that Miranda had made it to the top. Panting when I reached the roof's door, I opened it with a bang.

Miranda was there, standing on a broken step ladder by the edge of the roof, her back to me, staring into the distance.

"Miranda?" I said.

She did not respond. This was not good.

Afraid to startle her, I crept across the roof until I was close enough that I could grab her if she tried to do anything crazy.

"Hey, how's it going?" I said. "It was a beautiful funeral."

She didn't respond.

"I know it's been an upsetting day, but don't do anything crazy, OK? You didn't even like your cousin," I said. "And I'm sure your daughter will be happy with any type of wedding you can afford. Who needed his money?"

"What're you doing here?" Miranda said, her eyes glued to the horizon.

"I could ask you the same."

"Phil and I lived in this building when we were first married," she said, rising another rung up the ladder, now only one step away from the roof's parapet. "We were so happy in those days."

My heart racing, I looked over the edge. Then I exhaled and my palms stopped sweating a bit. In fact, I hopped up for a seat on the parapet. Only eight feet below was a patio for the top floor's apartment. At least there was no chance Miranda would die if she jumped.

"Get off," said Miranda. She looked at me directly for the first time.

"You get off," I said, folding my arms.

I knew, deep down, she had no plans to really jump. What would Mr. Binders, Lucky or Sugar do without her? Whatever Miranda was working through, it wasn't going to end in self-harm. Nonetheless, she was a wreck. Her oversized pearls rose and fell on her heaving, breast.

"I am responsible for Charlie Archibald's death," she said. "I'm not sure if I can live with that guilt."

I almost fell off the ledge in shock.

It was now my turn to breathe heavily. I slipped my hand into my coat pocket and felt my iPhone. I tried to remember how to call the police without dialing in case I needed to send out an SOS. Something about pressing the side buttons was all I could remember given how I was also trying to keep breathing.

I wanted to run. I'd been trying to find clues, trying to help Regina, but suddenly things were happening quickly. Too quickly. Aside from my phone, I was unarmed and alone with a woman who had just confessed to murder.

"The deli man knows we're both up here," I said. "Don't try anything foolish."

I was about to take a step back, but then I noticed she was wearing her large brooch. Of all the nerve. I decided to stand my ground. If I was going to be stuck on a roof with a crazed, dog-loving murderer, I at least deserved a full confession.

"I guess I'm not surprised," I said. "I saw your brooch the night of the ball. That was a very clever murder weapon."

"My brooch?"

"The clasp was long and pointy, just like the police said the murder weapon would be," I said. "It was brilliant, really. Stab him with it and then put it back on. No one realized you were wearing the murder weapon. But I have to say, it was cold to wear it to his funeral."

Miranda put her hand to her breast and ripped her brooch from her blouse in one swift move.

"Do you think I used my brooch to kill my own cousin? First, my brooch is magnetic," she said, her hand clutching the jewel. "I have rheumatoid arthritis, which is why I only wear clips for my jewels, including my earrings if you think those might have been a murder weapon, too."

"I don't," I said, but she wasn't listening to me.

"Even if I had a weapon to kill Charlie, I couldn't pull that off. He'd have knocked me over in a second. Trust me. I'd be the one on the floor with the dagger in my eye if I'd tried anything with him."

Miranda straightened her pearls and tsked.

"But, you said you are responsible."

"I didn't kill him directly," she said. "But I am responsible."

Here, her tears began to flow. I, on the other hand, felt the tension in my muscles begin to melt.

"And now our family is ruined," she said, wiping her coat sleeve across her nose. "Bethany's engagement will surely be called off, Phil will be in prison, and I'll be alone."

Miranda's sobs were loud and ugly. I let her cry it out for a bit as I digested her last statement.

"Why will Phil go to jail?" I said when I decided she could speak again.

"Because Phil is a saint," she said. "He knew I was furious with Charlie even before we got to the Holiday Ball. I'd told him how Charlie wouldn't let us invest in LaunchTech because we couldn't meet the minimum investment amount. At the same time, Phil knew how much I'd been fretting that we couldn't afford the wedding I wanted to throw for Bethany. I was horrible. I even called him a failure because he couldn't pay for his only daughter's wedding. But Phil, he took the high road. He said he'd talk to Charlie. I told him not to bother. I'd do it. And I did. I took Charlie out on the dance floor and gave him a piece of my mind. Phil was watching us. He saw Charlie wasn't going to budge. When we returned to our table, Phil stood to pull out my chair and I heard him let out a pained cry. That's how upset he was. He spent the rest of the night sitting at the table, looking so pained."

"None of this means he killed Charlie Archibald," I said.

"I wish," said Miranda. "But Phil knew I'd receive money if Charlie died. I lied when I told you we didn't leave the ballroom before Charlie was murdered. We both did. Before Phil excused himself, I saw him put a steak knife from the table into his jacket pocket."

"You think he killed Mr. Archibald with the steak knife?" I said. Miranda nodded.

"Did you ask him if he did it?" She shook her head.

"But I saw Detective Thorne at the funeral. I've been waiting for days for news that they'd recovered the murder weapon Regina Montague used, but they haven't found anything," she said. "You might not understand this, but Phil would do anything for me. I know I can be high maintenance, but he puts up with me. And for what? Charlie's fund was a fraud. And in his death, we have no inheritance. What a tremendous waste."

"So, you're up here because of remorse that you drove Phil to murder your cousin?"

"Well, I'm not up here for Charlie."

I folded my arms against the cold and thought about her story for a moment.

"It's a nice story," I finally said, "but how do I know that *you* didn't use the steak knife to kill Archibald? You left the ballroom, too. I saw you."

Miranda's eyes grew so large I thought they alone might fall from the roof to the street below.

"I would never," she said. "When I left the ballroom, it was to find Phil. I wanted to head home. I thought we could slip out."

"When you were outside of the ballroom, did you see Phil kill Archibald? Did you see the knife?"

"I saw Phil, yes," she said. "He was in front of the restroom. I told him I wanted to go home, and I also asked him about the knife. He said he didn't know what I was talking about. He didn't have a knife. I felt his pocket and he didn't. I was tired at that point and didn't really care. I told him I needed to go to the bathroom, which I did, and when I stepped out Phil had gone back into the ballroom, which annoyed me to no end."

I closed my eyes and sorted through the images I'd stored away, my own vault, you could say, to piece together Miranda's narrative with what I'd seen. The pieces all seemed to fit, except for one.

"Before you turn your husband in, I have one question," I

said. “The night of the ball, I noticed Mr. Headram was limping. Today he wasn’t. Did he have an accident?”

Miranda seemed as if she might burst into tears again.

“No. He was only limping at the ball,” she said. “I think after the presentations of the debs. Although when we left to go home, he’d stopped.”

I smiled.

“I don’t think Phil killed Archibald,” I said, remembering the cluttered tray with the bloodied napkin beside Regina after Archibald’s death. “I think the problem was that he’s worn the same dress shoes for too many years.”

“He has,” Miranda said. “One of his soles has worn through to a hole. I meant to get it fixed but I didn’t have time.”

“I also think the tack that protected your chair leg dislodged when Phil pulled out your chair and that he stepped onto it. Those are big tacks. When you heard him let out a yelp, it was probably because he had stepped on the tack where his sole had worn through. That can be a very painful thing. I think he took the knife to the bathroom to dig out the tack before you went home so that he could walk more comfortably.”

“And how would you know this?” she said.

“Because I saw the tack and the steak knife on a tray in the garden room after Archibald’s murder,” I said. “The tack was too short to have killed Archibald, but long enough to cause him discomfort. And, by the way, the knife had no blood on it.”

Careful to keep one hand on the ladder, Miranda managed to extract a handkerchief from her purse and dabbed her forehead. Then, she started to laugh.

“You are a clever one,” said Miranda. “Nothing gets by you.”

“I’m not so clever,” I said. “I just notice things.”

“That’s clever,” she said.

“Miranda, if I can help find the real murderer, will you get off that ladder?”

"My God, yes. I'm so tired," said Miranda. She stepped off the ladder and wiped her eyes.

When we said goodbye on the sidewalk a few minutes later, I think we were both ready for a stiff drink, but I had work to do. I headed back to my studio, checked on my grandparents, and started in on editing the photos I'd taken at the Delgados' baby shower.

It was a quiet time in the studio. I put on classical music to help me focus. Once I got into the rhythm, my thoughts roamed freely and returned to the Archibald suspects. Or my lack of suspects at this point. The Headrams were now officially off my list after today's meeting on the roof. I was also satisfied that Bill Topper and Felicity Cromwell had an alibi for each other that a security guard could confirm. Given the meeting taking place between Bill and Felicity, Anne had no time to set up a homicidal plan and execute it without having attracted their attention. Bill might cover for his wife, but Felicity would not. Bernie had vouched for Felicity's integrity, so I decided the Toppers hadn't bought her silence either.

When I finished Baby Delgado's portfolio, I was thrilled with the file I sent to my client through OneShot's private messaging system. My deal had been very generous, but it had worked for both me and my client. I decided there was no harm in keeping my offer up longer. I extended my Holiday Special Deal on OneShot, hoping to inspire new customers to check out my page.

It was getting dark, and I could hear my grandparents upstairs. Granny was baking. Poppy was looking for his Santa's hat. Christmas was around the corner, and we'd be heading to New Jersey for Christmas Eve and Day. We'd be packed like sardines in my parents' house. All of us were excited.

I decided to call Manjeet. I was sure we could put our heads together on the only two suspects I could not strike off with one-hundred-percent certainty: Donna Archibald and Elizabeth Everly. I wasn't sold on either of them as a murderer, but they were the last two standing.

"I have the juiciest story to tell you about me and Miranda on a roof," I said when he picked up. "You're going to die."

"Oh my God, it's been a nightmare," he said, distraught. "It's terrible."

"What's happened?"

"Regina was arrested this afternoon," he said. "For second degree murder. Thorne was at RMS with a warrant to look through her office. I'm sure it will be in the news tonight. I knew it was a bad idea for her to disappear like that, but she's so stubborn. If someone tries to flex some authority over her, she turns into a wild thing. Unless it's a client, of course."

"They found a weapon?" I said.

"I don't know, but they found out she has a record back in the UK. She was apparently part of some hoodlum group that raised hell in her town when she was a teenager. Shoplifting and mailbox toppling and dumb but destructive stuff. I mean, she was a kid in a small town doing stupid stuff, but they're stacking it against her. Thorne told me that he had received a tip that Regina said sirens made her nervous or something, so they spoke to some kind of forensic psychiatrist who said it's indicative of a disturbed mind. Are they kidding? Regina is the most honest person I know. Plus, he said there were photos where Regina was apparently staring daggers at Archibald during dinner at the ball."

I couldn't speak. In fact, I instinctively buried my face in my hands as I remembered that I was the one who had told Thorne that Regina didn't like sirens. I'd also taken the photo of her in the dining room. Unwittingly, I'd handed Thorne a tip and photos he was now using to strengthen his case against Regina, however circumstantial they might be.

"It also didn't help that Regina showed up in the Hamptons

at Archibald's burial. That's where they arrested her," Manjeet said. "Big news. Regina and Donna are lovers. I don't know how that one slipped by me. She was safe and sound at a Buddhist retreat. No phone or internet. But she had to go and blow it by seeing Donna. The crazy darling."

"I can't imagine Regina in an orange jumpsuit."

"She's not. Yet," Manjeet said. "She's using RMS as collateral to post bail. She must also stay with Donna, who's vouched she'll show up for her hearing. I hate to say it, but I think it's time we looked for new jobs."

Chapter 21

Three weeks later, it was Christmas Eve in New Jersey, and Nat King Cole's voice reassuringly filled my parents' home with cheer. My dad spent the afternoon outside checking bulbs on the multi-colored lights that framed our house. Eliza, beside him, attempted to make snow angels in the two inches of flakes that had fallen. My granny and mom took over the kitchen, baking a ham, while Poppy slept in front of the television.

Manjeet and Maria had showed up on my doorstep the morning after Regina was arrested, for an intervention about my investigation. My dear friend and colleague argued that I'd done my fair share in trying to help the woman who had helped me. I'd reluctantly, under protest, promised to forgo any inquiries into my remaining two suspects, if you could call them that: the unlikely-to-be-murderers, Donna Archibald and Elizabeth Everly.

I wasn't entirely honest with them, however. The truth was, I've learned as an artist that you sometimes need to walk away from a challenge for a while to get perspective. Like Thorne, I feared I'd gotten too caught up in my preconceived ideas. They weren't adding up. I needed to trust that in time, I'd see things in a new light. Meanwhile, I'd received a couple of requests for photo sessions based on my special holiday offer on OneShot. I kept busy.

Ironically, Liv Spyers Photography was still hanging in there, while RMS was now closed, indefinitely.

Christmas Eve dinner was outstanding, we all ate too much, and if it wasn't for the fact that Santa was coming, Eliza would have stayed up all night. Over ice cream and homemade pizzelle cookies, Maria called to say that one of our friends from high school was throwing a party.

"Come on," she said when I began to pass. "You need to get back out there. Jerry Spinoza will be there. Didn't you always like him?"

Although no one mentioned Harry these days, I was keenly aware of everyone's clandestine looks of sympathy, support, and stumped exasperation. It didn't help that Harry had sent a big box of Christmas candies from a high-end store on Madison Avenue that none of us had ever heard of. Despite our family-first loyalty, the gift had delighted and impressed my closest relatives, whose idea of luxury holiday confections is when Hershey's seasonally switches up their Kisses to red and green swirled foils. After Eliza popped the first of Harry's chocolates into her mouth, she'd finally voiced what everyone had been thinking: Why didn't I like him? Of course, I couldn't tell them the truth. Instead, I'd rolled my eyes, grabbed a caramel truffle, and left the room.

"You mean Jerry Spinoza from seventh grade?" I said to Maria.

"Well, if you don't want him, I'll take him," she said. "You're coming."

"I can't go out," I said. "I need to help with the dishes."

"Go!" my family said in unison, including Eliza.

"Majority rules," said Maria, hearing their pleas through my phone.

She hung up before I could protest further. No one would let me clear plates, so I went through a cardboard box I'd forgotten to take with me to New York to find something presentable to wear. My search produced a now somewhat tight, bright blue mini skirt with a small slit up the side, which I wore with my combat boots. To dodge any disapproval of my duds, from Maria or my family, I slapped on Ruby Woo red lips, swiped my eyelashes with my ultra-volume mascara wand, and popped on a Santa hat.

"Does this look OK?" I said, entering the kitchen, where my mom and Granny were making espresso.

They snapped up their heads, and I knew I'd interrupted a deep conversation.

"What?" I said, immediately aware that something was wrong.

"Nothing," said my mom. "You're looking good. It's nice to see you have some fun."

"Hello, Mrs. Spyers," Maria said, interrupting us by entering our unlocked kitchen door as if she'd never left. I was pleased to see she'd forgone her office suits for long, dangling earrings and a fur-trimmed crop top that did wonders for her figure.

Her entrance came to a halt when she saw the box of candy on the kitchen counter. "Oh my God. I've never seen so much chocolate. Are there caramels left?"

"Harry sent it, but Liv doesn't like him anymore," said Granny with a *don't upset her* expression I wasn't supposed to notice.

"Well, they're delicious. Put on some mascara and let's go," Maria said, handing me a bright pink tube and ushering me out the door.

Our old friend's party featured a hot tub, decorated with "Angels on High" cutouts that were anything but angelic. It overflowed with people in all states of dress, despite the cold.

I'll admit, it was a party that rivaled any of Manhattan's high-end extravaganzas from a photographer's point of view. I was particularly happy with a shot I got of two revelers, one dressed as Santa and the other as Rudolph, making out below an inflatable Holy Mother. On the con side, Maria quickly learned that Jerry Spinoza had a girlfriend. Following chit-chat with people we barely knew anymore, we gave each other the nod, grabbed our coats, and made an Irish exit.

"Wanna get a drink?" she said as we got into the car. "It's still early."

I thought about my mom and Granny in the kitchen.

"I think something's up at home," I said. "Maybe I should check in first."

We sat in silence as we passed home after home in lights, like a fairy land. "And you're sure Harry was bad news, right?" she said.

I turned to her indignantly.

"Um, what happened to *'who needs men'*? Don't forget. He lied to me about his job. And he told me I couldn't handle my investigation without him."

"He also helped you climb up a ladder to break into an apartment where a suspected murderer was."

"We didn't know that a suspect would be there. And he only did it because he knew I'd go anyway, and he thought it would be better for him to join in case something bad happened."

Maria didn't answer.

"He didn't tell the detective working on the Archibald case about me when I was breaking into Donna and Regina's apartment," I said. "I guess that was one redeeming thing."

Maria still didn't answer. I looked at my phone.

"He also told his Aunt Bernie about how I wanted to talk to Felicity Cromwell, one of my suspects. Bernie was at the funeral and made sure we sat together."

"Meh," she said.

"Well, not entirely meh," I said. We pulled into my driveway.

"Will you be long, or should I keep the car running?"

"Keep it running," I said, opening the door.

"Liv, I'm going to say one thing and then I'll keep my mouth shut. The guy is crazy about you. He's got your back. If I recall, he said that he never met a girl who went to such lengths because she screwed up at work, so I'd say he gets you. He watched you break into an apartment and still he liked you. *And*, I'm still tasting that candy he sent. It seems to me that the only real mistake he made was to be vague about his job and that's part of his job description. If you can't take it, that's your decision. But don't say that he blew it. He fessed up to everything and still tried to help you from behind the scenes with that Felicity woman and his aunt after you banished him."

"Jeez, Maria," I said—well, barked.

I got out of the car and banged the door closed, muttering to myself the whole way to my house. The light was on in the kitchen and the door was ajar to let out some of the garlic odor, so I walked right in.

"Granny, what were you two not telling me before?" I said to my grandmother, more sharply than I intended as I was still angry with Maria's uncalled for love therapy. Granny was seated at the kitchen table, rubbing her feet. "Is something wrong with Eliza?"

"No," said my mom, entering the kitchen.

"Tell her," Granny said. "She needs to know. Livia, come sit down."

I dutifully obeyed. Sensing things were getting serious, fast, I took off my Santa hat.

"Poppy had some tests a couple of months ago," my mom said. "We didn't want to worry you until we knew more, but he has Alzheimer's and it's progressing rapidly."

I blinked back tears and instinctively jumped up to hug

Granny, my anger disappearing. "It's going to be OK," I said. "I'll be there with you. I can help."

"You're sweet, *carina*," she said, "but the doctors are strongly recommending that Poppy go to an assisted living facility."

"No," I said, shaking my head adamantly. "He can stay at home. I can help more."

"He'd need a nurse and they are expensive," my mom said.

"Then I'll move back to Jersey, and you can rent out my space to someone else for more money."

"I gave you a good deal but not that good a deal," said Granny.

"We're going to look at homes next week," my mom said. "Poppy doesn't know yet. We don't want to scare him."

From outside, we heard Maria honk the horn. "Oh crap," I said. "Let me tell her to go on without me."

I didn't get into the details, but Maria could tell I was upset. When I went back to the house, everyone had moved to the living room. Eliza was asleep under the tree, and the annual Carrera tradition of watching *It's a Wonderful Life* had begun. I curled up next to Poppy and joined them. It was hard to enjoy the movie when all I wanted to do was hug him and tell him everything would be OK. I wished I had work to calm me.

I had jammed a bunch of gifts, last minute, into the bag I'd carried the last time I visited the Toppers. It had fallen on the floor and peeking out was Bill Topper's photo album I'd stashed in it. I'd been ignoring the book since I'd left, sort of wishing it would disappear because I was horrified to have taken it. Now, I crossed the room and picked it up. The old brown leather was soft, and the edges of the pages were yellowed. I brought it back to the sofa with me and began to browse through the story of someone else's life. Bill Topper, a young man on a trip of the world, enjoying adventures Poppy would never have. I'm not one for pity parties, but I leaned against my grandfather's shoulder and listened to his calm breathing. After a few minutes, Poppy looked over my head and joined me.

"I know that guy," he said.

"What guy, Poppy?" I answered quietly.

"That one," Poppy said.

He pointed to a man in one of the photos of a group of guys on the beach, all in brightly striped or flowered bathing suits à la the 1980s. Bill Topper had his arm around the man and Charlie Archibald stood beside them, holding up a fish. Bill had a lot more hair, although it was still spiked in little tufts. Charlie Archibald looked as polished as I'd seen him the night of the ball. The man Poppy had pointed to was a little softer around the waist than his friends, and he held a beer in a dark brown bottle.

"That's nice," I said. My heart broke a bit more. I knew that as Poppy's disease progressed, he would confuse faces and even begin to forget who people were. How long would it be until Poppy could no longer recognize me?

"He was the fellow who dropped off the safe around Thanksgiving," he said. I looked up at him, confused and curious.

"What was his name?" Poppy said. "Papillon—no, that wasn't it."

"Don't worry, Dad," my mom said, but I sat up very straight.

"Popolous?" I said, looking at the picture closely and starting to recognize similarities between the old man I'd met at the ball and the young man in the book. "Was that his name?"

"That's it," said Poppy. "Giorgio. Nice guy. A foreigner."

"With a beautiful cane?"

"I guess you could call it that," said Poppy. "We had a nice chat. He paid upfront, in cash, and said it would be tough to reach him but he'd swing by after Thanksgiving."

I hadn't solved the murder of Charlie Archibald, but I realized I had figured out what Harry and the Art Crime Unit had been up to when we met. They were after Giorgio Popolous. It didn't take me long to figure out why Bernie had invited Popolous to the ball. Over a social dinner, it would have been easy to gather information from him about how long he was staying and what he planned to do in the coming days. A lot could be accomplished over a meal. Like getting an invitation to Popolous's party. I also now understood why Harry had invited me to the roof party at Hudson Yards. While I was chatting with Elizabeth Everly, he had had his own work to do. I tried to remember details of the story he'd told me about his case, but I'd been so furious that night. All I could remember was that for a century it was rumored that the safe had housed a jewel belonging to the British royal family that had gone missing.

I had little to go on, but Google came to the rescue. As George Bailey was running home to Mary and the kids at the end of our movie, I looked through a list of the twenty biggest jewelry heists in history. The stories were amazing, and I found I didn't mind the slow work. The heists were as creative as they were dastardly, ranging from museum break-ins to hotel robberies to home invasions. There was a lot less bloodshed and a lot more cunning in the crimes, and I could see why Harry was drawn to the puzzle of figuring them out.

"What should we watch next?" my dad said.

"*To Catch a Thief*," I answered right away.

"Oh, I love that one. Is it on Netflix?" said Granny. "When Cary Grant tries to prove his innocence as the old cat burglar who stole all the jewels from the hotel?"

I scrolled down the page of jewelry heist stories on the list.

"That's the jewel that was in the safe that Popolous guy brought in," Poppy said and pointed to one of the stories on my phone. Now he was sitting up straight, too. "I can't believe it. Beautiful, isn't it?"

"You said the safe was empty," I said. "But do you think this might have been inside?"

I pointed to a photo of a jeweled pin. It was a diamond shape, encrusted with emeralds and rubies and sapphires and had a large diamond set in the middle. Three pearls dangled from the bottom of the piece to make it a both gorgeous and gaudy charm.

"That's the one," said Poppy.

"Are you sure?" I said.

"One hundred percent," he said. I studied his eyes, calm and clear and lucid. I believed him. One hundred percent.

I read the story below the photo. In a nutshell, during the 1920s a member of the royal family had an affair with a bright, young "it" girl from Greece. To impress her, he brought her to the Tower of London to play dress-up with the family's jewels. After her visit, however, the beloved and priceless Crown Badge of Love had disappeared as did the young flapper, back to her homeland. The royals sent their wayward young relative to the army while a discreet investigation was undertaken into the jewel's whereabouts. The trail led back to Greece, and to a green safe housed at the estate of the wealthy Popolous family. When the British ambassador came to investigate the rumors, he was informed that they had neither a jewel fitting their description nor a green safe. Unconvinced, the royals offered one thousand dollars for its recovery, lest there be a Popolous family member willing to turn it over, but no one ever did. Since then, the jewel had never been found.

I realized that Poppy had sent the ACU in circles. My hunch that my grandfather had found something in the safe, lost it, and had been trying to find it was true.

"Do you still have the jewel?" I said to Poppy. If he did, my grandparents might be in danger.

His eyes became wet, and he closed them. I could see he was working hard to remember what had happened. He'd been searching alone, but now he could talk to me.

"I found it. I thought I was losing my marbles, but now that I see the photo, I know I found it. I thought it was beautiful, but not Granny's style," said Poppy. "I'll tell you, honestly, I thought I put it back in the safe and locked it up. I wrote down the combination on a Post-it and left it on the safe. I could swear it. But a couple of days later, you were there, and the safe was open, and the jewel was gone. I've been looking and looking but I can't find it. What did I do with it?"

Poppy put his head into his hands.

"What are you saying to upset him, Livia?" my mother said.

"Come on, Antony," said Granny, pushing herself off the sofa. "It's time for bed. We can watch the movie tomorrow."

"I want to watch football tomorrow," Poppy said as she led him to my parents' room, where they were spending the night.

"OK, football is good, too, my love," I heard Granny say as the door closed.

"There's no football tomorrow," my dad said in a whisper.

"What did you say to Poppy?" My mother was giving me the eye.

"Nothing," I said. "He's tired. Me too. Merry Christmas?"

I gave my parents a kiss and retired to my toasty fold-away bed in the small WFH space my parents had created after I'd moved to New York. Crawling under the covers, I knew I had to tell Harry that Poppy had found the lost jewel in the safe. I also thought about what Maria said about Harry "getting me" and blah, blah, blah. She had made a couple of points in Harry's favor, but I wasn't ready to trust him again so easily.

I called him.

"Hey," he said after one ring. "Merry Christmas."

"You too," I said, happier to hear his voice than I wanted to be. "First, thanks for the candy. Eliza has been in heaven all day. Second, I have something important to tell you."

He didn't get worked up while I told him what I'd learned, and he listened to everything before reacting.

"I'm so sorry your grandfather has Alzheimer's," Harry said when I'd finished. "I didn't realize his fogginess was that bad."

"I didn't either. It's been happening slowly, but I've been noticing the change for a while. He didn't mean to mislead you," I said. "He got confused. He couldn't remember if he'd opened the safe and found it empty, or if he'd taken the treasure and lost it. That's why he was in my apartment that night. He was looking for it."

"Don't worry," said Harry. "We'll figure it out. We're going to have to look around your grandparents' house for the brooch."

"It's probably in his box of old keys at the store," I said. "They will be so frightened when they find out the police are searching their house."

"Shhh," he said gently, and I'm sure he could hear my throat catch on a tear. "I understand. I do, I do. How about we work on this together? Bernie and I can look around before your grandparents get home, just the two of us, and I'll keep you updated. I won't let anything upsetting happen to them. OK?"

I buried my head in my hands, my worries for Poppy overwhelming me. The last thing I wanted was to be vulnerable in front of Harry, but I was moved by his offer.

"Thank you," I said.

"Are you kidding? Thank you. And thank Poppy. Don't give up on that guy," Harry said, so kindly. "He may have just helped us solve a hundred-year mystery."

At that I let the tears flow and laughed through them. Harry's support of Poppy took a hundred pounds of weight off my shoulders. I wouldn't give up on my grandfather. Never. It was nice to know, however, that someone outside of our family had not either.

"It's a big coincidence, don't you think?" I said, recovering.

"Popolous drops the safe not far from where Donna Archibald was moving?"

"You're not thinking murder again," he said.

"There's no crime in thinking about it," I said.

"It's definitely a coincidence, but no more than that," he said. "Your grandfather has a good reputation. Popolous needed someone skilled yet low-key for his plan to work. It was a perfect match."

"True, but photos tell stories," I said, undaunted. "Through the photo album, we now know that Popolous and Archibald and Topper knew each other when they were young. At least for a short time one summer."

"And most of the people at the ball that night had crossed paths at least once in their lives. It's a small world," he said.

"But Donna and Angela said that Archibald had to climb his way into society, starting with a scholarship to Yale. I'm sure at his age that summer, he was looking and learning and soaking up everything he could. Archibald had that magnetic charm. Maybe over a lot of drinks one night he even got Popolous to talk about his family and then, wham, he hears about this myth of the stolen jewel that surrounds the Popolous clan. He might have thought it was a myth as well until one day, thirty years later, he's walking down the street in Greenwich Village and there's Popolous, older but still recognizable to him, lugging that old safe up the stairs. Archibald remembers the story and realizes it wasn't a legend after all. The jewel was in there."

"Why would Charlie Archibald be walking around Greenwich Village in the middle of a workday?"

"There could be a reason," I said.

"Even if your theory is right, there are a lot of dots to connect between your story and murder," Harry said. "I know it must have been hard for you when Regina Montague was arrested. It wasn't the outcome you wanted, but I can't see how the Crown Badge of Love and the murder are connected. Thorne didn't either."

"Me neither," I admitted.

"What worries me right now is the location of the brooch."

We were both quiet for a bit.

"Night," I finally said.

"Night, beautiful," he said. "See you soon."

I pulled the covers over my head and quietly screamed into my pillow so as not to wake Eliza and have her think Santa had arrived.

CHAPTER 22

Waiting for news from Harry the next day, I threw myself into gifts and food and caroling, but the wheels had begun to turn again. At four o'clock, my phone rang.

"Well?" I said.

"Nothing. We looked everywhere."

"Is the place a mess?"

"They'll never know we were there," said Harry. "I think we're going to need your help."

"I can be back home tomorrow," I said.

In the early morning after Christmas, I lay in bed, thinking about Regina in prison for Archibald's murder and wondering if I was crazy to connect the missing brooch to his death. I still couldn't imagine Regina in prison orange. I thought of Regina at the ball, her fabulous outfit, her jewelry . . .

I sat straight up and opened my laptop. Quickly I searched my photos from the ball. "Oh. My. God."

I looked at my photo of table eight's group picture, where Regina was standing in the background. The one Angela and I had looked at, where she was staring darkly at the company from beyond. In it, as I had recalled after visiting the Headrams, she was wearing a brooch. But not just any brooch as it turned out.

"What the *f*—" I said.

The brooch was the Crown Badge of Love in all its glory. It had been right there at the party, in front of Harry and Popolous and anyone else who cared to see it. If only Popolous had not been late to the ball, he might have seen the jewel that his family had been hiding for a century, on the event photographer. I remembered clearly now how it had dazzled against Regina's emerald-green dress when we had begun the night with the debutantes. The jewel had been competing with her dangling earrings and jangling bracelets. On anyone else, the sheer size of it would have attracted attention from across a room. On Regina, however, it looked like a second skin. It was as if the jewel was made for her.

I flipped through the photos from the end of the night, desperately looking for another photo of her. I'd been beside her at the discovery of Archibald's body, and I trusted my eyes completely, but I needed tangible evidence to support what I was looking for. When I arrived at the series I'd taken of the debutantes and their friends leaving for their after-parties, I finally found one where Regina was once again in the background. She looked as if she herself was trying to disappear with the group and I knew it was to have a smoke outside. I zoomed in once again on Regina's image.

The brooch was gone.

The question was: How did Regina get the jewel? And, what had she done with it? Regina was already deep into one mess. Before I got her into another one, I had questions.

I was meeting Harry and Bernie at noon, but I knew there was an early train back to the City. I threw my stuff into my bag, wrote a note to my family, and called an Uber for a lift to the train station. It was still only a little past eight in the morning when I arrived at the bright blue front door of Regina and Donna's apartment building with coffee.

I pressed the button and waited. "Hello?" said a sleepy voice.

It was Donna.

"It's Liv Spyers. I'm sorry to show up like this, but we need to talk," I said. "It's about Regina."

A moment later, the building's front door buzzed to let me in. When Donna opened her own door for me, I handed her a coffee.

"I need to speak to Regina," I said.

"What's going on?" she said, letting me in.

"Happy Boxing Day." Regina yawned and entered the living room wearing a furry purple robe and matching feathered slippers. For someone who had bailed herself out of jail, she looked good. "I'm all for festivities, but if I'm not allowed to go to work, I was bloody well planning to sleep in."

"Here's a coffee," I said and sat down. "Regina, the night of the ball, you were wearing a brooch. By the end of the night, it was gone. What happened to it?"

"Liv Spyers?" she said, shading her eyes from the morning light with her hand and squinting hard to make sure she was seeing straight. "What are you doing here?"

"You gave me the opportunity of a lifetime. Not only do I owe you one, but I also don't think you killed Charlie Archibald. This is the time for the people in your life to roll up their sleeves and help, but I need some answers."

"You would do that for me?" she said and sat on the edge of the club chair across from me. "You sweet, bloody fool."

"I told you she felt bad," Donna said.

"I need to know about that brooch," I said.

"What does a piece of jewelry have to do with anything?"

"I'm not entirely sure."

"I can't say anything about the brooch." Regina looked at Donna and then down at her slippers as if they were the most interesting shoes in the world. Observing her evasiveness, my heart sank.

"If the story isn't investigated by someone who believes you are innocent, Thorne will twist it to make you look more guilty," I said, giving her one last chance to share her side of the story. "That brooch was big. If you opened the clasp, you could have used its long, pointy, metal fastener to stab Archibald in the eye."

"The truth? I threw it out at the ball, during dinner," Regina said. She looked at Donna. "I'm sorry, honey. I found the jewel in our apartment the morning of the ball. I was so touched. It suited me perfectly. I thought you'd be happy to see me wear it out that night, but you did not notice. You were all over Charlie, and I know you were doing it for Angela, but I couldn't help it. I got blindly jealous. When I saw you kissing him at dinner, that was the final straw. I took off your beautiful gift and threw it in the trash. I hope you can forgive me."

"Reggie," said Donna. She reached out and held Regina's hand, shaking her head as she did. "I never bought you a brooch. I don't know what you're talking about."

"Yes, you did. I found it in my tea tin," she said. Regina grabbed a cigarette, lit it, and tapped her foot. "And there's something I didn't tell you, Donna. Charlie saw me wearing the jewel at the ball and he wanted me to give it to him."

"Did he confront you?" Donna said, forgetting about the mysterious brooch and looking deeply upset that either of them had had words with the other.

"He sent me a text," Regina said. "It said that I had stolen his wife, but I wasn't going to steal anything else from the Archibalds."

"Did he mention the brooch specifically?" I said.

"No, but I knew what he was talking about," said Regina. "I caught him looking at it when you were taking the table photo during dinner. His eyes practically flew out of his head when he saw me wearing something so expensive. Something I could never afford on my own. Donna, I thought you had told him about us, and I felt so ashamed to be angry with you. I went to the bin later to fish the thing out, but it was gone."

"Before the debutantes made their presentations after dinner, I saw you cross the ballroom, Regina. You said, '*You'll never get it back*,' and you were typing into your phone. Archibald tried to bully you, but you didn't back down."

"That text is one of the things Thorne is holding over me," Regina said. "Donna, I hoped you wouldn't ever have to find out."

"But the brooch wasn't Mr. Archibald's," I said, as much to myself as to Regina and Donna.

"He sure acted like it was," Regina said.

"Wait a minute," I said. "You threw the jewel into a trash bin?"

"I know, it was stupid of me," she said.

"No, it was brilliant," I said. "I think I know where the brooch is."

"She's got a sharp eye," Donna said in response to Regina's bewildered look.

I sent a text to Jinx.

My colleague responded moments later with a picture of herself in bed, looking unhappy to hear from me.

I acknowledged her text with a single question.

"Regina, you made it clear to me before I started working for you that Team RMS has to cover each other's backs," I said. "Jinx did. She told me the ins and outs of how to work these parties, including about the perks. She even told me the story of how she had seen someone chuck a piece of jewelry. I thought at the time that she meant in the past but I realize now she'd seen it happen that night."

A message from Jinx popped onto my screen. I opened it.

Let me go back to sleep was written below a photo of a diamond-shaped brooch encrusted with emeralds, rubies, and sapphires, with a large diamond set in the middle. Three pearls dangled from the bottom.

"That's the brooch," said Regina, peering over my shoulder. "Jinx, that little gnat. She grabbed it out of the bin after she saw me toss it."

Don't be mad, but I'm sending someone over to pick it up. It's real, not a copy like you thought, I told Jinx.

I knew it was too good to be true, Jinx responded.

"I've never seen that piece of jewelry before. What does any of this mean?" Donna said. "I don't see how it can help Regina."

"I need to make a phone call," I said, finding Harry's contact information while my heart pounded. "Can I use your bedroom?"

"Make yourself at home," Regina said, looking a bit exasperated. I closed the door.

"Hi!" Harry said on the first ring. "What's up?"

"You don't have to come over today. I found the brooch." I was so excited to spit it out I could barely contain myself.

"You did what?" he said, sounding equally excited.

I told Harry what I'd learned. He cursed joyfully. I joined him.

"I knew you were good at this," he said. "You've put the ACU and a hundred years of investigation to shame."

"I told you," I said, sharing his enthusiasm. "My eyes are my secret weapon."

"You can say that. I'll send someone over right now to recover the jewel from Jinx. You're going to make the British royal family very happy."

"Pish," I said, borrowing a phrase from Regina. "I'm more interested in getting Regina off the hook. Don't you think it's *very* odd that Archibald behaved as if the jewel was his? And that Regina found it in a tea tin, a place that Donna would never check? What if there was something shady between Popolous's treasure and Archibald? Couldn't that have led to murder?"

I was expecting a word or two of supportive enthusiasm for my progress, but instead, Harry was quiet.

"Except you only have Regina's word to go on," he finally said. "I hate to tell you this, but it sounds more like Regina might have known Popolous. Otherwise, how did she get the brooch? I know she told you a story about how she found it at the apartment, in a tea tin of all things, but Donna denied the whole thing. As for Archibald, can we be certain he was even talking about the brooch in his text to Regina? As you said, he didn't spell it out clearly. Like it or not, Regina's at the center of your discovery."

"But why would she throw it out if she was helping Popolous?"

"I could make up a slew of reasons. Thorne will definitely question her extensively about it."

Once again, I was about to get Regina into deeper trouble.

"I feel like this is an awkward moment to ask," said Harry, "but I was wondering. Would you be opposed to me still coming by today, even though the brooch has been found? I feel like we should celebrate."

"I have work to do."

"I wouldn't have it any other way," Harry said.

I couldn't deny it. I'd been looking forward to seeing Harry, too. I inhaled and took the plunge.

"I'll see you at my place," I said. "But I'll warn you. I'll still be thinking about Archibald's murder, and the fact that Popolous and Archibald knew each other, among other things that I've learned from my suspects. I'm not like Detective Thorne. I don't make up my mind until I've seen everything.

After a point, coincidences become opportunities to see facts from a new angle."

"I will expect you to bring it on," he said.

I hung up and opened the door to the living room. Donna was the sole occupant of the room.

"Regina threw her coat over her PJs and went to get fresh milk for my coffee," she said. "I can't drink black."

I looked out the window to check, but I didn't see her. Whatever my photos had told me, Harry's version of the story was a solid one, too. I was beginning to spiral into damning thoughts when, to my relief, the front door opened, and Regina returned with milk.

"I remembered something," she said. "I always do my best thinking when I take a walk and have a ciggie. I would quit, but then where would my inspirations come from?"

"What is it, honey?" Donna said, taking the milk to the kitchen.

"For what it's worth, I told your husband that he'd never get the brooch, but what I didn't tell him was that I'd tossed it. I remember how flustered Charlie looked when he realized I wasn't wearing the brooch. I was arriving to the ballroom before the presentations of the debutantes began and he was in a deep conversation with the Greek guy, Popolous. First he tried to block me from entering, and then he just looked shocked. And he wasn't able to confront me about it because we started to hear the guests make their way to dinner. It wasn't a good moment for him to risk me making a scene. Not in front of people. Shortly after that I got the text from him that he wanted it back."

"He was talking to Popolous?" The floodgates were opening. Giorgio Popolous was suddenly popping up everywhere. I had been curious the night of the ball to know who Archibald was speaking to when he deposited me at the ladies' to fix my dress. He had transformed from a smiling, charming host to a sinister figure. What had he said? *I have a business proposition for you.*

"But what's the point of all this?" Regina said.

She ripped the cellophane off a new pack of Gitanes.

Regina was right. What was the point of the pieces I'd been putting together about everyone's whereabouts that night?

Chapter 23

About an hour later, I was back in my studio, thinking through the entrances and exits of those last moments of Charlie Archibald's life. While I waited for Harry to arrive, I printed out some of the key photos I had taken at the Holiday Ball; the two photos of Regina, with and without the brooch; the group photos of the Archibalds' party; and the photo of Popolous with Harry and Bernie at table three. I also cropped photos to produce a single image of each of my original suspects, my version of mug shots, you might say. Even if I had written off most of these individuals, they had all played a part in the events leading to Archibald's murder, even if, like Jinx, unwittingly.

When I heard a knock on my door, I was almost afraid to look up. It was the first time I'd see Harry since he'd confessed his real identity to me. To keep cool, I waved at him through the window. He waved back, looking equally nervous. I opened the door.

"We found the brooch," Harry said to kick things off. "Jinx had it, she was forthcoming about the story, confirmed she saw Regina toss it. She even confessed to having worn it dancing one night. The Crown Badge of Love was sent to the British embassy this morning. It's heading back to England under heavy guard tomorrow."

"That's great," I said, standing aside to let him in. "Case closed. Congratulations."

"Until this morning, it had become a cold case again," he said. "You did some great work."

I raised an *I told you so* eyebrow. He gave one right back to me.

I sat on my one kitchen stool while Harry settled into the guest chair by my desk.

He was in sweats and a T-shirt, hadn't even had a chance to shave with all the action of the morning, and if he was trying to drive me crazy, he was doing a good job of it. I'd forgotten how much he affected me, so the stool across the room from him was the safest place for me.

"There's another thing, too," he said. He leaned forward, his elbows propped on the chair arms, and pressed the fingertips of each hand together in a way that seemed serious. "I've been thinking about what you said about Popolous being the murderer."

"Because you think it's a possibility or because you feel badly that you keep telling me to lay off?"

"Can I say both?"

"Because I've learned something else. While you and Bernie were eating dinner at the ball, Popolous and Archibald met, right before the presentations. I know you invited him to fish around for information. I'm sure you weren't expecting any sneaky business from Popolous that night. But now we can put Archibald and Popolous together. And, yes, Popolous left the party to go home before Archibald stormed out of the ballroom, so, like Felicity Cromwell, he wasn't on anyone's suspect list. But he did stay until the bitter end for his doggy bag."

A smile crept over Harry's face. "For once, you have to let me do the talking. This is important."

I pressed my lips together and sat on my hands.

"My answer should be no, Popolous couldn't have killed

Archibald, because I was outside the Pierre by then, waiting for him to leave, and when he did, he was not covered in blood, nor did he look shaken. I followed him all the way to his apartment, where he nodded to the doorman and went upstairs. When Thorne and I spoke later, we noted the timing was a little bit close, but we dismissed Popolous because he had no connection we knew of to Archibald, and which you only uncovered in Topper's old photographs. And, to your point, Thorne was insistent that the killer had known the victim and was trapped at the hotel after your discovery. He also believed, given the clues, that we were dealing with a crime of passion, that the motive was love."

"So, you're sticking with no?"

"Actually, my answer is"—I felt a drum roll—"*maybe.*"

"Really," I said, genuinely amazed and appreciative that he was willing to keep an open mind. It wasn't a yes, but it was much more than a no. "It's because of the brooch, right? It's a big coincidence."

"That, and—"

"And the two of them had words earlier in the night?"

"And because I know that Popolous enlisted in the Hellenic Army not long after that summer trip around the world where he met Archibald and Topper."

I wasn't expecting that one, although I recalled Popolous's military-style gait when I'd walked him to his table.

"His service was nothing special because it's a requirement for most men in Greece to join for at least a short stint," Harry said, "but Popolous was in a special division that worked with swords. More for ceremonial occasions than battle. He had been a fencer in college. He was dismissed because he had anger issues."

"So, he might have known how to kill someone quickly and with little blood using a long, thin, pointy metal object."

Harry nodded.

At that moment there was a knock at my front door. We turned our heads to find Granny's smiling face bundled under a scarf and hat in front of the studio. She waved to us both and raised a pan covered in tin foil that she was carrying. I knew how upset she was that Poppy would have to move into a home, by the amount of cooking that was coming out of her kitchen. A lot. I had eaten every morsel to make her happy, but each bite was tinged with her sadness and an abundance of calories. I opened the door and put my arm around her shoulders as she brought the pan to my counter.

"Harry," she said. "Is that you? I didn't realize you were here."

She was the worst liar on the planet, but Harry let it slide. He gave her a warm hug and asked her how she was doing as she headed straight to my kitchen counter and prepared two plates of chicken parmigiana.

"Nothing to complain about," she said. What a tough old broad. I loved her so much. "Tell me what you think."

She handed a plate to both of us. It was just after ten in the morning, but we dutifully began to eat and I'm now a convert of enjoying the meal for breakfast every now and then. It hit the spot.

"What are these?" Granny said of the photos I had laid out.

"They're just a project Harry and I are working on," I said over a nice cheese-to-chicken ratio.

"This one, he looks familiar," she said, pointing to the picture of Charlie Archibald.

"Probably because he's been in the news a lot," I said. "He was murdered. He's the guy who stole money from a foundation so that he could keep his business afloat."

"Strange project you have going on," she said. "But that's not it." Granny picked up the photo of Archibald and studied it more carefully.

"I've got it," she said, smacking the image decisively with the back of her hand. "He was a customer. I can't believe I ever met such a crook."

"You met him?" I said.

"He came in a couple of days before Thanksgiving," she said. "I made a key for him. One of those tricky Bowley lock keys. I remember because he was admiring that safe Poppy was hired to open. That, and he complimented the aroma of my coffee. He asked if I didn't mind going back to the kitchen to get him some. What could I say?"

And yes, I almost fell off my stool.

"It doesn't surprise me to learn he was crooked. Look at that smile." She poked Archibald's face. "It's too nice. Like your cousin's face, God bless that poor wife of his."

Granny was no slouch when it came to reading a room either. When she noticed Harry and I staring at each other as if we'd been hit by a freightliner, she cleared her throat.

"You kids look busy, and I have a lot to do so I'll get going," she said, heading back to the door. "Have a good day, you two."

"Thanks for the food, Granny," I said, slowing my brain long enough to give a kiss to her wrinkly, soft cheek.

I closed the door behind her.

"Regina and Donna's building uses a Bowley lock," I said. I dialed Donna.

"Sorry to bother you again," I said when she answered. "Do you have your key to your new place on you at all times?"

I put the phone on speaker so Harry could hear.

"Yes," she said. "Ever since I lost the first set. That's why Regina came to your shop that day. She was making a copy of her key for me. Honestly, we were afraid Charlie had found out about the apartment and had taken my key. A couple of days before the ball, I saw him in the neighborhood. I was so freaked; I turned on my heels and walked the other way. Does this help?"

"It might," I said.

"There's a knock on my door," she said. "I have to go."

"I think we're at the point where there's one too many twists," Harry said when I hung up.

"Archibald stole the brooch. He was desperate for liquidity to rebalance the books at Lion's Mane and the Archibald Foundation."

"You raise an excellent motive for the robbery," Harry said. "The jewel was worth a fortune. But how would he pull it off? He's not a safe-cracker."

I had my photos in front of me, but not everyone I needed to put the story together. I hopped into my bedroom and returned with a photo of Poppy and Harry in front of the safe. I laid it on the counter.

"Exhibit one," I said. "Poppy opened the safe, found the jewel, decided the smartest thing to do was leave it where he'd found it. He closed the door back up, and then wrote the combination on a Post-it, which he stuck onto the side of the safe. See? Look at the picture. The combination was right there."

I grabbed the photo of Bill Topper and put it above Poppy.

"Exhibit two: From Topper's photo album, Poppy and I learn that Archibald, Topper, and Popolous knew each other."

Harry put Charlie Archibald's photo beside Poppy.

"Meanwhile, Archibald is planning to scope out his wife's new place," he said.

"Yes," I said. "Where's my photo of Popolous?" Harry handed it to me, and I put it beside Archibald.

"On the way to Donna's apartment, Archibald sees Popolous, after all these years, bringing the safe into the shop. My old theory holds up that everything came back to him about the brooch and how valuable it was. He went into the store, where Granny met him and asked for a copy of Donna's key, killing two birds with one stone. Now, he can go to Donna's any time he wants, which might come in handy if their divorce gets tricky. Plus, he sees the Post-it Poppy left on the safe."

"Dark, but true, about the keys," Harry said.

"With the combination right there, I hate to say that robbing the safe would have been easy," I said. "He sent Granny off for a cup of coffee, and the rest was easy work."

"The ACU must have just missed him. Our information came quickly, but not quickly enough."

I picked up the photos of Regina and Donna.

"OK," I said. "After he steals the brooch, he panics. He goes to Donna's place and finds them out so he hides it there, in the tea tin because he knows Donna doesn't drink tea. Sucks for him that Regina does. With a little cultural sensitivity about the Brits and their tea, he might still be alive today. Weird."

"Weird."

"But why not keep the jewel on him?"

"I've got this one," said Harry. "I've seen it before. Thieves are always looking for a safe place to stash their loot. That jewel was hot, and even more exquisite in person than he probably expected. I'm sure he decided to hide it nearby rather than risk being found with it. He had the key to the apartment and knew he could retrieve it at the right time. A guy like Archibald probably saw that apartment as much his own as his wife's. Of course, he made a mistake using a tea tin as a hiding place."

"Meanwhile, Regina finds it, thinks it's a gift from Donna, wears it to the ball and all hell breaks loose there," I said.

"Stay specific," Harry said, now deep into his investigative mode. His concentration reminded me of how I am when I'm editing a new piece of work. "How did all hell break loose?"

I looked at my other photos, but Harry was a step ahead of me. He moved the photos of tables three and four side by side.

Popolous was there, Regina was frowning, Archibald was eyeing the jewel with a mixture of fury and excitement.

"During dinner, Archibald sees both Regina wearing the brooch and Popolous at a table not far from him," Harry said.

"Worlds collide."

"But he's a clever businessman and he sees opportunity. He decides to blackmail Popolous. It's much safer than trying to sell such a significant piece on the black market. Of course, Popolous was the worst person to blackmail."

"He seems to have assets, judging from that apartment."

"Popolous's family was very wealthy, but with each generation there's a little less to go around and Popolous has never been an ambitious type. He married money, but when his wife died a few years ago, most of their wealth was gone. He's tried to make a living speculating in real estate, but it's not bringing him the kind of income he'd like."

"Wow. Detective Thorne said Archibald's murder was a crime of passion. You said Popolous had a temper. Maybe one thing led to another. Popolous lost his temper when Archibald tried to blackmail him, and killed Archibald. Once he realized what he'd done, he snuck out. He got lucky because Felicity and Bill's crisis distracted the guards for a short time. I guess Archibald had the last laugh though. By killing Archibald the brooch was now gone for good."

"Hmm," said Harry. "That's quite a temper for an old gent like Popolous."

I placed the photo of Anne Topper next in line.

"Anne Topper said she heard someone say *'what arrogance,'* when she was heading to the restroom. When Bill explained that he was meeting with Felicity, they thought the comment had to do with Felicity staying behind at the ball. Now, I'm thinking it was Popolous telling off Archibald while they met to discuss the details of the jewel's handoff."

I placed the photo of Felicity Cromwell beside Anne Topper.

"Shortly after, Felicity heard someone say *'you'll have to pay first,'*" I said. "That was likely Archibald, buying time because he'd lost the brooch, at least for the time being. He probably planned to search for it at Donna's place the next day."

"That helps," Harry said. "No one was a particular genius that night, but it holds together."

"We have a suspect who had the skill to kill someone with a long, sharp, metal weapon, along with a motive to support it. Do you think we have enough to call Thorne?" I said.

Harry rubbed his chin.

"Under any other circumstance, I'd say yes, but Thorne's very excited about the recovery of the brooch and we don't have a murder weapon. I have a feeling Thorne was the one knocking on Donna's door when you called her. What you and I have is highly compelling, but still circumstantial. What Thorne has is a valuable jewel last seen on Regina. He'll come up with his own version of the story that leads to Regina rather than Popolous."

Harry returned to his chair and I to my stool.

"Which leaves one challenge: How do we prove it?" he said. "We need something concrete before we get Thorne involved."

"We?" I said.

Chapter 24

"I think we make a good team," Harry said. "That's all."

"We are only good if you can promise not to lie to me again," I said.

"How about we have a sign when I'm leaving details out," he said. "Then you'll know when it's the job."

He put his finger by his nose.

"That will never work in the long run," I said, "but it will do for now."

"Then we are officially a team. We know where we stand," Harry said. "And now that we worked that out, let me grab the bottle of champagne I brought that's been cooking in my coat pocket."

I cleaned off the two wine glasses I own and Harry popped a split of champagne.

"I brought this to celebrate finding the Crown Badge of Love," he said, pouring the bubbly.

He raised his glass.

"To teamwork," I said.

I took the glass, clinked it with his, and downed it in one swig.

"Back to work, partner?" he said.

"Work?"

I guess they always say to be careful what you wish for.

"Right," I said, putting my glass down. "You said to stay specific. Tell me this. Why did Popolous want to sell the brooch now, after all these years?"

"He found the safe," he said, putting a foot up on my desk and tapping a pen against his thigh while I paced the room. "We found out because one of his family members got nervous and tipped off an ACU informant. The family has staunchly denied their involvement for so long that their family's reputation is tied up in it. It's like an albatross."

"And why bring it to New York?" I said.

"He came by boat, where it was easy to hide his stash. And selling the apartment was a good cover. While you were questioning Elizabeth Everly at his party, I spoke with the real estate broker. He said the seller was motivated and open to offers. He was under pressure to broker the property quickly, which was why he threw the party. No one made an offer, by the way. Popolous went home without the jewel or a sale of his apartment."

"He's left town?"

Harry nodded.

"It's going to be hard to prove anything with him out of town, don't you think?"

"That's why you're the right person for the job," he said. "We need creative thinking."

An hour later, we were still tossing ideas around. We'd finished the chicken parm completely. I threw a couple of ice cubes in our wine glasses, and we finished the split as well. Harry's attitude remained professional, and I won't lie. It was driving me crazy. I guessed Maria was right. I was the one who had blown it. We were now work pals. Finally, I had to send him to the liquor store for another bottle of anything, just to catch my breath.

"Think big. Think big. Think big," I said, trying to come up with a big idea.

I heard my phone buzz and saw a message from Jinx.

Working these days? I have a gig with RMS's competitor for last deb ball of the season. LMK if you want a job.

Harry opened the door I'd left unlocked. We might be trying to catch a killer, but I was still open for business.

"You have an idea," he said, pointing to my excited smile.

I nodded, afraid to speak in case it sounded ridiculous aloud.

"Spill it," he said, popping a new bottle.

"First of all, do you think the British embassy would let you keep the jewel in New York for a couple of days?"

"I'd need a compelling reason to ask them," he said. "Do you have one?"

"What if people, many people, like hundreds of people, saw how desperate Popolous is to get his hands on the brooch?" I said. "What if these people witnessed Popolous lunge for the Crown Badge of Love?"

Harry poured for the both of us. I could see he was thinking.

"I mean, if he was in America and it became public knowledge that he is after the stolen jewel, that would be great. Combined with our other leads, Thorne might be inclined to get a warrant to test his tuxedo for Archibald's blood. Even if it was dry cleaned, there would still be traces of DNA that forensics could pick up."

"And at this moment in time, who has knowledge that the brooch was recovered?"

"The ACU, the British embassy, the royal family," he said as if that was an everyday kind of list for a cone of silence. "What are you thinking?"

"Do you think you could change the story about how you found it? Can you ask your highfalutin' ACU guys back in Greece to circulate a story that the brooch might have been found by a guest at the Holiday Ball, and it's still missing?"

"Well, there's highfalutin' and highfalutin'. I guess there are some guys who are falutin' enough over there, yes," he said. "The royals don't need publicity, so I'm sure they'll be amenable to holding the story. But I'm still not following you."

"If Popolous is inclined to return to New York to find his missing jewel, we could lure him to a large gathering, one where he'd need to wear his tuxedo, and trick him into showing his hand," I said.

"What are you thinking?" he said. "Like a benefit?"

"Better. Jinx told me there's one more debutante ball of the season. I'm sure many of the guests were also at the Holiday Ball. What better gathering for Popolous to find his treasure?"

"I see where you're going," he said, nodding enthusiastically. "Bernie can wear the brooch to the ball."

"Think bigger," I said. "We need everyone, including Popolous, to focus on the brooch at the same time."

Harry took my champagne away from me.

"No," he said. "We can't ask a civilian to be a sitting duck. I'm not going to ask one of those girls to wear the brooch during her presentation. We could never be sure what he might do."

"I'm not asking you to draft one of the actual debs for help," I said. "But I'm sure Bernie can sneak me in."

"Not going to happen."

"You still don't trust that I can do this?" I said. "What happened to partners?"

"That's not it," Harry said. "I absolutely think you can. But the truth is that there's a list of debutantes and you can't slip into their fold unnoticed."

I looked through my studio's window, thinking about the Holiday Ball's program.

Drinks led to dinner, then to the presentations and partying. It was likely that the next ball would be the same.

"If you can ask Bernie to invite both me and Popolous to her table, I can take care of the rest."

"How?"

I pulled Harry from my desk and led him to my door.

"You need to get word to Popolous and talk to Bernie. I need to work out how to make an entrance. The less you know the better. I don't want Bernie on the line for anything that will blow your covers."

I was already dialing before the door closed behind him.

"I need to borrow your super-high heels and your sexy black dress from last New Year's Eve," I said to Maria when she answered. "I'm going to another ball."

"Yes!" she said. "And wear the extra mascara. Work or play?"

"I have a date," I said, pouring myself another glass of champagne. I decided I would need to get used to the stuff if I was going to be a debutante.

"Is this a date with Harry?"

"Nope," I said. "An old Greek man."

"Oh, Liv," she said. "What am I going to do with you?"

When we hung up, I called Manjeet, who gladly agreed to help. Then, I decided I had one more call to make, but it was a delicate one.

Given the short period of time until the ball, however, I wasn't sure who else to turn to.

I dialed Angela Archibald.

"Hello?" she said.

"It's Liv Spyers," I said.

"I've been meaning to call you. Thank you so much for the photo of me and my dad. I've put it in a frame by my bed. My mom was home last night, and it made her cry."

"I'm glad you like it," I said. "I was wondering, are you going to the last debutante ball of the season?"

"Not to be presented," she said. "I could never do that again. But I am going with some of the girls to support our friend Lee. I promised her. She said I didn't have to face the music because of all that's happened, but I can't hide. But if it's too much, I'll leave."

"I think you're very brave."

"Will you be working the party?" she said.

"Actually, I'm going to be a guest of Bernie Andrews," I said. "I know this is going to sound crazy, but would you consider helping me find your father's real killer, because I have some ideas about how to do that, but I can't go it alone. And, full disclosure, I can't give you all the details about the plan up front."

"I'd do anything to hunt that killer down. What can I do?"

I was ready to catch a killer. I felt thrilled and terrified, but mostly thrilled.

CHAPTER 25

Three nights later, I entered Cipriani 42, the venue of the last debutante ball of the season. It was right across from Grand Central Station, so I'd walked past the building countless times. I'd never realized that inside was filled with marble columns, inlaid floors, and, at least for tonight, flower arrangements I could never carry home as they were taller and heavier than me.

I entered the palatial space alone, among the well-heeled crowd already sharing air kisses with each other, and feeling small under the event room's sixty-five-foot ceiling. In doing research for the night I planned to expose Giorgio Popolous, I had learned that a sixty-five-foot ceiling is taller than the Hollywood sign, or fifty bowling pins stacked on top of each other, or twelve times as high as Napoleon Bonaparte, although he probably would have looked completely at home here.

Fortunately, I was dressed in Maria's black velvet gown, coordinating black clutch, and her stiletto heels. My hair, blown straight, fell to my shoulders with small braids around my temples held back with delicate, dried baby's breath and one rose bud. The flowers weren't glittery, but they added a festive flair. If practicing law didn't pan out for Maria, she would be a top-notch stylist.

"Would you like a glass of champagne, madam?" a waiter

with a tray of sparkling glasses said to me as he moved among the crowd. He had a trimmed beard, wire-framed glasses, and wore the burgundy uniform of the dozens of servers who rotated among the party. Harry had done a magnificent job disguising himself.

"Thank you," I said and took a cocktail napkin and drink from his tray.

"You're very welcome," he said. "And might I say, you're looking particularly sexy tonight."

"Watch your tongue, young man," I said. "Or I'll have you fired on the spot."

He gave me a wink as he turned to the couple behind me to offer a welcoming beverage.

My first instinct was to give the nod of fellowship to the photographers and waiters, but I reminded myself that I was an invited guest. I wouldn't be bounced. The first hurdle of my plan was behind me.

I switched my social interactions to friendly nods and smiles with the other party guests and casually made my way to a table filled with small cards and found the one with my name and table number seven. As a guest of Bernie, I had a prime table by the dance floor. I was more interested, however, in the names of other guests for the night. Felicity Cromwell's name was absent, as the well as the Headrams and Donna Archibald, none of which surprised me. There were table cards for the Toppers, however, despite Lion's Mane's scandals.

"I believe I am the luckiest man at the party tonight," I heard a heavily accented voice say, too close to my ear. "I see we are sitting at the same table."

I turned to find Popolous beside me. He wore his velvety tuxedo and carried the fancy walking stick he had worn at the Holiday Ball. Tonight, it was his eyebrows that caught my attention. They were thick and dark in comparison to his trimmed, silver hair.

He waved his number seven card at me and then engulfed my wrist with his hand as he had done the night of the Holiday Ball. The only way I can explain his effect on me is to say that I now knew how Red Riding Hood felt when the wolf came upon her.

"Good evening," I said as he began to usher me toward Bernie's table. "What a beautiful night."

We approached table seven, where Bernie had assembled a small party of ten. She was hugging and greeting her other guests, but I would not be focused on them tonight.

"What a lovely dinner partner I have, Bernie," Popolous said, kissing our hostess on both cheeks. "Thank you."

"Giorgie, you be on your best behavior," she said. "Liv, how goes it tonight? You do look lovely."

"Thank you, Bernie," I said. "You do too."

"Ah, you Americans," Popolous said, pulling a chair out for me to sit. "Cannot an old man have a little fun? Come, my dear. Tell me all about yourself. I am Giorgio Popolous."

Not that I expected it, but I was still amazed that he had no recollection of me from the Holiday Ball.

"Liv Spyers," I said, sitting down beside him. "Of New Jersey."

"New Jersey?" he said, removing a crisp linen napkin from my place setting and putting it on my lap, where he let his hand linger. Politely, I lifted it and put it on the table. "How do you know Bernie?"

"Bridge," Bernie and I said in unison. We had practiced a few tricks to ensure that my relationship to Bernie was convincing. I learned that little things, like answering a question in unison, would help.

"Interesting game, I hear," he said. "Although a young woman like you should be out and about, rather than playing cards with the old matriarchs."

"That's very kind of you but I enjoy the wisdom of Bernie and her friends," I said.

"I am not familiar with the Spyerses of New Jersey," he said.

"You need to spend more time in our country instead of Greece," said Bernie. "The Spyerses are the key to many homes."

"Impressive," he said.

"You're from Greece?" I said. "I've always wanted to go there. I bet you have a beautiful home and gardens. Do you have pictures?"

Popolous puffed his chest and produced his phone.

"It's lovely," I said as I scrolled through his pictures of quite a setup.

"Let me see," Bernie said.

I passed the phone to her.

"Perhaps you can visit one day," he said, his focus still on me.

"If you are abroad most of the time, you must have missed the big excitement at the Holiday Ball," I said, ignoring his offer but meeting his eyes. "I wasn't there, but the head of Lion's Mane was murdered, in front of everyone."

"Ah, yes," he said. "The photography lady had a lovers' spat, correct?"

"That's what they say." I leaned into him. "But some think there was more to it. There are rumors a woman found a brooch that was once owned by the British royal family. I wonder if she's wearing it tonight. I know I would."

"Do they know who found the jewel?" he said.

"Gorgeous house, Giorgio," said Bernie, handing Popolous his phone. "As far as the jewel, I agree with Liv. She'll probably be wearing it tonight. This is a great event to debut it."

"Yes, it truly is," Popolous said. I could see he was scanning the room for the brooch.

I opened my purse and extracted a small vial of perfume. Opening the lid, I dropped it onto Popolous.

"Oh dear," I said. "I'm so sorry."

"Not at all," he said, coughing at the strong scent that now covered him.

He bowed his head graciously, but I could see he was furious. He rubbed his napkin into his lapel, but it only served to grind the scent deeper into his tuxedo. In a short span, I had begun my second goal of the night, which was to make him feel generally unhappy, uptight, and put out. The more I could stir the pot, the easier it would be later, when I needed him to lose his temper.

I stuck to Popolous like gum on a shoe, and even stayed on his tail as the entire gathering formed a reception line to meet and congratulate each of the debutantes in person. The ritual was endless, and my feet were killing me by the time we returned to our table, but I managed to keep an eye on Popolous the entire time. Dripping in perfume and drowning in the sound of my chitchat, I could tell he regretted his flirtations with me when we arrived.

Throughout dinner, I kept up the pressure by talking incessantly, leaving him no time to study the room or talk to others. Bernie helped, too. She shared a long recitation of how sad Archibald's funeral was. By the time she finished, Popolous's face was bright red. I felt sure that we had picked the right man. It was terrifying to know that I was dining with a murderer and talking his ear off, but I was excited to see justice done.

At nine thirty on the dot, my phone quietly buzzed against my thigh. The presentations would begin in thirty minutes.

"Excuse me," I said. "I need to use the restroom."

"Let me escort you," Popolous said, probably seeing his first opportunity to mingle with other guests while I was indisposed.

"You stay right where you are, Georgie," Bernie said. "I have a hundred questions about the real estate market and you're the only one I trust for the inside scoop. My nephew thinks it's time for me to settle in Florida. I can't think of a place more different than New York, but I try to keep an open mind."

While Bernie continued to confine an increasingly impatient Popolous at her table, I discreetly slipped away and headed toward the ladies' at the far end of the room, which felt about a mile away. On my way, I made a slight detour and passed Angela's table, where I knew I should find her at her seat. When I arrived, I saw her chair was empty. I took a deep breath and continued. My stomach began to make little butterfly flutters, but I kept moving.

It was only when I reached the ladies' room that I realized I'd made my first miscalculation of the night.

The line of women in gowns waiting to use a toilet went out the door. I estimated a several minutes' wait ahead of me, time I didn't have.

I put my hand over my mouth in a not very ladylike move, but I was desperate.

"Excuse me," I said, pushing to the head of the line. "Emergency."

The women parted like the Red Sea to let me in, all looking nervous that the girl who had not paced her drinks would lose it on their dresses.

I rushed through the door, adding a dry-heave noise à la Regina to my performance, and headed directly to the last stall, one of those big ones you find at the end of the line, where I saw two feet in flat satin ballet slippers. I stopped and tapped lightly on the door, three times.

"Hey," Angela said to me, opening the stall and letting me in.

"Hi," I said. "How are you feeling?"

"Like I want to kick some ass," she said. "I wish you'd let me do this. I have a few strategic punches I'd like to throw."

I took Angela's hands in mine.

"Promise me you won't," I said. "Promise me you can stay at your table." Angela nodded.

"Promise?"

"Yes," she said.

"OK, let's go," I said.

I grabbed the hem of Maria's beautiful dress and tugged it gently over my head. Angela unzipped a garment bag hanging on the door's hook and produced her white dress from the Holiday Ball.

"Hold my arms while you step inside," she said, her hands around the skirt of the dress. "Otherwise, you'll trip."

I leaned my half naked body to Angela and grabbed her arms. There was a knock at our door.

"Is everything all right in there?" I heard a lady say.

I made a gagging noise. Angela picked up a glass of wine someone had left behind on the toilet paper roll holder and dumped it into the bowl for acoustic effect.

"Be out in a minute," I said in my shakiest voice.

"We're fine. I have her," Angela said, seamlessly coming to my aid.

While a few disapproving comments echoed on the other side of our stall, I stepped into the dress and turned around. As Angela zipped me up and then began to fasten what must have been one hundred tiny buttons up the back, I allowed myself a moment to feel the luxury of the white, satin, strapless gown against my body.

"Good thing I have weak ankles and I always need to wear flats," Angela said. "Otherwise, this would be way too long on you. Fortunately, there's still enough length that the dress covers your black heels. That's a huge no-no. Whatever you do, don't raise your arms too high. If anyone sees your shoes, your cover will be shot. "OK, turn around."

I turned around, feeling like a princess.

"You look the part," she said.

"I need to remind you," I said. "If things go right, this beautiful dress might bite the dust. I can't promise anything."

"If you hadn't needed the dress, I would have burned it myself, no matter how beautiful it is," she said. "Do what you need to do."

I handed her Maria's dress and purse, which she hung in the garment bag.

"Good luck," Angela said.

"Thanks," I said. "Ready?"

She nodded and we opened the door, looking fresh as daisies.

"All good," I said to a few women who looked us over.

We washed our hands, checked our faces, and walked out with our heads held high. Without further acknowledgment of each other, Angela went one way, and I went another.

My journey took me in the opposite direction of Bernie's table. I headed to the kitchen doors, where I leaned against the wall, grateful for the semi-darkness of the nook. I probably lingered for no more than a minute, but every second felt precarious. I'd known that to make my plan work, I'd eventually need to have all eyes focused on me, but I quickly learned how sharply the light shown on the debutantes. Even in this quiet area of the ballroom, anyone who passed by nodded and had a friendly comment to make. I did my best to graciously acknowledge my admirers, but I could practically feel my hair frizz with the stress of my impersonation.

"Cocktail?"

I heard Harry's voice beside me.

"Thank you," I said, turning to him without making eye contact.

I reached my hand to the tray where the Crown Badge of Love was waiting for me. I lifted both it and a glass. Harry nodded and walked away. I downed my champagne for a little fortitude, put the glass on another passing waiter's tray, and then stole a peek at the jewel in my hand. The sheer weight of it told me how valuable each of the gems must be, and even in the dim light its gems sparkled as if by magic. I thought of the young Greek woman who had stolen it all those years ago, and honestly, I was a little more forgiving of her risky behavior than I thought I would be.

The music rose in the ballroom and the guests quickly took their seats, even those who had been stuck in the bathroom line, as everyone immediately began to quiet down. I pressed myself against the wall and listened as a man greeted all from the dance floor and then began to announce the long list of names of the evening's debutantes as they were presented. Each young woman entered the dance floor to make her bow by descending a set of stairs from a loggia above that served as the evening's staging area. I counted each name, all of which I'd memorized. When the last names reached the letter Y, I took a step forward to a dance floor entrance near the band that was still cast in shadow.

The next part of the debutantes' program included two short dances led by the women alone, without their escorts. This was not something I had seen at the Holiday Ball, but it worked perfectly tonight. The spotlight would be shining on all the women, and I would be able to join their throng now that the formalities of names had passed.

I was about to make my entrance when I felt a hand grab my arm. Before I could turn around, I also felt a pressure on the back of my neck. It reminded me of a long, metal, pointy item. I inhaled deeply, but there was no scent of the perfume that I had poured onto Popolous.

"What the hell do you think you're doing?" said a female voice. I tried to step forward, but Elizabeth Everly ground her heel into the back of my dress.

CHAPTER 26

"Hey, Elizabeth," I said as calmly as I could. "How's it going?"

Elizabeth wasn't in the mood to chat. She pushed me against the wall instead. Face first.

I remembered the long scissors from her clipboard and decided not to fight her.

"I knew there was more to the story with you," she said. "Suddenly you're everywhere. Partying at Hudson Yards. Cornering me at Archibald's funeral. I hate to break it to you, but you're dealing with the wrong person."

I raised my hands to show her I was unarmed. "You can let go of me," I said.

"Like hell," she said. "I see you're wearing Angela Archibald's dress, too. And even in the dark your bling is blinding. But black shoes? I saw you from across the ballroom. Whatever you thought your plan would be for tonight, it's not going to work."

In the background, I heard the debutantes start their dance. I hoped that when Bernie and Harry saw I was missing from the stage they would know to come find me. In the meantime, my best bet was to keep Elizabeth talking. I decided a murder confession might help, too.

"You won't get away with this," I said. "I know all about

you. I don't think you want to mess with me. There are eyes on me all over the place."

"You think I'm going to stay with you here?" she said. "Walk."

"Where?"

"Toward the kitchen."

I raised my hands again and walked to the kitchen door, not more than a few feet away.

"I know you need money," I said. "But is that why you did it?"

"I think that's a question I should be asking you," she said. "In all my years of working these balls, I've seen a lot of wild things, but no one has ever tried to crash the debutantes' presentation."

I stopped. "Wait," I said.

I made a bold decision and squirmed my way to face Elizabeth. "Is that what you think is going on?" I said.

Elizabeth raised her hands, her weapon making wild circles in the air, and shook her head as if it might fall off her body.

"What the hell else could be going on?" she said.

"To be clear," I said, "you didn't kill Charlie Archibald?"

"Are you crazy?" she said.

The music was ending. The ladies had finished their dance. There was only one more to go before my window of opportunity closed.

"I'm curious," I said. "If I was to tell you I wanted to crash the debutantes' last dance to catch Archibald's real killer, what would you do?"

Elizabeth lowered her scissors.

"What do you mean?" she said, quietly, and with a new sense of urgency.

"I don't have time to get into details," I said. "But I need to get out there, now, if I'm going to help solve Archibald's murder."

"Regina Montague did it," she said.

I shook my head.

"No," I said. "One of the guests out there did."

Elizabeth burst into tears. They were more surprising to me than the feeling of metal against my neck a moment ago.

"I loved him," she said, her shoulders beginning to shake.

I'd known there was something Elizabeth was hiding, but she had done a great job of keeping her love life to herself.

"And he loved me, too," she said. "At least I thought so until I heard about Regina. But all Archie did was steal my money and cheat on me."

"Regina wasn't involved with Charlie, she was involved with Donna," I said.

"What?" Elizabeth said, clearly confused.

"I'm sure he loved you, but we don't have time to unpack it all right now. Maybe tomorrow, over coffee. Jinx is a good listener, too. But right now, you must let me out there."

"He loved me?"

I nodded my head a thousand times in one second.

"Go get the bastard," she said, releasing me.

"If you could make sure security doesn't interrupt anything that's about to happen, that would be great, too."

Elizabeth nodded through her tears, and I took two steps toward the side entrance to the dance floor.

"Wait," Elizabeth said.

She pulled a small bouquet of roses from the back of her sash, like a magician pulling a rabbit out of a hat, and handed it to me.

"You need this for the dance," she said. "All the girls have them."

I looked at the flowers, then her, and scooted off. From my spot in the shadows, I watched the women weave across the floor in a choreographed wheel of billowing white and red roses. They formed a circle and then floated toward the middle of the floor in a tight group. I waited for two beats of music until the circle opened wide to the edge of the stage and made my move. I stepped forward and scooted into the ensemble. I could immediately see from my peripheral view that the women on either side of me were stunned, but I looked right ahead as if I'd always been there, and after a moment, they must have decided I wasn't worth making a scene over because I noticed them smile at each other and even laugh a bit. Immediately, I felt a sense of camaraderie, and I raised my roses into the air.

I also wasted no time in making eye contact with Popolous.

Contrary to the plan, he did not see me. I wondered if Bernie and I had overdone it by keeping him at the table all night, because now he was looking everywhere but the dance floor. I heard the music reach a climax and knew there was no time to spare. Raising my flowers to the air once more, I did a ballet twirl across the floor and to the middle of the open circle. I must have done a good job, because the audience applauded.

This was it. All eyes were on me. All except Popolous's. Undeterred, I continued my twirl until it brought me, somewhat dizzily, to the edge of Bernie's table. There, I bowed as deeply and as graciously as I could.

"Fingers crossed. Fingers crossed. Fingers crossed," I said to myself.

When I looked up, I made instant eye contact with Popolous. He knew. And I knew he knew. His eyebrows knitted together. His nostrils flared. His lips pressed firmly together. Imagine a bull getting ready to charge. It was just what I wanted, and I took a few steps back to the middle of the room.

As I did, Popolous rose. Carefully, he pushed his chair into the table and rolled his shoulders back and forth. Then, he turned and walked the other way. I looked at Bernie, who casually sipped her wine. No way was she blowing her cover for Thorne's case. This was on me, but I had no idea what to do.

As my mind was racing, the lights suddenly went out.

If Popolous's plan was to throw us all into darkness while he grabbed the brooch off me, he was in as much trouble as I was. The fact was, each dinner table had at least ten different candles glowing. When the lights went out, the glow of the flames was breathtaking. I realized, however, that Popolous had done a little planning ahead. A man walked toward me, sans cane, in a hoodie thrown over his head.

"Liv Spyers," Popolous said when he reached me. "You shouldn't have used your real name. Hand me the brooch carefully because I know where you live. That grandfather of yours seems rather delicate. If I could kill Charlie Archibald, I can surely get to your grandad."

My fingers immediately fumbled for the jewel. Popolous's back was to everyone, and I knew no one had heard him. I also knew as I handed him the brooch that no one saw him take back the jewel, but I was not going to risk my family's safety. The man was a murderer.

"Here," I said.

"Have a good night," he said.

Popolous turned to make his escape. I looked for a security guard but remembered that I asked Elizabeth Everly to keep them away from me. A scream probably wouldn't do much good, either. The band had stopped playing, but the crowd was in a tizzy from the darkness. Finally, I saw Harry. I could see he had been watching what had transpired.

I also knew that if he tackled Popolous, dressed as a waiter, in front of everyone, it would ruin his cover and career. Harry didn't seem to be worrying about that. He was heading toward us at full speed, but Popolous had too much of a head start in the grand room.

Thinking quickly, Harry bent his arm back and hurled the round, disc-like tray he'd been holding across the room like a Frisbee.

We watched the disc fly through the candlelit room. Its trajectory seemed perfect, but then I realized that, although the direction was spot-on, the height did not take into consideration the altitude of everything around us in a sixty-five-foot-high room. The tray began to head to a now empty bar station that featured a sculpted figure of Eros, sparkling in ice.

"Oh!" I said, marveling for a split second at the statue and remembering the photos of the exact same ice sculpture on Anne Topper's table. Her donation of this work of art must have been the committee job she'd told me about.

The platter hit the god of love, whose poor head flew off and landed on the floor.

The lights went back on.

"My ice sculpture!" cried Anne Topper, running to the headless cherub.

"Oh, how pretty," a woman in a bright blue dress said as the head rolled to a stop at her feet.

"Hey," said Bill, rising from his seat. "Who did that? My wife loves these ice things."

Harry, however, was gone. I realized I was the last soldier standing as Popolous's figure exited through the ballroom's doors and out on to Forty-Second Street.

"That woman isn't a debutante," I heard someone say at a table not far from me.

It was time for plan B.

I lifted my dress, tossed off my heels, and made a dash for it. I noticed that Popolous had dropped his walking stick, so I grabbed it in case I needed to defend myself. At least I knew it was sturdy. As I rushed across the dance floor, I noticed two young girls about twelve years old running beside me. The Toppers' twins had joined their parents for the evening's festivities.

"Go!" Peridot said to me with a collusive fire in her eyes.

"We've got this," said Jade.

I had never seen them look so happy. Jade grabbed the icy head from the woman in blue. She rolled it across the floor like a bowling ball toward the security who were heading to me. I had no doubt in the girls' abilities to pull off a disruptive deed. I was only happy to be on their side for once.

I flew through the exit, shoeless, holding up my dress in one hand, and brandishing the cane in the other.

"Where is he?" I said when I exited.

Manjeet stood on the sidewalk and held open the door of a red Ferrari 488 GTB, compliments of the Classic Car Club. This alone is why I stand by my goal to win any and all party prizes. You never know when they will come in handy.

"That way," said Manjeet, pointing down the street.

"Hop in," I said.

I jumped into the driver's side and put on my seat belt while Manjeet popped in beside me.

"Here," I said, throwing my phone to him. "Bernie connected Popolous's Find My Phone app to mine when she was looking at pictures of his house. Fortunately, he doesn't believe in passwords. Can you follow him?"

"Got it," he said as I pulled out into the city traffic and sped ahead.

"He's heading to the West Side," Manjeet said. "I guess it didn't go well?"

"Popolous has the brooch," I said. "No one saw him take it."

As I took a left, I felt the warm slobber of a tongue across my cheek.

"Miranda was delighted to let me babysit her dogs tonight," he said. "But if we don't get them home by midnight, I will lose my job with her. Turn here, turn, turn."

I turned.

"You planning to become a full-time dog walker?"

"If your plan doesn't work out, I will. He's getting on the FDR. You're catching up to him. Oh, look!"

Manjeet's attention shifted from my phone to the cane. "My great uncle used to have one of these," he said. "Uncle Baba used to threaten me with this when he wanted me to get him cigarettes."

He put his hand onto the bottom of the cane and yanked off the brass tip, the spot where Poppy puts his tennis balls for balance. What remained behind was a long, pointy metal tip.

He'd found our murder weapon.

"Put the cap back on, put it on!"

"Jesus, you're giving me a heart attack, Liv."

I continued dodging through heavy traffic with cars, signs, and lampposts all a blur.

Manjeet yelled directions and the dogs yapped behind him.

Popolous forged ahead, I had no idea where to, until I finally saw a sign for Westchester County Airport.

"Call Detective Thorne and tell him where we are," I said.

I pulled off the highway, not slowing, as I entered the airport drive and continued onto the tarmac. Ahead of me, a plane was parked, and Popolous was heading toward its stairs to climb aboard. His gait was confident, as if he had not a care in the world. The airplane idled. A flight attendant waited at the plane's entrance with a courteous expression.

I pulled the car to a screeching halt and opened the door.

"Wait up," I said, spilling out of the car before I remembered to hold up the hem of my dress.

Popolous turned to me, and I could see he was genuinely shocked I'd held on this long.

"Hand me the cane," I said to Manjeet. "And wait for my signal."

"What's the signal?" he said, but I was already running.

Popolous's smirk disappeared as he saw me holding his serpent-headed cane. He instinctively moved his hand to his side, in a motion that reminded me of the day I'd lost my camera on the subway. I knew he was experiencing that horrible moment when you realize something important to you is missing. In his eagerness to recover his brooch and get back to the safety of his country, Popolous had forgotten it. I raised the cane aloft, as I had earlier with my roses. Popolous waited for me.

"I think we both have something the other wants," I said, slowing to a jog as I reached him. "I have a feeling if I hand your cane over to Detective Thorne, he might find incriminating evidence."

Popolous looked back to the attendant who was still politely waiting for us, curious about the woman in the wedding dress and a cane. If I were in her shoes, my imagination would have been running wild. Most importantly, however, I knew that Popolous could not attack me in front of this witness.

"Hand it over," Popolous said.

"You first."

"You are very childish," he said.

He slipped his hand into his jacket lapel and retrieved the Crown Badge of Love. "You have no idea how powerful my family is," he said.

"You have no idea how crazy mine is," I said.

He reached his hand out to the cane.

"Change of plan," I said.

I put my fingers behind my back and gave Manjeet a thumbs-up. Within a moment, Mr. Binders, Sugar, Lady, and several other pups I'd never learned the names of came barreling down the tarmac toward Popolous, who was still dripping in the perfume I'd poured all over him. It was the alluring scent of their dear mistress, Miranda Headram. Without pausing to confirm it was she, the dogs barreled onto Popolous and began to lick and hop on him. Their army was small in size but mighty in spirit. The more Popolous pushed them away, the more manic the dogs became until they had their man fighting for his freedom. Not even the sounds of the cavalry coming dissuaded them from their mission.

When the sound of the sirens reached the tarmac, Manjeet pulled out Miranda's whistle and blew. Immediately, the furry gang quieted and pattered obediently back to the Ferrari, where Manjeet waited with a snack for each of them.

"Put your hands where I can see them," Detective Thorne said to Charlie Archibald's killer.

CHAPTER 27

The next morning, when the news of Popolous's arrest hit, my grandfather spent a good hour looking for amusing headlines such as ART IS MURDER. I was overjoyed that order had been restored, and justice served, although I felt it was a crime that the ACU had withheld the details of their hand in the story and instead gave the credit all to Thorne. As for me, I insisted my name be kept out of the official statements and press releases. I feared the GoFundMe account my parents would start to send me back to the safety of New Jersey if they knew what I'd done.

Instead, I spent the morning in my studio taking portraits of Miranda's dogs. They were the heroes of the day, too, and the best way I could repay Miranda was to give her a free portrait session. I even persuaded her to join in a couple of photos of the dogs, who doused her with love as she rolled on the floor with them. It was her best look, I thought. Angela joined me for the shoot as my assistant and Maria circulated the studio with more champagne. This was, after all, a celebration of sorts.

When we were finished, Miranda began to get into details about my upcoming gig shooting Bethany's summer wedding. The bells above my door jingled. Regina and Donna stepped inside. I was happy to see Miranda and Donna greet each other warmly, and to see Angela hug Regina. After the clamor of the puppy parade left, Regina reached her hand out to me.

"I don't know how I can ever thank you," she said.

"You'd do the same," I said.

"I like your optimism," she said. "But rather than promise I'll one day throw myself into grave danger to save your ass, which is unlikely as at the end of the day I'm really a wimp, can I offer you a job? Full-time? Perks and all?"

At that moment, my phone buzzed on my desk. "Hold that thought?" I said and grabbed it.

I smiled at the message that greeted me. Baby Delgado had joined the world and she was ready for her first close-up. I was ready for the job. I hugged my phone.

"Thank you for the job offer," I said. "But can I negotiate?"

"Well, that's new," Regina said, lighting a cigarette. "What're you thinking?"

"Freelance," I said.

"On two conditions," she said, dropping ashes on my floor. "One, you promise to keep working on these street portraits over here. Brava to them. Two, you let me paint your front door something more colorful. No one is going to roll in off the street to do business with a photographer who has peeling paint to greet them."

"Deal," I said, trying to contain my excitement and play it cool.

To celebrate the outcome of my first job with her, we finished the bottle of champagne. And so, it was with a couple too many drinks in me when my door rattled again with another visitor.

"Hi," said Harry. "Is this a good time?"

"We were just going," Maria said, grabbing her coat and shooing my remaining company out the door with her.

"Toodles," Regina said. "Don't mess up or I'll fire you. Just kidding!"

The door closed behind them. Harry took his seat in my desk chair. I headed to the safety of my stool.

"Big night," he said. "Are you feeling OK?"

"Oddly," I said, "I've never felt better. I can see why you like your job."

"I can see why you like yours," he said.

"I have something I should give back to you."

"Really?" he said as I disappeared into my room. I came back with his hat.

"Now that I know this is an official detective's hat, I think you should hang on to it," I said and put it on his head. "For good luck."

"Before we start arguing about who should wear this hat," he said, "I have something to tell you. Bernie's been working on it, but it took a few days to formalize."

"Sounds big," I said, returning to my stool.

"It is. We told the British ambassador about your role in finding the Crown Badge of Love. He, in turn, told the royal family. Here's a letter from the palace."

I took a letter with a royal seal from Harry and opened it.

"Aww," I said, clutching the letter to my heart. "They want to give me the reward for finding their brooch. That's the sweetest. One thousand dollars would be awesome. But you should get half of it, right?"

"I'm an officer of the law," Harry said. "I was only doing my job, which was to follow up on a tip. I can't take a penny."

I could see he was trying to contain his excitement about my good fortune. I appreciated it even though I felt badly that he couldn't take a penny.

Harry left the desk chair, took my hands in his, and smiled. I decided to take him out to dinner with some of my earnings. Somewhere nice, but also cozy.

"The reward was one thousand dollars one hundred years ago," he said.

"It's OK," I said. "I'm happy with anything."

"You don't understand," he said. "Do you know what the present value of one thousand dollars is?"

I shook my head, suddenly afraid to ask.

"About three hundred thousand dollars," he said, and I swear to God there were tears in the man's eyes that were about as bountiful as mine suddenly were.

"They're going to give me three hundred thousand dollars?" I said, barely able to get the words out.

"Yup."

"Why?"

He shrugged and laughed.

"Trust me," he said. "That's a small percentage of what the Crown Badge of Love is worth. They're getting a good deal."

The tears were really flowing now.

"I can get a nurse for Poppy," I said. "He can stay home."

Harry hugged me. I let him. I let his arms wrap around me and his cheek rest against the top of my head and I stood up and hugged him right back. As I looked up into his eyes, I realized one more marvelous thing.

"I can go back to college, too," I said. "Maybe take a couple of classes next fall."

"Back in Jersey?" he said, tugging me closer. "I was thinking City College," I said.

"I like your thinking," he said.

My phone buzzed between us. Very awkward. I moved it to the counter and noticed a message.

"It's from Bernie," I said.

Good work. If you have time, I might have more jobs for you. A good photographer is hard to come by.

Harry put his hat on me.

"Let's not fight about who can wear this," he said.

"I'm not arguing," I said. "It'll be our partner hat."

"About that. I don't want to take advantage of this moment, but I really want to kiss you. Would I be violating the code of our partnership if I did that?"

"As long as you're not after me for my money," I said.

Acknowledgments

There are a few photos I wish Liv Spyers could snap for me in her studio; those that capture the brainstorming, pep talks, *ah-ha!* moments, and back-to-the-drawing-board days that contributed to the creation of *Photo Finished*.

Photo One: The Official Team (from Left to Right)

Christina Hogrebe: Agent Extraordinaire. Cheerleader. No-Nonsense Hero.

Norma Perez-Hernandez and Elizabeth Trout: Kensington's Dynamic Duo editors who generously share their creativity and support no matter the day or what the world looks like.

Larissa Ackerman and Jesse Cruz: The team behind Kensington's magic formula of cozy reading fun.

The Kensington Design Team: Because, to be honest, I'm framing their stunning cover for my apartment, my parents, my therapist . . .

Jonathan Putnam and Michael Bergmann: Who are also representing my friends at the *New York Society Library*. They might be surprised to see their names here until they read the book. I hope it brings back some memories.

Photo Two: The Friends Who Make It All Happen, Clockwise

Alysia Macaulay: Thank you, my dear friend, for the early read. You made sure Liv is a true photographer.

Olivia Cleary: Whose creative spirit I know Liv would love. Her artistic eye and creative zeal is infectious.

Jill Furman, Valerie Steiker, Gretchen Eisele, Alicia Cleary, and dozens more friends whose smiles and encouragement lift me every day and help believe in myself. Anyone would be lucky to have one of you in their life. Without you, there's no way a gal could get up, kick ass, and repeat.

Team Deb—rest in peace, my friend. I am grateful for your love and light and strength, Deb. May those of us you called to help you, aka The Harem (only you could pull that off!), continue to cherish each other and nurture the bond which grew like magic out of our collective love.

Photo Three: The 24-by-36-Inch Family Portrait for Over the Sofa

Thank you, my lovely, loving, and wise Shanahan family. As my mom, always my first reader, says: A family who can laugh together can handle anything. I hope this book gives you a few smiles and chuckles. Including all the inside jokes.

My Granny and Papa, who taught me how to make puns, tell stories, and shop for food in every borough.

And, lump in my throat, Caroline and Tommy. You are my inspiration for everything. Thank you and I love you.